PEOPLE ON OUR ROOF

SHEFALI TRIPATHI MEHTA

olive turtle

NIYOGI BOOKS

Published by
NIYOGI BOOKS
Block D, Building No. 77,
Okhla Industrial Area, Phase-I,
New Delhi-110 020, INDIA
Tel: 91-11-26816301, 26818960
Email: niyogibooks@gmail.com
Website: www.niyogibooksindia.com

Editor: Arunima Ghosh
Layout: Shashi Bhushan Prasad
Cover Design: Misha Oberoi

ISBN: 978-93-89136-70-8
Publication: 2021

Printed at: Niyogi Offset Pvt. Ltd., New Delhi, India

To my father from whom I came to know and understand those, who are 'not all there', and my mother, who let me be that a lot

PROLOGUE

'It is a deep, dark blue—dusted with gold, *sona*! Like the night sky studded with stars.' At 'stars' he raises his hands towards the sky and flowers open his fingers. The many rings on his fat fingers glint as they catch the late afternoon sun.

'From far away—Afghanistan.' He stretches the word and with his right index finger, loops the air to indicate distance. '*Badakhshaan*.' His voice soars. 'Or from *Roos*—Russia. It is called Lapis—brings *shaaanti*.' The elongated 'sha' softens his tone. Stealing a look at Nani sitting beside him on the front steps of the porch, their backs to the house, he whispers, 'Healing—*aarogya*.'

Nani, in her cucumber green cotton saree, drawn over her shoulders, sits like a small dhobi-bundle on the steps, and beside her, in a well-worn khadi kurta, this huge man, an afternoon visitor whom only she meets. Always outside.

He turns his ruddy face towards Nani, the coiled string of hair springing from the flat of his bald head, undisturbed. 'This chakra here? he points to his brow, 'Fate! Where the *teesri aankh*, the third eye, is—our *hosh*, consciousness—*this* is the door to our thoughts, our dreams and emotions.'

Nani's silence is unusual. She is always quick to respond to Bajpayee *ji*.

'The dark blue crystal will release serenity into her mind and body—*especially* her mind.'

That's what she's always waiting to hear—a cure for the mind. But today, Nani seems far from enthralled.

'Lapis lazuli is the stone for spiritual healers and kings. It *connects* us to our deepest truths—our fears—' he clears his throat, 'and the flaws in our karma.'

He falls silent. Then, tries again, 'It stops psychotic attacks by blocking evil energy.' He's now holding an imaginary brick in his hands, that he pushes away, as he says, 'Like a powerful mantra, it stops and sends it back.'

'The most potent is the darkest blue with golden streaks. Like a river of gold flowing in the night sky.' He intones again.

Nani stoops over, resting her chin on her open palms, her elbows digging into her folded legs. Bajpayee *ji* sighs. He sounds a little resigned as he continues, 'Otherwise, I also have the yellow sapphire—*pukhraj*.'

'Make her wear it in the left hand, on the third finger. Make it in gold and the demons of the mind will stay away.'

Bajpayee *ji* rambles on, but Nani is only half-hearing because she is very afraid that Nana will return home any minute and find her doing what he had said he would not allow *as long as he lives.*

'Amethyst of a violet hue? *Jamuni*?'

She does not respond.

'It will bring peace of mind—prevent accidents and there are other benefits. Mata *ji*?'

'Bajpayee *ji*, can you come another day? I cannot decide.'

'*Fikr! That* is your enemy, Mata *ji*. Leave your worries to me. She is innocent and guileless—a gift of the merciful God. Just her mind—it is in a thick fog. We will clear it by and by.'

As a little girl hiding behind the main door, Naina had watched this scene play out on the front porch of her grandparents' home, her home now, on so many afternoons that if she closed her eyes, it ran in her head, frame by frame, like a much-watched film.

I

New Delhi, 1997

A dinner party had been arranged on the lawns for her Nana's best friend from school, a renowned neurosurgeon in England. Many friends of theirs were expected.

The bungalow seemed to be puffing up with activity; so, when in the evening, just as the sun was setting and its doors and windows were opened to the still summer outside, it gently tipped itself into the small garden in the front. Out came everyone carrying tables and chairs, plates and glasses. They carried the big folding table from the storeroom and pulling out its legs, set it up at the far end of a slightly damp lawn. Nani came out clutching her treasured white damask rose-patterned tablecloth. It had been laundered and bleached so that only she, who knew where the curry stains had been, could spot those with a very close look. As the sky dimmed its light, the whites—the tablecloth, the mogra buds studding the bushes, and the lace curtains that billowed in the windows—began to glow. When the lights inside were switched on, they fell out through the windows in long, warm rectangles. Nani smiled as she placed the dahi vada platter on the kitchen counter and sprinkled roasted jeera powder over the creamy curd. Two of the cook's teenaged daughters, who had come to help, dashed in and out of the front door, carrying plates and counting cutlery, giggling and whispering into each other's ears. One of them wore a blue dupatta edged with *gota* that glinted as she moved in light and shadow. Naina wanted it with all her heart. She would tell Nani, later.

At 7, Papa called and spoke with Nani. When she placed the receiver back on the cradle, Nani's happy, dahi vada platter bearing shoulders seemed to flop and Naina felt as if 'the voltage has gone low' as the elders would say when the lights suddenly dimmed.

Nani started to hurriedly dress Naina, pulling the white organdie frock over her head impatiently, propelling her firmly around to tie the belt into a bow at the back, a tad too tight. The comb furrowed Naina's head as Nani parted her hair in the centre and fastened it with ribbons into two pigtails. Then she sent her off to be socked and shoed by the maid. Naina forgot Nani's low voltage when the maid rolled the lace socks that she loved, up her knees.

Just before the guests arrived, Papa came with Amma and Tara. Amma did not look at anyone. Tara was sleeping, her head bobbing on Papa's shoulder where a steady thread of drool was forming a wet patch on his lemon-coloured shirt. They went into the guest room, where Amma sat down on the bed with her feet up and her back very straight. Papa settled Tara next to her, arranged pillows on the other side, and hurried into Nana's study. On his way out, he saw Naina watching them from the door and only lightly patted her cheek.

As the evening slowly filled up with guests, the aroma of food and perfume, the tinkle of ice in glasses of squash, and soft chatter, Naina pushed away thoughts of her glassy-eyed mother and baby sister in the guest room, and wove her way among the guests, hiding into the folds of Nani's crisp saree when people spoke to her. She received kisses, pats, and much praise for being 'such a quiet little girl', but soon everyone got busy with grown-up talk and Naina was left to amuse herself.

When no one was watching, she withdrew behind Nani's chair and slowly moved to the *madhukamini* bush that stood outside the guest room window. Sitting at the edge of a water-filled flowerbed, she was completely engrossed in setting the fallen blossoms a-sail, prodding them around with a twig, when she heard a shrill cry, and turning around, saw Amma in the lawn.

Amma without her clothes. Perfectly still. Like a photograph.

No one laughed.

Except her.

Naina giggled at the sight of her mother naked. The only other sound was that of the empty glasses that clanked on the tray the cook's daughter held. She put it down on a chair and taking off her *gota*-edged, blue dupatta, tried to cover Amma.

Papa and Nani caught Amma by her arms and led her away, inside. The *gota* shimmered against Amma's brown body.

It was all over in a couple of seconds, but the silence stretched for seemingly long moments, until some voices, punctuated with nervous coughs, floated up—someone asked for a drink they did not want, someone complimented another on a saree they did not really care much about, someone cracked a joke that prompted feeble laughter—and everyone joined the pretend game of 'nothing happened', the adult make-believe.

The forever changes in their lives were triggered off that evening. Papa stopped coming to the dinner parties. Naina would be left with Nani for days. Whenever he came, they squabbled—he and Nana-Nani. Those times, he referred to Amma as 'your daughter' instead of Naintara. When he thought she was sleeping, he would kiss Naina. She would be awake, but would not dare to move, too scared to upset anyone and conflicted about which side she was supposed to be on.

Naina held Tara responsible for all this. Ever since Tara had come into their lives, Amma had started behaving strangely.

Awake before dawn, lying in bed, unable to stop herself from slipping into the black hole of memories, Naina looked out the window of her room that was once the guest room where her mother sat with her feet up, not looking at her. How things had changed in the two decades since then, and yet, how little they had—like the *madhukamini* outside the window, a keepsake from another time of which so little remained—no lawn, no laughing people in cane chairs, no zinnias and dahlias, like upside-down ballet dancers. But it was the stillness of the once-bustling home that was the most palpable. Fewer doors opened and closed, the doorbell and the phone rang rarely, no feet scuttled in the lobby outside, no one called out to the *subziwala* or the *bartanwali* from the kitchen window. Of the four that lived in the house, only two had words to communicate with; none to laugh, joke, or tease.

A slight breeze blew in the citrus fragrance of the *madhukamini* blossoms that she could not see yet. A new day lay before her—she could still turn things around. She sat up and, picking the notepad from the bedside, began to write her to-do for the day in small, squat letters.

Run
Check vacancies
Copy-test
Interview
Tuition 1
Tuition 2

At 6—she had to wait till 6 to feel safe outdoors—with streams of sweat running down the sides of her face and her soaked tee stuck to her back like butter paper, as she sprinted past the bus stop, she heard him holler.

Just another among the morning sounds—the emerging cacophony of the day—unobtrusive if you did not focus, but if you did, each very distinct: the grinding halt of milk lorries, the screeching roll of store shutters, the gentle thump of newspaper bundles being dropped off at street corners, the clip-clip of stray dog feet on empty pavements, an occasional tinkle of bicycle bells.

His cry rang out clear—two words that could mean much or nothing at all. She did not think he was directing it to her. He was, like so many on Delhi's streets to whom this came as naturally as pissing on the walls—calling out to a passing woman, brushing past her in a hurry, squeezing a breast, whispering a lewd something into a little girl's ears, just venting. It was not her problem. Nor anybody's. She was venting too. Running like this.

Late again. Releasing her sweat-soaked hair from the grip of the band with one hand, she lifted the gate open with the other and saw Amma sitting on the stone bench in the empty, craggy lawn with her back to the house, holding a mug of tea between her palms—still as a photo.

'Amma!' Willing cheer into her voice, Naina walked up to her, 'You got up early today? Had tea?' She sat down next to Amma on the cool bench. The air was dense with rain that was swelling up in some unseen layer of the sky. It could be days, even weeks, before they got some temporary relief from the humidity. 'Amma, today I have two interviews. It is an important day. I will first go to this ad agency...' She was used to talking for two—to say something, imagine what a mother would say, reply to that, carry on till it felt like a conversation, and end when her heart tired of it.

Amma turned slightly to look at her and lifted one finger to her lips to quieten Naina.

'What happened?' Naina whispered.

'Shhh—those people.' Amma raised her eyes slightly in the direction of the roof.

The people on the roof. The people that no one but Amma could see or hear. On some days, they assailed Amma's mind to the depths of fear; on others, they quietly watched her from their perch. These days, they did the latter.

'Why don't you come inside with me, Amma?' Naina waited for a few moments for some reaction, and then added, 'Okay, Amma, I am going to get ready. You don't worry about them. They will leave. Come inside or Tara will get late, okay?'

She gave Amma's hand a squeeze and got up. Turning towards the house, she looked up at the terrace. A cloudless monsoon sky sat over the straight line of the parapet wall. Naina hurried inside.

Tara was in the hall, gently rocking her chair to the soothing strains of the Gayatri mantra—her morning ritual.

'Good morning, Tara!'

Tara did not look up. She never did. Her whole world of talking, listening, thinking, and loving was inside her. Those that mattered to her could listen to her unspoken word, respond to her silent enquiry. She kept to her neatly ordered life. Like Naina ran, just focussing on one foot in front of the other, one at a time, Tara too looked at each task at hand as though through a fire lens. Her days were neatly slotted into tasks. She would move from one to the other only when the last had been put into place, like pieces of Legos. Everything in her world was in order, in the particular order that she had everything set in her head.

This was her time to rock with the chants of *Oṃ bhūr bhuvaḥ svaḥ...*

Raju handed Naina a cup of tea and the carefully folded newspaper. Over the years, there had grown a silent understanding between the two. Ever since he noticed Naina's anxiety over the Wednesday newspaper with its jobs supplement, Raju had made it a point to bring it in first thing in the morning and keep it carefully folded in the kitchen.

Taking the newspaper and tea from him, Naina shut herself in her room. Sitting on the cold floor, she began to skim through the vacancies—three columned attention-calling ones, as well as the tiny-boxed, money-per-word-counted ones. Nothing too relevant showed up, but she noted down the address of one place she could pop in if she had time after the two appointments that were scheduled for the day.

By 8:45, she was ready to leave, when she heard a familiar voice boom, 'Naina, where are you, *beti*?'

'God! Not Ajit Mama today!' She panicked as she quickly tied her hair and grabbing her bag, rushed to the drawing room.

As long as Nani was alive, Ajit Mama had pestered her to divide the house and will a portion each to him and Amma. But Nani had declined. A roof over their heads was all she could leave the three, rather four, unfortunate souls with, she had said.

'*Aao*, *beti*. Come, come,' he said and smiled. Amma was sitting next to him and Tara, at the dining table across from the hall, was lingering over milk from her yellow cup and slices of bread, the sides of which has been sliced off carefully—every speck of brown removed.

'Mama *ji*, I really have no time now. You know how desperately I'm looking for a job. Today, there are several people I have to meet. I must hurry.'

'What to do, *beti*, you are always busy, either rushing somewhere or not at home. I've even waited for you till late in the evening, but...'

'Please don't start all that again, Mama *ji*,' she cut him short.

'*Arré*, what did *I* say? You also know it's not alright for girls your age to stay out so late in the night. People don't look upon such girls with respect. They talk. What did *I* ever say?' he turned to Amma for support.

Amma seemed uneasy, frowning at a spot on the carpet.

'*Ab dekho*, Didi, see if *I* don't think of you all, who will? *Woh sala...*'

With that, Ajit Mama had tried his luck with Amma too far. As he spoke those words, Amma's expression changed. She got up, caught hold of his arm and started to lead him out the front door.

'Didi, why are you getting angry with *me*? I am telling you, this girl will ruin our family name. She has already brought shame to the family, *badnaam kar diya*! I can still salvage our reputation. If you don't listen to me, you will all be ruined. You will be out on the streets! Let me rent out the back portion, just two rooms, Didi. I'll pay you some money too—every month.'

But Amma was not listening. She was gesturing to him to leave, like one would a tramp who had got to the front door. Naina walked past them to still try and reach her first test in time, by 9.

The ad agency was in the basement of one of those posh bungalows that one knows are posh because of how completely hidden behind tall walls and iron grilles they are.

Naina sat staring at the paper in front of her, the silence inside the room completely distracting her. Each time a door opened, each time someone coughed or turned a page, she was startled, losing all threads of thought. Ajit Mama's words boomed in her head. She needed so badly to do this copy test well, but she knew it was not a day for writing headlines for washing powder. Reluctantly, she turned in her answer sheet and came out knowing she would not be called back in there again.

The other agency was familiar. She'd been there a hundred times, or so it felt. Every time she went, the creative director was busy. Finally, yesterday his secretary had confirmed that she could meet him.

When she arrived there at 12:30, after changing two buses, the receptionist asked her to wait. Naina waited for forty minutes and finally, the creative director decided to speak with her on the phone from his cabin somewhere on the upper floors of the building.

'Yes?' his officious voice shot in from the other end as she stood in the lobby, speaking self-consciously with three other waiting faces looking intently at her.

'Mr Pandey, this is Naina. You called me for an interview today,' she hoped, he remembered. 'At 1 pm,' she added nervously.

'Okay.' That was all he said. It did not mean no; so, she figured, she should wait.

At 1:50, a middle-aged man came down the stairs and the receptionist, on a phone call, mouthed 'Mr Pandey' and pointed one long, scarlet-nail-painted-finger at Naina. Naina looked at Mr Pandey's expressionless face and her heart began to beat in her ears as she stood up to meet him. He nodded to her hello and walking straight across to a small cabin, held the door open for her. The moment they were seated, he began, 'Okay now, there is this one manufacturer, who has produced 40,000 cups—disposable cups. These were made for something, but are now—say—surplus. He has to sell these. What you have to do is, find buyers for these cups. You have to think what these cups could be used for, who would buy them, and how you will sell these through your print ad. Okay? You may go now and think over it. Whenever you're ready—tomorrow, next week, next month, six months later, you can come back.'

Even before he finished speaking, he was on his feet, holding the door open again. In a daze, she got up and walked out. Six months! This man does not need a copywriter. She watched him dash back upstairs, climbing two steps at a time, and had an irrepressible desire to go after him, three steps at a time, and punch him smack in the face. He'd wasted so much of her time. Angry and humiliated, she came out of the office.

The sun dripped down furiously. Against her better judgment, she stopped at a dingy tea stall and asked for a Pepsi. The man at the stall called out to a little boy with a mop of haystack hair, 'One Campa!' When she looked at the only other customer, a man wearing a tie and blowing smoke through his nostrils, he winked at her.

A rag-picker was walking around the garbage dump next to the tea stall, rummaging through it. Tea, coffee, cold drink, soup, ice-cream, jelly, candle holder, planter—the uses of disposable cups on her mind, Naina saw him pick a soiled, squashed pack of Frooti from the sweeping expanse of rot and without a moment's hesitation, suck from its straw. Nauseated, she looked away.

The bus to Maharani Bagh inched ahead. Near Ashram, a burly Jat got in stomping a heavy lathi and plonked himself next to Naina. As a few other women got in, the conductor mustered enough courage to ask him lightly, '*Tau*, sit there comfortably,' pointing to the vacant seats.

'Why?' he boomed threateningly and in a brazen show of clout, squared his shoulders moving closer to Naina. Naina kept her head turned towards the window. The bus had stopped at a traffic signal and two little girls outside in colourless salwar kameezes, their necklines falling off their bony shoulders, were jumping up to touch her arm. They implored her to buy the garnet roses in cellophane cones they were carrying. 'Buy one for your Sa'ab, your mister,' they said.

Rose Day.

The bleak winter afternoons hurtled hastily into dark evenings. Their second semester exams were due in a week. She had taken the week off from the tuitions and spent the afternoons before class, studying in the library.

One evening, Professor Chopra's lecture continued over the next hour and it was 7:30 when he finished. The girls were talking excitedly about something, milling around the exit. Threading her way out, Naina overheard someone ask if there would be classes the next day. Looking around for a familiar face, she spotted Lata and asked.

'No classes. It's Rose Day, no? There's a party in the basement. You didn't see the notice?' Lata asked.

Naina remembered then: she had seen the girl-boy-waltzing poster while copying the exam schedule, but had not cared to read the details after she glanced at the entry fee. Three hundred rupees per person. She could put her time and money to better use. Besides, the aftertaste of outings was familiar—guilt and shame.

However, the next afternoon she was torn, unable to decide whether she should go to the library or just stay back home and study. If she went, she was sure to bump into someone and then it would be difficult to explain why she was not attending the party. Also, Deepak would be there with other girls. It was best to stay away.

Finally, it was curiosity in the garb of nonchalance that made her leave for the library at 3 pm. For over an hour, she sat reading distractedly and making notes. When she finally could focus, she missed the 5 pm deadline she had set for herself to leave. The party was in the adjoining building and she would have to go past it to get to her bus stop. She almost ran out, hoping no one would be around so early, but just as she crossed the gate, she heard a loud 'Naina!' that was impossible to ignore without seeming rude. She turned to look.

'Hey, where are you hurrying away?' Aman was walking up to her. Behind him, a large group of her classmates hung at the entrance. Of all the people crowding there, she spotted Deepak. While she spoke with Aman, everyone else came and stood around too. She lied that there was a family function to attend, aware of Deepak in the outer periphery of the group. They offered her several excuses to give the family function a miss, including 'say you died—no one in the family will bother, really'. But finally, she managed to politely extricate herself from them, and was on her way.

'Can I walk you to your bus stop?' She had hardly walked two steps when she found Deepak beside her.

They talked about the professors, the chai-bun at the shanty across the road, the assignment he had not completed. They talked like people talk, people who meet by chance and discover common things to talk about. But all her senses were alive only to a faint aftershave, an endearing hint of a childish lisp, of round-toe, brown leather shoes, and the two times that he turned to look shocked-embarrassed-incredulous at men, who brushed past her on the pavement not yet crowded.

Surprised at how completely at ease she was with him, she had no hesitation as they approached her stop, to turn to look straight at him and say, 'I think you should return to your party now.'

'Okay,' he said and clicked his heels.

'Enjoy yourself,' she said, meaning it sincerely.

'You too,' he raised a hand in a salute, walked backwards two steps, looking at her, tilted his head to the right once, then turned and sprinted away.

The 'family function' she came home to, relieved her of the delirium, instantly.

The ayah appeared as soon as Naina entered the Malliks' dining room, and placed glasses of milk before the children. 'Good evening, Didi,' she said and on cue, Rahul and Rukmini repeated after her. Naina's plate on the table was also laid out and tea brought in.

For a long time, she had resisted being part of this ritual. Late afternoon, when she reached their bungalow in Maharani Bagh, the

Mallik kids would be having their evening snack with their mother and the maid would lead her straight to the dining table. Naina tried coming in a little late, embarrassed by a situation where she was asked to join in out of politeness, but they had insisted on it by either prolonging the snack time to fit her in or by sending in a tray for her in the children's room, later. She was less awkward now. Today, buoyed by the Rose Day memory, she chatted with the children happily as they munched on fat slices of a gooey ginger cake.

Should she ask Mrs Mallik for an advance? It would take care of some bills. She would still need to withdraw more money this month. Should she just withdraw more from the bank? Mrs Mallik was not home anyway.

Mrs Mallik entered, just as Naina was leaving. She was at the door, looking for something inside her handbag and did not see Naina. Before her mind could flip again, Naina spoke, 'Hello, Ma'am, I needed a favour.'

'How are you, Naina?' Mrs Mallik's matt-pink lips curved into a smile on her luminous face. 'Are the brats giving you much trouble, my girl?'

'Not at all. Ma'am, can I have my salary in advance?' Anxious, she blurted out. Mrs Mallik seemed to want to ask her something, but did not. Withdrawing some notes from her handbag, she thrust them quietly into Naina's hands with an assuring smile.

'Rahul got into the school football team; did he tell you?'

'Wow, that's wonderful. No, he didn't.'

Even as she said that, Naina knew Mrs Mallik was only trying to put her out of her awkwardness. 'See you, ma'am,' she said and walked out.

A short walk away was the Agarwal Villa. Even the sight of that name in elaborate gold letters outside the gate made her cringe. The Agarwal boys, Vinay and Mohit, were bratty and barefaced show-offs.

All their mother talked of was money and yet Naina knew, if she ever asked her for a paisa in advance, Mrs Agarwal would not loosen her purse strings. Naina despised their flashy lifestyle.

She pushed the ornate gates open and saw the servant boy about the same age as Vinay and Mohit carrying their school bags from the parked car, inside. Disgusted, she wished in vain that she did not have to go inside. Someone pressed the remote and the car chirped twice before locking itself in. The sight of the red Ford made her smile. One day, after tuition, the Agarwal boys were going her way and offered to drop her to Nehru Place where she was to meet Deepak. Seeing the red Ford with soft toys of all imaginable shapes and colours stacked at the back, Deepak had asked, 'A toy shop came to drop you?'

She swayed synchronously with the others packed into the 427 from Ashram to GK, as the bus veered left and right. Usually quick-eyed and sharp-elbowed, she had given in to the pushing and jostling, hanging from the handrails. The woman standing next to her was carrying in her arms a girl who did not need carrying—she was easily seven or eight. She was wearing a gauzy pink frock and a matching frilly hairband. Maybe it was her birthday. Catching her stare, Naina winked at her. Suddenly shy, the child buried her face into the woman's shoulder, peeping at Naina the very next instant, doing it over and over. But Naina was too tired for games.

She too had worn a pink frock on one of her birthdays. Her 8th birthday in March that had fallen so close to Holi that year that Nani had made her wear the same new frock on both the occasions—a coral pink shift dress with gold buttons and black lace all the way down its front. The buttons did not open; Nani said they were for 'show'.

Immediately after, she had come to stay with Nani along with Amma and Tara. No one had said anything, but Nani had cried a lot and Naina somehow knew that this stay would not be like those before, when after having spent the day at Nani's, she would fall asleep lulled by the hum of the grown-ups talking, waiting for Papa to come. When he came, he would pick her up and she would wrap her arms and legs tightly around him, her head with its sleep-tangled hair bobbing on his shoulder which gave out that Papa smell, he would carry her home. Nor was it going to be like those other times when Papa did not come for several days and Nani told her to be a good girl and to not keep asking for him, because he was taking care of Amma who was not feeling well.

It was clear, he would not come—not that day, nor ever.

The bus was stuck near Nehru Place for close to half-an-hour. She had been terribly delayed at the tuition. Vinay and Mohit did nothing on their own; she was expected to help them write each answer, each essay, and correct all their homework. Today, Mohit had been extremely distracted—brazenly yawning and looking at the clock. It had required all her patience to get him to complete his schoolwork.

The bus started moving and everyone was relieved when the still air inside was displaced and the sweat that ran in streams down their faces and back began to cool their bodies. The bus was racing towards her stop when, suddenly, the driver hit the brakes and the jolt threw her over a man whose hand lingered suggestively on her back.

'Bastard!' she spat out, repulsed, and scampered off the bus even as it was pulling away, realizing only later that she had got down two stops ahead of hers.

Darkness lay crouching in the distance between the streetlights. Naina kept a close watch. The game her shadow played—of leaping ahead of her as she crossed one lamp post and following her in quick strides as she approached the next, kept her alert. When she was right under a streetlight, her shadow dropped at her feet. Like a heap of clothes. Stripping her naked. Like Amma did on evenings when she was late returning home after a long, rough day.

Walking around the park to the end of the lane where her home stood, she crossed Gupta Aunty's house and caught a glimpse of the family gathered in the drawing room watching loud TV and talking louder. Her own house across the street was in shadows, characteristically quiet. She lifted the latch to open the gate that had slumped on its rusted hinges, but it still grated on the loose gravel—a familiar sound that made Raju peep out. She saw him framed in the dim yellow light of the kitchen window and then disappear. The porch was in darkness. She looked up at the terrace—the straight line of the parapet was sharply silhouetted by the moon rising in the east, behind the house. A crack of yellow light grew into a wedge on the dark porch as Raju opened the front door noiselessly. The look on his face told her that things were okay. Okay was enough. Nothing needed to change just as long as all was status quo.

'Why don't you switch on the light in the porch?' she scolded him under her breath.

'I did, Didi,' he pinched his throat.

'Shhhh.' Naina, tired of the confrontations every night that she was late, tiptoed across the lobby to her room. Amma and Tara were watching TV.

She walked straight into the shower, eager to wash the day off. The water was cool, but fell sluggishly on her shoulders, reminding her that the shower head needed to be changed too. Nothing had changed for her since she had stood under the shower in the morning or last night…or the innumerable mornings and countless nights before. She could have just stood under this shower and made no effort. It would all have remained the same. Status quo. Deepak had again not taken her call. 'Sir is busy,' she had been told. She had waited for him at the bus stop too, but he had not come.

There was a gentle knock on the door as she quickly dressed.

'The bania asked for money.' Raju placed the tray with her dinner on the table by the bed, turning to leave, he hesitated before adding, 'Milk bill is also due.'

'Have you all eaten?'

'*Han ji*,' he replied and left.

A bowl of dal, rice, two chapattis, and aloo-baingan—suddenly ravenous, she ate everything. It was her first proper meal of the day. She had dinner in her room when she was late; otherwise, it drew Amma's attention. If Amma came to check, she would find Naina in her room and had no means of knowing when she had returned. It was cheating, Naina knew, but it was harmless; another attempt at maintaining peace.

She drank the cold water Raju had left in a jug on the table, and then, lay down on the bed with the light switched off, listening to the muffled sound of the TV. A straight line of yellow light that came in through the edge of the door, fell prostrate on the floor beside her bed. She closed her eyes and waited.

The sound of the TV broke off suddenly and the house seemed to hold its breath in the quiet that it released. Naina looked at the clock. 9:45. There was a thump of a heavy foot as Tara got off her rocking chair. A click as the drawing room light was switched off. Another as the dining room light was switched off. One more—that of the kitchen. No more. She knew it. He had not switched on the porch light.

She heard light footsteps approach her door, then turn away. She waited another few minutes, so that Amma would get into bed. The medicine Amma took helped her sleep soundly.

Click.

One more light was switched off somewhere. The porch?

Quietly, she opened her door and stepped out. The night light in the lobby threw a sinister shadow of her on the wall as she carried the tray back to the kitchen. Raju was sleeping in the hall on a mattress on the floor, and Amma and Tara in the room they shared. Walking past Nani's room, she looked in instinctively. Nani would have sensed her presence and called out from her bed next to the open window, 'Go to sleep *laado*, all will be well tomorrow; the night is but a shadow.'

A broad staircase led to blue-grey double doors with no signboard and when she pushed one open, Naina was right inside the workspace. There was no reception desk, no formal cordoning off of the work area from that of the visitors. Like visitors never come, she thought and stood wondering what to do next when a passing person stopped to ask.

'I'm here to meet Dilip.'

'Hey!' he shouted turning towards the hall, 'For Dilip!' He pointed a thumb at her over his shoulder to people at large and walked out of the blue-grey door. *Baam!*

The people before her stopped staring and dipped their heads back into work and conversations, only when Dilip walked up to her in hurried, definite strides.

'Naina,' she said as he shook her hand and conjured up two folding chairs that creaked as they sat down. He stretched his hand for the portfolio she was carrying. Without a word, he flipped through it. Like a stick, he reclined, and the headrest seemed to bore painfully into his neck as he straightened his back and stretched his legs straight in front of him. His uncomfortable posture made Naina doubt his earnestness in looking at her work. This might be my last chance, she thought nervously as she watched him turn the pages. Then, as suddenly as he had appeared, Dilip stood up and excusing himself, disappeared.

He was back in five minutes.

'You're in.'

She stared at him, speechless with disbelief, as he continued in his brisk manner, 'You know there's a slowdown and we cannot afford to hire new people. So, we can't pay you. If you like, at best, we can reimburse your commuting costs.'

'On submission of bills,' he added, deposited the portfolio back into her hands, and walked away.

All through school and college, she had lived one dream—to be a part of *Dimension 3*. Hours took wing as she burrowed into old magazines, flipping through their exquisite black and white print ads. Every year, as they swept away the coveted advertising awards, she gloated in it as if it was her personal achievement. One whole year had passed since graduation, but Naina had found no job. It was then that she took up tuitions and joined the part-time diploma. Mornings she studied; afternoons she taught tuitions; and in the evenings, attended classes.

Deepak had joined the course late.

They were engrossed in making a media plan for a cold crème brand during Prof. Chopra's third class on Media Selection, when the front door creaked open. The whole class turned in tandem to look, as a lanky, young man, with curly hair, entered. He dipped his head slightly in the direction of the professor and walked straight to the back of the classroom, inconspicuous once again in the shadows.

Naina despised latecomers; they displayed an inherent disrespect for others. After the lecture, as she walked out of the main gate, she saw the latecomer zoom past on a motorcycle. Another moneybag to bear with in class, she thought. How was she to know then? How fast everything had happened.

For one of her course assignments, Naina had interviewed D3's Creative Director, Samar Ahuja, and the Copy Head, Dilip Bose. Both had answered her questions patiently over coffee and were generally obliging, smiling indulgently at her 20-point questionnaire. The meeting buoyed her confidence and she began to dream of being a part of D3.

Today, she was back. Not for the first time though. She had come before, on the day after her last exam. And again, twice, but had not been able to meet either Samar or Dilip. She had left messages for both, but neither had called back. She had then started applying for other jobs. Now, two months after the course, she still had no job. Today, Dilip had agreed to meet her. Samar was no longer with the agency, which had suffered a huge setback and had recently moved from its posh M Block address where she had first met them, to this warehouse sprawl in Okhla.

A woman with oversized sunglasses entered the restaurant and walked straight up to Naina's table. She kept her big sunglasses on indoors too. She pulled up a chair and sat down at Naina's table. Naina's heart sank.

The waiter came with the cupcake Naina had ordered. The rose-pink swirl of icing made the cupcake look like the head of a brown man wearing a pink turban. The taste of sweetened buttercream was bursting in her mouth, but the big woman's presence paralyzed her.

Big Woman drew the plate to herself. She picked the spoon placed before Naina and ploughed it in right through the pink turban and into the equally yielding brown cake. One half of the head fell—the pink turban lay splattered at the edge of the plate.

Big Woman quartered it with the grace of a queen on a banquet table and began to eat. A tiny blob of pink cream, the size of a bead, stuck to her left cheek just where her lips met. Naina wished she would wipe it away, but Big Woman did not seem to care. The pink mole moved precariously as her mouth worked. Naina watched the pastry disappear in bites, its taste slavering on her own palate.

Blood had begun to ooze from where the pink mole was. A steady stream of scarlet ran down Big Woman's chin and onto her sequined saree. Naina watched horrified. She wanted Big Woman to go away.

An army of little green people—midgets, suddenly appeared. They were wearing pink turbans and formed a circle around Naina and the pastry-eater, holding hands and laughing, paying no heed to the blood that was forming a pool at their feet. Fear caught in her throat, Naina watched the blood rise. She lifted her feet in the air, but the ocean kept rising and soon there was no air. No air to breathe.

Naina bobbed out of sleep, gasping for breath.

Drenched in sweat and still swimming on the blurry brink between sleep and waking, Naina remembered the woman from her dream. Returning from D3 after her meeting with Dilip, she had seen her again. In a magenta, sequined saree and bright, blotchy lipstick, she had stood holding a suitcase in one hand at the busy intersection, paying no heed to the staring eyes of passers-by. Naina had often seen her there, near the Bhairav temple. Who was she? Why does her family let her roam the streets like this? Does she have a family?

Her sleep had run into *godhuli*, the sunset hour. How Nani would chide her if she slept at this time. The gloaming is full of delusions, she would say. When the meeting of the day and the night is obscured by the dust raised by cows returning home, it is inauspicious to sleep.

'All that you dream of will come true.'

'Isn't that nice, Nani? For dreams to come true?'

'What if you dream of death?'

Naina splashed water on her face. The house was quiet. The last light of the retreating sun filtered through the big and small rectangles of the lattice of the lobby and laid out the dying day on the floor.

Across the darkening lobby, the front door was slightly ajar. Amma, Tara, and Raju must be sitting outside as they did at this time every day, she thought. She went into the kitchen and was pouring water into a glass to drink when she heard Raju's frantic call from outside, 'Naina Didi, *jaldi*! Quickly, please!'

Naina bolted out of the front door, her heart in her mouth.

Raju was leading Tara in through the gate with blood running down her face. Amma was hysterically shouting and cursing a bunch of kids on the street. *Pagal! Pagal!* the kids were chanting, calling her mad. They ran away when they saw Naina. Blood was streaming down Tara's face, down her neck, and soaking her sky-blue tee. It was oozing out of a gash close to her left eye. Taking her inside and straight to the washbasin, Naina splashed water on her face to see. The half-inch cut exposed the bone and she knew immediately that Tara would need stitches. Wringing out a towel soaked in water, Naina handed it to Amma, 'Hold this tight over the cut.' Then, instructing Raju to get an auto, she ran inside to fetch her wallet.

Waiting outside the Emergency as the doctor sutured Tara's cut, Naina could feel the needle going in and out of her own flesh. She peeped in and saw Tara lying quietly, staring at the ceiling. Her heart wrenched with a sudden need to gather Tara in her arms and hold her close; so close that it would somehow fill the abyss that she thought was created in Tara's heart by the love she had been denied.

In the autorickshaw going back home, Tara, sedated by the analgesic, fell asleep on Naina's lap. Naina ran her fingers through Tara's curls that fell on her face, something she could not do when Tara was awake. Why anyone would want to hurt this innocent, harmless girl, was beyond her reasoning. The cut was so close to the eye, what if it had hit her eye? Cowards!

Even from the distance, she could see Amma's silhouette at the gate and as they went closer, her worry-ridden face. She began fussing over the half-asleep Tara, and while Naina helped Tara to bed, Raju hurried into the kitchen and came back with a glass of warm milk with haldi.

The smell hit her. Turmeric boiled into milk.

Bhabhi was handing the glass to Deepak as he sat up in bed, his right hand in a bandage and bruises all over his right side. His bike had skidded as he tried to avoid colliding with a child who had suddenly come running across the road. Deepak fell under the bike. He had called Naina at the Agarwal residence from the hospital.

'Hey, Naina, good I could catch you here. Hey, I had a little accident. It's nothing—just some bruises. But the doctor says I've to rest for a few days. Sorry, I can't pick you up today.'

'Where are you, Deep? Are you hurt?'

'I'm fine, just a few scratches. I'm at the nursing home with Bhaiya. We have seen the doctor. Just managed to sneak in a call to you. Should be going now, Naina; Bhaiya is already downstairs waiting for me.'

Much against better sense, Naina decided to visit him. It was the second time she was visiting Deepak's home. But this time, unlike the first, she had little to worry about the impression she would make. Again, it was Riddhima who opened the door. She looked at Naina with surprise and mumbled a greeting; moving aside, she let her in. Naina believed that secretly Riddhima was on her side, only too scared to oppose her Bhabhi who had brought them both up—Deepak and her. Riddhima shut the door behind Naina and vanished inside. Nervous as she was, Naina sat in the hall, waiting until Bhabhi's voice from somewhere inside rang out. It was directed at her.

'You rest here. You have my *kasam* you will not move out of bed for the next three days—for anything or *anyone*. *Whoever* wants to meet you can come and meet you here.' Then a derisive—'People have no shame these days.'

Though the little speech was meant to convey her scorn for Naina, Bhabhi's words heightened her anxiety about Deepak's condition. Without waiting for anyone to ask, Naina walked towards his room. Bhabhi was standing in the doorway, glaring at her accusingly, as if she'd been in some way responsible for Deepak's accident. She stomped away when Naina lowered her head in a namaste.

Deepak looked at her dreamily, the way he did, the way that made every broken, scattered piece of her world come together to wrap her in a warm cocoon. He sighed dramatically to show that the accident did not warrant so much worry, but his big smile said he knew and had hoped she would come and that there was nothing more that he had wanted.

'Hey, Nain! Hey, I'm fine. Why do you look so worried? Let me get up and show you.' He attempted to rise. Naina smiled even as tears were beginning to sting her eyes. He was the only one to whom her feelings mattered. She sat on the bed beside him and touched lightly the fingertips of his right hand that seemed swollen over the thick bandage. Deepak began to recount the accident sounding all heroic and Naina relaxed. She was laughing when Bhabhi came back with a glass of warm, turmeric milk that she thrust in Deepak's left hand and snorted angrily as she walked past Naina. The moment she left, Deepak turned to Naina, 'Hey, Nain, hate this stuff. You drink it, please. There's no getting away from it with Bhabhi.' He put the glass in front of her. The smell of uncooked turmeric rose to her nose and Naina grimaced, making him laugh.

And again, there arose in her, a deep, aching desire to have nothing more to do than spend her entire life sitting next to him, listening to him talk. But Bhabhi's warning struck again, 'Deepak, you should rest now.'

Naina was being asked to leave.

'Stay for a while more.'

'No, Deep, they must be waiting for me at home.' She did not want the embarrassment that he hid behind the plea to become obvious.

'Feel better soon.'

'Take care, Nain. I'll call you later.' He tilted his head to the right and as she got up to leave, he reached out and squeezed her hand. Quickly, she hurried out of his room and walked through the dark and empty hall, opening the door to let herself out. How different this was from that Holi, when all of Deepak's family stood at the doorway waving when she left.

With a rag and a mug of water, she stepped out into the hushed morning and soaking the rag in water, began to rub off the letters written with coal.

Naina had seen it when she was returning from the hospital with Tara, but she had learnt to wait out the first rush of rage. She could have asked Raju to clean it, but she knew if he had seen it first, he would have done it quietly without letting her know. It was her turn to spare him this embarrassment.

Pagalkhana. Madhouse. The letters were gone, but the wall would forever remain smudged.

The slow whirring of the fan that was slicing the day away, stopped completely—another power cut. Instantly, several generators in the neighbourhood roared to life, filling the still, stifling air with the odour of diesel.

What are my options? Naina sat thinking. She had not heard from any employer yet. Dilip's offer was without remuneration. She needed money. Nani had left them with two fixed deposits and a monthly income plan with which she managed the household expenses. But very often, like this month, it had already run out; so Naina had to dig into the annual fund she got from Nana-Nani's insurance policies. Expenses were mounting—Amma and Tara's medicines, Tara's centre fee, the running of their down-at-its-heels home. For some years now, she was also handing out a thousand rupees every month to Raju. Last month, however, Raju had declined, saying, 'I'll ask you when I need it.'

Homeless and orphaned, Raju had been with Nani since he was a child of eight or nine. Ramprasad, the mali, had brought him to fetch milk from the milk booth, every morning. Gradually, he was handed a few rupees and asked to get vegetables, bread, or soap from the corner shop. Once his integrity was established, he was allowed into the house to sweep first, then to wash, and gradually he took over the kitchen, learning from Nani's cook. Now he was family, and with Nani gone, it was reassuring for Naina to have a trustworthy man in a household such as theirs.

This was perhaps her chance to live her dream. There was always the possibility that they may offer her a position, at some point. She would have to continue to go to the Malliks and the Agarwals after office. This meant she would not be home before 9, perhaps 9:30, and the thought of the daily drama that was sure to play out was distressing, but there was no way Naina could forfeit the tuition money, nor the opportunity to work at D3.

Sharp at 9 am, on the first day of work, Naina dressed gracefully in a white salwar kameez climbed those dusty, wide steps again. Once again, she pushed open the big, blue-grey door and took a deep breath to suppress her nervousness.

The place appeared more uninspiring at the early hour. Most of the tables were unoccupied and the few people that were about, seemed too busy to take notice of her. She asked for Dilip to the first man who walked past. 'Not in,' he replied and walked away. Naina pulled up a chair slightly away from whoever's desk it was and sat down with her bag and papers on her lap. After another ten minutes, a man in a broad, egg-yolk yellow tie and hair plastered from one side to the other in flat half-inch bands that showed a bald pate under, came by, and asked her, bending down to her level so his tie touched his knee.

'Yes?'

'I—I'm waiting for Dilip.' Hesitating, she added, 'I'm joining today.'

'Okay!' He straightened up and his tie fell back on his shirt. 'Then why don't you come and sit with the others? Dilip doesn't come in this early.'

He was already leading the way. She followed him through the maze of randomly arranged tables to the end of the hall. 'My name is Raj. And you are—?'

'Naina.'

'Naina, glad.' He shook her hand and pointed to a chair. 'You can sit here. This is where the Creatives work.' Then just as suddenly as he had appeared, 'Ciao, best,' he said, flashed a thumbs-up, and disappeared.

She looked around. Two young men were bent over some drawings; one smiling, plump man sat looking at her from a corner.

As the place began to stir, the least action seemed to be in her section. A few smartly dressed women walked around self-importantly, holding papers, speaking on telephones. Men in ties rushed about greeting others, sipping from cups of tea and coffee. Nobody stopped to talk to her.

Yellow Tie looked her way once and smiled at her and she smiled back. After five minutes, when she looked up again, to her utter mortification, she found herself staring at him again. He raised his coffee mug to acknowledge.

'Would you like to read something?' The smiling man in the corner was standing next to her. He did not bother with intros.

'Yes, please.'

'Come, I'll show you.' She followed him to where the two men bent on the drawings sat.

Bookshelves covered one entire wall. She started looking for something to flip through, and Smiling Man went back to his perch in the corner, but continued to look at her. Quickly, she grabbed a book and returned to her seat. She mouthed a 'thank you' to the man who continued to smile. The book was on Mughal architecture, one she could flip through without appearing either frivolous or pretentious.

At around 11, a small boy with a misshapen wire carrier, precariously balancing glasses of tea, came by. He stopped at each table and handed out a glass. At hers, he stopped and looked.

'Chai? *Kaafi*?'

'Chai.'

He deposited a conical glass filled with tea before her and moved to the next table, but he kept looking at her. It was 11:30 when Dilip walked in.

'So, you're here,' he said. It sounded more like a surprise than a greeting. 'Let me introduce you to the gang.'

'Hey,' he patted a curly head on the back, 'This is—you are—?' He turned to her.

'Naina,' she flushed.

'I'm Arjun,' Curly Head said pleasantly.

'Naina is joining as apprentice copywriter,' Dilip said to each person. Almost everyone said something to the effect of a welcome, the pleasure of meeting. Intros done, Dilip pointed to the bookshelves and said, 'Pick up a black book from there and read.' Obediently, the first-day-apprentice-copywriter fetched herself a black book and was soon engrossed in it.

Around lunchtime, Smiling Man came back, 'Are you staying for lunch?'

'Yes.'

'The *chaiwala*, Chhotu, gets meals too. But you have to tell him beforehand.'

'That's okay, I'm carrying my lunch.'

He returned to his corner.

Naina flipped through more black books after lunch.

A glossy, green-skinned toad sat on a wide aquatic leaf. So real, it could leap off any moment. She ran one finger over its back, but felt another texture, from another time. Rubber.

A small rubber frog with a spring inside its belly.

She was sitting on the floor playing with it, pressing it down with all her baby might, and then releasing her hold to watch it jump. Lost to everything around her, drawn completely into her play, one time she pressed it so hard that the frog's plastic body was squashed flat. Either it was angered by that or hurt from being pressed on the cold cement floor, the frog leapt in the air and Naina's gaze followed as it landed on the silver-haired woman in a flesh-coloured salwar kameez chopping slimy bhindi, bits of which were hanging from the knife and from her fingers in trembling threads.

Angry eyes looked up from the big bhindi bowl resting on her bony thighs. She placed it on the sofa next to her and quietly wiped her fingers on a kitchen towel before getting up. A heavy palm landed smack on Naina's cheek. She was holding Naina by her shoulder in her gaunt fingers and had raised her hand to hit again, when Papa walked in. He caught hold of the raised hand and stared angrily into her face.

Bua let go of Naina. Papa walked out. No one spoke. Bua left their home that evening and never returned.

Papa had *abandoned* them—she had heard Nani tell the school principal, Sister Anne. She looked it up in Nana's Oxford dictionary. 'Abandon—leave a place or person permanently.' *Them* would be Amma, Tara, and her. What about Nani, Raju, and Ramprasad? Papa had also abandoned…left…them permanently. That made six of them. Papa's crime was compounded.

From a government flat in Moti Bagh, Amma, Tara, and Naina came to live in Nani's spacious home in Kailash Colony. It was not a big change for her—on most days she came out of the school gate to find Ramprasad waiting to take her home to Nani's. She would run to him excited at the prospect of not having to go home to unpredictable scenarios—the front door locked and no sign of Amma, or Amma sitting outside in the sun, her hair on her face, her rumpled clothes not covering her, talking to herself and very often, just staring at a spot of sunlight, refusing to respond to Naina. Ramprasad would lift her up and set her down on the front bar of his rickety bicycle and walk beside her for some time and then climb the bicycle to slowly pedal home. It was a two-kilometre distance, but there was always so much to talk, so much to tell him about.

'Ramprasad, you know it was Teachers' Day today? Everyone had brought flowers and cards for Miss. But Amma did not give me anything.' Or 'Ramprasad, today was the white uniform day and I went in blue. The principal made me stand on stage during assembly.' 'Why does Amma forget, Ramprasad?' Ramprasad would be quick to divert her attention, 'You know what Nani has made for you, *bitiya*? Pooris and kheer! Aren't you happy?' And all the little heartbreaks would be forgotten as he regaled her with the imaginary fights between the cook and the maid or how the milkman was chased by the neighbour's dog till his dhoti fell.

A siren went off in a nearby factory. She looked at her watch—6 pm. As workers spilled out of the factory gates in their navy overalls, Naina too got up to leave, to catch a bus to Maharani Bagh. Only Smiling Man responded to her bye. The Creatives had begun to work.

Reaching home at quarter to 10 after the tuitions, Naina found Amma waiting, sitting still on the divan. Naina had no energy for a confrontation. Amma did not say a word, but looked furious. How could Naina explain to Amma? Would Amma understand that she had taken up a job that would not pay? Would she understand that for just this once, Naina wanted to live this lifelong dream of hers? Naina knew that the timing was all wrong.

After two days of flipping through the black books, Naina was finally given work. Dilip decided that she could write mock ads. He would give her a brief and she would write the copy. He would then look at her work making a great show of the effort it involved, making it seem like her constant bothering was keeping him from the important work he was doing—reading *Zen and the Art of Motorcycle Maintenance.*

One day, she got to edit a brochure and on another, she wrote the copy for an actual client brief. Dilip made her write it again and again and with every iteration, it was a crisper, cleaner copy. Finally, Dilip rearranged her words and sent it to the client.

Soon he seemed to run out of ideas for pretend ads. One morning he said, 'Why don't you get a book from home to read?'

'I can do that at home,' she almost blurted out, but swallowed her indignation. Once again, she sat looking at the glossy pictures in the black books.

The winter sunlight was weak on the day she first spoke to him. They were sitting in the lawn in groups discussing the presentation each group was to make. He sat two people away. His voice was calm, his ideas clear. After the discussion, as they walked back to the classroom, Naina found herself walking alongside Deepak.

'You joined late?' she asked to diffuse the awkwardness.

'I was travelling on work. I work with my elder brother at his travel agency. Wanted to study advertising, but had no time. This seemed like the perfect opportunity. And you? What do you do?'

'Same as you. Work in the day. Less glamorous though. I give tuitions.'

'Dilip, please give me a brief,' scribble-pad and pen in hand, she stood before him like a schoolgirl. It was her day thirteen in D3. Dilip was still reading *Zen* and had his feet up on the table. Without looking up, he took the pad from her hand and scribbled, 'A premium whisky'. Dismayed, she said, 'But what would I know about whisky?'

'You don't drink?' He looked at her with a smirk on his face. 'Then you're in the wrong profession.'

Oh god! Such conceit! Naina fumed. As she sat doodling whisky bottles in her scribble pad, Arjun came by.

'Care for a chai?'

She looked towards Dilip who had *Zen* for his head.

They climbed down the stairs and came to sit on the last step. The air was still and muggy. The paint on the wall was cracking with heat and there was dust on the side of the steps.

'Chhotu *ji*, two chais—special,' Arjun shouted towards the big hall on the ground floor, his voice booming in the emptiness beyond.

'So Naina,' he turned to her, 'what's eating you?'

'Hmm...nothing,' she smiled politely.

He pulled out a pack of cigarettes and offered her one, smiled when she declined, and then lit it up. He kept puffing at it, but did not speak. It was like he was waiting for her to tell him something.

'I was reading this very nice book...' she began.

'What is bothering you, Naina?' he asked.

'Was just wondering why I'm here; if I've taken the right decision.' It came out on its own accord. She paused for his reaction, but he kept taking deep drags on his cigarette, without looking at her.

'I joined this place for the experience. I'm not being paid and there's nothing to learn.' Suddenly it felt very liberating to tell someone that she was working for free.

'It's not just you. We're all going through this. There is little work coming in. There won't be enough work for all of us for a long time. Do you think you'll get to write the copy when work comes? Don't kid yourself. I do my work here and I also freelance, so I'm okay, at least I get a pay-packet and I don't have to worry about sitting idle.'

They fell silent when Chhotu came with the tea. Naina was beginning to arrive at a decision. They finished the tea in silence. Arjun took the empty glass from her and leaving the two glasses by the side of the step, got up and extended his hand towards her, 'Chal'. By evening, she was sure. The dream had soured. The decision was difficult, but after making up her mind, Naina felt immensely relieved.

Monday morning, she called up D3 at 10, 10:30, 10:45, and again at 11. She wanted to get it over and done with. Though she had felt annoyed with Dilip, she could not overlook the fact that it was he who had given her this chance to live her dream, however brief.

At 12:05, when Dilip reached office, he took her call.

'Dilip, this is Naina. I'm sorry, I won't be able to continue. I wanted to thank you for everything—for giving me this chance,' she paused for his reaction.

'Okay.'

Okay was all he said. He had hung up. Naina stood listening to the silent buzz. Why did he take me in at all? But now she had no time to waste. She needed to look for a proper job. A job that paid.

Let us go, through certain half-deserted streets,
The muttering retreats
Of restless nights in one-night cheap hotels

She followed the sound of her own voice.

And sawdust restaurants with oyster-shells:
Streets that follow like a tedious argument
Of insidious intent
To lead you to an overwhelming question...

Jai was sitting alone in the classroom, listening. Naina tiptoed from the rear door and sat two benches away, careful not to make a sound. Jai sat listening, his unseeing eyes staring blankly ahead, his head occasionally swaying from side to side.

Oh, do not ask, 'What is it?'
Let us go and make our visit.

In the room the women come and go
Talking of Michelangelo.

The yellow fog that rubs its back upon the window-panes,
...

Jai always taught her something new. He knew so much. When they sat talking, time took wing and she always regretted when either of them had to leave. Within a week of joining college, they were discussing lessons after class. She read out to him whenever time permitted. Sometimes, she read into his cassette recorder. Being with the courteous and gentle Jai was restful. He did not ask her probing, personal questions like the others.

On winter afternoons, they sat on the sprawling lawns of the college and she read out texts to him.

One day, after she had read out *Ode to Autumn*, Jai remarked, 'It's beautiful. I like the softness of your voice.' A little awkward at the personal allusion, she searched his face for some trace of some other fleeting expression—there was none. To Jai, it was just an honest expression of his feelings, nothing more.

On days when the sky stayed sooty and the sun's weak rays did not reach them, they walked up to the college canteen to warm their freezing hands around tumblers of tea. Often, she noticed students whisper and smile on seeing them together. She often caught comments like, 'a good catch' or 'the blind got himself a beautiful stick'. Initially, it would infuriate her, but with time, she learnt to ignore such remarks. She did feel uneasy if the comments were within Jai's earshot. He maintained a stoic expression, but sometimes she could swear she saw a shadow cross his face.

Weird, *pagli*, crack pot, mad, crazy, idiot, abnormal, *khiski hui*—there was an endless list of names people called Tara. Being only four years older than her, Naina was not aware of how and when Tara's disability came to light, but as far back as she could remember, Tara had been like this. A blue plastic file had come along with their belongings, which did not proclaim in words, *Tara's Records* or *Tara's Medical Reports* or even, just *Tara*. Was it because, in writing, Papa was afraid to give the uncertain certitude?

Two months after he did not report to work, there came a letter from his office asking them to take away their belongings from the flat. *Vacate the flat*, it said.

So, Nani went there with Raju to *vacate the flat*. They came back with a tempo full of trunks and bundles of things tied in old bedsheets. How could Nani decide what to pick and what to leave behind for cleaners to take or laugh at? Could she leave behind her daughter's discoloured wedding lehenga? Or Naina's amputated dolls? Tattered picture albums? Books, diaries, or yellowing letters? How could she pick and choose from a family's trove of memories, the only proof that they were once a family?

After they shifted to Nani's, Naina had continued at her school and Tara at Sparsh, the all-in-one school for kids with disabilities. Sparsh was not a place where kids with disabilities were given specialized care or training so they could make sense of their surroundings and live life with the degree of dignity and independence each could. It was more a place they were sent to, away from their homes each day, so that their families could live with dignity and independence; go about their businesses of life normally.

Jai had an above-average IQ, as was revealed in the test they took in the first year of college. He always topped the class and remained well ahead of the rest. But this too was seen as a *side-effect* of his disability and not his personal achievement. *These people*, because they have one sense less, the other senses are sharper—and such was said. Bullshit, she wanted to tell the professors and students who repeated this self-importantly. Had they never known any blind student trailing in class or wallowing in self-pity, or worse, trying to live off and take advantage of others?

She first saw Jai on a swing, swinging high and laughing aloud—a pure, throaty laugh that plumped up on its own gladness to come out in a splutter that embarrasses adults. Waiting for her bus, she sat watching him. How oblivious he was of all the stares, the restraint and smugness of grownups. This simple joy of chuckling with delight eluded them. Her bus came and she left with the image of Jai laughing on the swing.

Did it help that he was born blind? Did it help that he had never seen, so he did not know what he missed? Did he miss anything at all? Jai reminded her of Tara. Was the unresponsive Tara capable of such joy? Did joy tied in a bundle, lie in a corner of her heart, awaiting release?

The blue plastic file contained an Assessment Card.

Name: Tara
Class: Pre-school 'A'
Father's Name: Advaith Singh
School: Blossoms Primary School
Montessori Apparatus: Needs practice. Confused.
Numbers: Needs help.
English: Confusion with phonetics. Needs constant encouragement.
Hindi: Confused with *swars*.
Adjustability: Does not mix with other children.
Punctuality: Satisfactory.
Cheerfulness: Unsatisfactory.
Creativity:________________
Promotion: Not promoted.
General Remarks: Refer to the letter attached.

The yellow card contained a letter.

Tara, a very lovable child is diagnosed with several characteristics of slow learners. Please consult a specialist. A special school for children with learning disabilities will be more suited for her needs. We hereby request you to proceed with the school-leaving formalities. We wish Tara a bright future.

It was signed, in elaborate loops by Mrs Kalpana Kapoor, Head Mistress. Yellowing, dog-eared, fold-marked; it was as if Papa had tried different folds hoping to somehow erase all this from their lives, hoping someone would tell him that his Tara was normal, or just about; or at least, with treatment would be.

A few other notes in Papa's immaculate handwriting were all that Naina had to understand Tara's condition. There was a letter from Dr Sumit Kumar addressed to Papa. The letterhead was of the Chicago Children's Hospital.

Dear Mr Singh,

From the details that you have provided about the condition of your daughter and the reports of Dr Mahajan of AIIMS, I am quite certain that your four-year-old is autistic.

Autism is characterized by repetitive routines and actions, lack of communication, and social awareness. The severity of autism varies. She might be able to do well in school and even lead an independent life when she grows up. She may even display an extraordinary talent in a specific area, such as art, music, or numbers. Although there is no cure for autism, appropriate intervention programmes can provide a positive impact on your daughter's development.

My advice to you is to place her into an appropriate intervention programme with a proper treatment plan with the supervisors there, at the earliest. Involve your family. Please do not hesitate to write to me for any other questions that you may have.

Best regards,

Dr Sumit Kumar

Naina remembered how Tara would sit in the front porch and spin the rear wheel of Ramprasad's old and green Atlas cycle that stood precariously on its stand, its rear wheel suspended. Sometimes, Tara would spin the wheel so fast that Nani worried the cycle would fall on her, but it never did. Tara would sit there for hours not feeling hungry, thirsty, or tired. Some days, if the cycle was not there, she would begin screaming. Naina did not like anything that Tara did. Tara would line up coins on the floor of the lobby along the line of the tiles and if Naina moved any, she would begin screaming and banging her head with her fists. Gradually, Naina learned to stay out of Tara's way.

On hot summer afternoons, when Tara preferred to stay on the porch rotating the cycle wheel, Nani would tell Naina, '*Laado*, go and see if Tara is okay.' Irritated, Naina would reply, 'I will not go; it's too hot.' Nani would say, 'She's your sister, Naina. Poor soul. God knows what wrong she has done in her previous births to deserve this.' Then just so Nani would not begin the long tirade about misfortunes—Tara's, hers, or Amma's—she would reluctantly go and peep out from the small crack in the door. Sometimes, she just made a pretence of going and instead of going to the door, took a round of the kitchen to come back and tell Nani, 'She is okay.' The same story was repeated every evening when Naina got ready to go out to play. She loathed to go tell Nani that she was going out, for invariably in reply, Nani would say, 'Naina, take your sister with you.' So, she devised new plans each day. She would call out from somewhere far from where Nani was. 'Nani, I'm going out to play,' she would shout and, before Nani could say anything, bolt out of the front door.

Naina was playing house with Anjali. They had tied the four corners of an old bedsheet to a pillar, two chairs and a tree in the porch and in the cosy hideout under it; they had set up their kitchen sets and dolls. When Nani sent out a plate with biscuits and two glasses of Rooh Afza, the two girls came out to sit on the steps.

It was a hot day. The plate with the orange crème biscuits sat on the steps beside them as they looked at the garden through the rose-coloured water, holding the glasses to their eyes. Tara who had been inside and who Nani had promised she would keep an eye on and not let out until Anjali left, suddenly appeared on the other side of their Rooh Afza glasses.

Tara walked straight to the plate of biscuits and after first arranging the biscuits into two straight rows, she picked one, opened to lick its cream and then stuck it back together and placed it neatly back in its place on the plate. She began doing this to all the biscuits.

Anjali looked at Naina. Naina quickly picked two biscuits Tara had not licked and handed them to Anjali.

Very calmly, but persuasively, Tara, without looking up at either of them, wrenched the biscuits from Anjali's hands and placed them back on the plate. Anjali tried to pick one again, but Tara pushed her hand away.

Anjali got up in a huff and started gathering her dolls and her beautiful blue tea set. 'I'll get you biscuits from inside, okay?' Naina pleaded with her, but Anjali left without a reply. At the gate, she turned around and called out, 'Naina, I will never come to play with you. Your sister is mental.'

Naina ran inside in tears, took out one of Tara's pictures from Nani's grey photo album and pierced a safety pin right through her heart. She wanted Tara dead. Anjali had told her about this when Sister Elizabeth died. Anjali had asked her to cross herself and swear to not tell anyone that Ayesha, who had been punished by Sister, had poked her mother's hairpin through Sister's photograph in their annual school magazine.

Carefully, Naina had read the notes in the blue plastic file. At four, Tara's autism was confirmed. The facilitator had ticked on a checklist:

- √ Echolalia: repeating something heard
- √ Lack of interaction with other children
- √ Preoccupation with hands
- √ Extreme dislike of certain sounds
- √ Extreme dislike of touching certain textures
- √ Desire to keep objects in a certain physical pattern
- √ Repetitive behaviour (preservation)
- √ Islets of competence—areas where the child has normal or even advanced competence
    1. Drawing skills
    2. Musical skills
    3. Arithmetic
    4. Calendar arithmetic
    5. Memory skills

At ten, the affliction was referred to as Rett Syndrome by one doctor friend of Nana's, who was visiting from America. But very little was known about it and it was considered convenient to continue as before.

Tara would spend the whole day at Sparsh. A van came to pick her up in the morning and dropped her back at 5 in the evening. After returning home, Tara spent most of her time in her rocking chair watching TV. She loved music shows. Nani visited the school sometimes to speak with the volunteers and the staff and to find out if everything was alright.

When Tara was thirteen, a volunteer at Sparsh suggested a new specialized centre for autism which happened to be at walking distance from their home. Tara was admitted to the Sunshine Centre.

Jai was completely independent. He could manage all his work without help from anyone. Would Tara be able to do things on her own? Some things? At home, they were always helping her. No one had the time or patience to help her learn. It was always easier—and faster to do it for her. After meeting Jai, Naina began to spend more time with Tara. She waited with her as she washed, cleaned, brushed her teeth, dressed, and ate on her own.

It was Holi. Their final semester exams were just two weeks away, but Deepak had insisted on taking her to meet his family.

Naina chose her clothes with care. She would have asked Reeta Bhabhi, Gupta Aunty's daughter-in-law, if she was around. But Reeta Bhabhi was visiting her parents. There was no one to ask. Red or blue? Pearl or silver? Studs or drop earrings? Too much? Too austere? How should one dress to visit the family one would be married into? What should she talk to them about? Should she make the effort to appear vivacious so they like her, or should she be quiet, so they like her? Most importantly, was it okay to go? Who could Naina ask? She was her own mother, sister, friend, and confidante.

At precisely 6 in the evening, she stood waiting on the main road. She had worn her green and maroon ikat kameez, a small maroon bindi, and had let her long hair open. Deepak's bike came to a silent halt in front of her and the way he looked at her, made her feel better about the effort she had made to look good.

Deepak stopped at the crowded parking lot of their Alaknanda flat and waited for Naina to alight, so he could fit his bike into its narrow slot between other two-wheelers. Naina suddenly felt very conscious, aware that someone may be looking out at her from his flat—from a balcony she could not see, from some window, from behind a chink in the curtains—scrutinizing her already.

They climbed up a flight of stairs. Just as he pressed the doorbell, Deepak sought her hand and squeezed it, murmuring, 'Relax, they're going to love you.' He tilted his head to his right and smiled. Riddhima, his sister opened the door and led them into the drawing room to meet Deepak's Bhaiya and Bhabhi. Their twins—Kunal and Karan were beyond themselves giggling and throwing teasing glances at Deepak.

Of the polite conversation they made, Naina could not recollect a word later, because Deepak sat across from her refusing to look away. Bhaiya spoke little, but was warm. Bhabhi appeared aloof and mostly did not look at her directly while talking. It was very clear that the household was wound around her manicured finger. Riddhima brought in the tea and as long as everybody sat in the hall—talking, gorging on delicious sweet and savoury snacks, and sipping hot tea, it went smoothly. Then Naina got up to help Riddhima clear the table. Once she entered the kitchen, the probing began. As she turned to return to the drawing room, Bhabhi stood blocking her way. Very sweetly, she asked, 'Naina, what does your father do?'

'He's not there,' Naina replied, not lying.

'Oh! And mummy?'

'She stays at home.'

Naina could imagine the questions forming in Bhabhi's mind.

'Doesn't keep too well.' She added.

'Who else is there?'

'A younger sister.'

'Studying?'

Before she could reply, Deepak was in the kitchen, 'Kohli Uncle and Aunty are here.'

Fast as a whip, Bhabhi turned to Riddhima, 'Riddhi, make sure you introduce Naina as your friend and Deepak, *you* be careful! I don't want the whole neighbourhood to start talking about *you two*.' Her voice was very stern. It struck Naina then, how quick her reaction to save their family's 'reputation' was and how insensitive where Naina's feelings about hers were concerned. But this was Deepak's family and she had decided to not judge them. She was still very happy that day after she returned home.

But Deepak was not there for her anymore. She wanted him now—this very moment, she wanted to be in his arms and wanted him to tell her again, 'Nain, everything is going to be alright. You are the bravest girl ever. I'm there for you, always.'

Always.

That is why she runs—to keep herself together; mind, body, and soul.

Naina got down at the Triveni circle and started looking for the address.

It was a nondescript building under the bridge, a five-minute walk from Bengali Market. Beyond the entrance, there was a long, dark corridor. A lone guard sat on an upturned tin, scraping with the back of his thumbnail, tiny mud flecks off his trousers. He saw the address in her hand and pointed to a narrow alley that led to a flight of stairs going down to the basement. Naina took the steps; the staircase was not lit and she hesitated. Looking back at the guard for reassurance, she saw him spitting phlegm into a potted plant. She hurried down the stairs. The luxury of not appearing for a job interview was not hers. Once at the bottom of the staircase, the surroundings altered dramatically. Entrances at both sides of the staircase led to plush offices. She chose the one on the right. Pushing open the glass door a crack, she peeped in and asked.

'Excuse me, I'm looking for Digital Wizards.'

A glum lady behind the reception desk nodded and Naina stepped in, waiting for her to look up again.

'Hi, I'm Naina, I have come for the interview.' The glum lady raised her chin to point towards a chair. Naina sat down, portfolio and handbag on her lap.

It was a tiny space with chairs on one side, the reception desk next to the entrance, one door leading to the workspace and another door right opposite where she sat now, probably the office of whoever headed the firm. Through the glass partition, she could see the workspace—straight long rows of worktables with computers and young people about. Most of them were barefoot and relaxed. Some of them looked back at her and their mouths moved to words that did not reach her. Then, two young men came out to the reception at the pretext of some work, stealing glances at her. She was wearing a red *bandhni* kameez and dupatta with a white churidar. Red was the colour of confidence, she had read somewhere.

The closed door opposite her opened as the peon took glasses of water inside and it remained open long enough for her to catch a glimpse inside. Two men sat behind a big table, neatly arranged with regular office-table paraphernalia—table calendar, clock, and pen stand.

The corridor was long and quiet at the hour. The only sound was that of their feet and of insects dashing their alien heads into the tubelights. Papa's call to the chowkidar was stern, the voice of authority that he assumed the moment they entered his office building.

Late into the evenings, bending over his work, Papa would suddenly want some file or paper and Naina would tag along with him to his office. The chowkidar would scamper through the corridors and with a '*shalaam*' to Papa and an exclamation for 'Baby *shaab*!' turn the keys in the huge padlock. He would then push open the collapsible grille shutters and switch on the tubelights one by one in the hallway leading to Papa's office. The door of his room screeched where it rubbed on the cement floor, streaking it with new quarter circles each time. Papa would immediately start flipping through papers. As soon as the chowkidar retreated into the shadows, Naina would climb into Papa's office chair. Round and round she would turn till all the things in the room—bookshelves, windows, curtains—became threads that wound around her so fast that even when she stopped, the room kept spinning around.

The glum lady slid her eyes from Naina to the door and said, 'You go.'

Naina sat quietly before the two men, as they skimmed through her resume. This is what she hated about walk-ins—the awkwardness, as each party was clueless about the other. They were pointing at certain things in her resume and talking softly. One of them underlined something, which made her very nervous. Scriptwriter—a writer of scripts. She was sure she could write.

'So, what have you been doing, Naina?'

'I was working with D3 as an apprentice copywriter.'

'Interesting. Why do you want to leave such a prestigious agency?'

'I have already left it. The working hours were a little—erratic. I have some personal commitments. I can only keep regular hours—they usually began work when it was time for me to leave. Besides, they do not have much work coming in now and I was not really learning much.'

'But is your interest in ad copywriting? Advertising?'

'I thought I wanted to do that, but I would love to do any form of writing.'

'We are looking for a scriptwriter and you don't have the training or experience for that.'

Wrong place.

'I can write well. If the job demands that, I can handle it. But if it requires me to have some other specific skill or training, I'm sorry I have none.' With nothing more to lose, she felt better being upfront.

'Have you ever written anything? Published anything? We'd like to see.'

Naina slid her slim portfolio across the table. It contained a few newspaper articles, some copyrighting assignments that Prof. Rajan had given good remarks on and the rare copy she had done at D3. The two men leafed through it.

'We'll get back to you' had the ring of 'sorry', she thought, as they got to their feet to shake hands.

It was 4 in the afternoon when she returned home, disheartened and drained. There was a look of surprise on Raju's face when he opened the door, and it immediately turned into that of relief. She heard voices coming from the hall.

Amma and Ajit Mama were sitting on the sofa and he was talking in a low, patronizing tone. Amma saw her first and her eyes widened with a strange mixture of dread and hate. When he saw her, Ajit Mama hurriedly stuffed some papers into the cloth bag he always carried.

'Namaste, Mama *ji*.' Naina sat down on the divan opposite them. Today she had to deal with this.

Ajit Mama smiled. '*Jeeti raho*'.

Naina's good looks, combined with her fondness for dressing up well, made her vulnerable to malicious gossip by people such as him. Neighbours too plugged suspicion into Amma's frantic mind. Naina wondered if looking plainer or dressing more inconspicuously would save her some trouble. It was only Amma's opinion she cared about. How she wished Amma would trust her more. Here was Amma, looking at her with disgust. Naina wondered what stories Ajit Mama had fed her today.

'Where are you coming from?' he asked, the confidence that Amma was on his side, clear in his tone.

Why does she dress up to attract attention? Why does she stay out so late? Why does she not have a decent job to show for?... She knew what was coming.

'How come you're here again today, Mama *ji*?'

'*Jawaab do*!' Amma suddenly thundered.

Naina had been pushed too far. The volcano had been dormant too long.

'Why should I answer? Who is he to ask me? What has he done for us? Has he ever tried to help us? I don't care what you think, Mama *ji*! I know why you come here. The day Amma signs those papers, you will throw us all out of this house!'

Amma sprang to her feet and slapped her hard across the face.

Stunned and humiliated, Naina stomped away. Let them do what they want! Who cares! We can live on the streets like dogs. This isn't much better, is it? She banged her bedroom door shut.

It was late evening when she came out of her room to find Amma and Tara watching songs on TV. Raju was sitting in a corner, peeling potatoes.

'Amma, I'm going to the temple with Tara. Will you come?'

Amma did not respond.

'Get up, Tara. Get your slippers. We are going to the temple.'

Tara got her slippers. Naina straightened her shirt and they came out.

It was a cool evening and the market was bustling. Inside the temple complex, people were coming and going, some sat in groups, talking. The evening *aarti* was long over. It would soon be closing time. Naina and Tara sat in the atrium where a cassette recorder played mantras. Tara hummed along incoherently, her fingers swirling the air. Tara loved being in the temple at this hour. It was a ritual they both loved. From the temple, they would go to the sweet shop, where Tara would eat her favourite *malai cham-cham*—neatly devouring the cream on top and then the succulent sponge of the rasgulla.

The cassette player was switched off and the murmur of people leaving rose to fill the sound vacuum. Then the brass bell rang out and its lingering reverberation seemed to hang in the air with the last scent of incense. The lights were being switched off one by one. The gods needed rest from the troubles of the world. Reluctantly, Naina got up. Tara was already walking towards the shoe-stand outside. They walked out, and holding Tara's hand, Naina walked past the mithai shop. She did not stop. Tara's hold on her arm tightened. Naina turned to look at her and burst out laughing at Tara's perplexed expression. Tara turned to go inside the mithai shop. Naina followed her and sat watching her relish her little treat.

'Come Meow, come drink the milk.' The skin on Nani's face bunched up around her eyes when she shut them so tight. Naina looked around for Meow. Perhaps Meow likes Horlicks; she hated it.

'Meow, my eyes are shut. Come and drink the milk. Let me see who drinks first—Baby or Meow.' Baby was me, was not it? Naina looked around, fearing that a big, black cat would emerge from under the curtains and standing on its hind limbs, begin to drink from the glass Nani was holding in her hand. She moved closer and wedging herself securely between Nani's knees, looked closely at her face. Little slits opened and shut right back.

Naina turned to look at Nana. He winked and swayed his head to one side in the manner of 'go on'. Naina understood then. Without taking the glass from Nani's hand, she started to drink, carefully looking at Nani's glass-holding hand tilt until the milk was over and then like a magician's, Nani's eyes opened wide and the face lines fell smoothly back in place.

'*Arré wah*!' she squeezed Naina into a tight hug, '*Lo*, this is finished! Where did the cat go?' Naina giggled and pointed to the window.

It was only 5:10 am. She was lying in bed looking out of the window at the dark sky.

'This *ghar*, Mata *ji*,' Bajpayee *ji* would tell Nani conspiratorially, 'is faulty. *Galt hai*! It lets in the evening sun, the last dying rays. What you need is the healing energy of the rising sun. But you have blocked it out.'

The main door was in the north, but the house faced west—if that's what he meant.

It was a sprawling house, now badly in need of repair—its exterior stucco walls seemingly held together by moss; the patch of tiled floor that ran around it isolating it from the unkempt vegetation surrounding it.

But not too long ago there was a velvet green lawn in the front, its edges studded with mogras; sturdy rows of hollyhocks and cannas camouflaging the boundary wall; carefully nurtured roses and lilies in neat flowerbeds; and the *madhukamini* that still stood outside Naina's window, had along with a *raat-ki-rani* infused the summer nights with its intoxicating fragrance.

At 7 in the evening, the cane chairs would be brought out in the lawn. Nana and Nani hosted elegant dinner parties. Naina, and often Papa too, would meet their guests there. Amma preferred to stay indoors, sometimes peeping from the windows and sometimes suddenly emerging to take them all by surprise.

Visitors would be served iced orange squash in tall glasses. Nani in her crisp cotton sarees would bustle in and out of the house. She would go into the kitchen to supervise the cooking and inquire if ice-cubes were aplenty. Naina would sit in a chair as long as she sensed eyes upon her; then, would wander off into the shadows—to the fascinating muddy rows of the white mogra blossoms—playing imaginary games until someone noticed her absence and took her inside to eat on the small cards table in the kitchen, which hoisted, on its crossed legs, a green rexine top that was fun to peel off when no one was looking.

The front porch opened into the lobby running the entire length of the house. The drawing room on the right had an ink blue Persian carpet and fawn-coloured wallpaper; from its high ceiling, hung fans with elongated stems like upturned flowers. Reprints of Rembrandt and Monet hung on the walls. Naina's favourite was Renoir's *A Girl with a Watering Can*. As a child, she had stood and looked at it for hours, imagining the life of a girl who had gold coloured hair like her doll, Sweety's. The more she brushed Sweety's hair, the frizzier it became, and the comb seemed to have more and more coils of yellow plastic in its teeth every time she sneaked it back into Nani's bedroom. Finally, when Sweety grew completely bald—Naina stood before *A Girl with the Watering Can* and wondered if she too would grow bald and have a neat line of holes around her pink skull.

The dining room on the left had a long teak table which sat eight. Most of the glass panes on the matching sideboard were now broken, letting in layers of dust into Nani's carefully collected crockery and cutlery. It was too much effort to keep them clean. No one visited them anymore and they had no use for fancy things.

Next to the dining room was the kitchen. Big enough for Naina to play carrom with the servants during the quiet hours of Nana-Nani's siesta. There were three other rooms along the lobby. Amma and Tara slept in one, and the one across from it was Naina's. It overlooked the garden and the *madhukamini* bush leaned on her window. Nana-Nani's bedroom and Nana's study at the far end of the lobby, which remained unused now, were the ones Ajit Mama wanted to be given to him.

The other end of the lobby opened into a concrete courtyard, which wound off towards the front of the house. A part of this was once a thriving vegetable patch that gave them tomatoes, brinjals, and succulent baby carrots. There were also papaya, guava, and pomegranate trees. The broken-glass-spiked boundary wall had a small rusty gate at the back, which suited Ajit Mama, who saw no reason why the house could not be divided into two with a separate entrance at the back for 'his portion'.

All ties had been broken with Ajit Mama. He had been taken in by Nana-Nani when his parents, Nana's second cousin and his wife, died in a train accident. Ajit Mama was ten years old, then. Legally adopted, he was, like the kids of Nana's other colleagues, sent to the elite boarding school in Dehradun, where Nana too had studied.

Like so many other family matters—the matter of Ajit Mama's fall from grace was also fuzzy—something Naina had only a vague idea about—enough for her to assume a manner of response that was in keeping with the general opinion about him at home—distant and cold. Later, growing up, Naina caught wisps—mention of his falling into bad company, of drugs, of bullying others at school, of stealing money. By the time he finished school, he was supposedly reformed. He did his BA while staying with friends because he needed 'his space'. Of course, he was home when he needed money, which was often. Later, he could not stick to any job. Nana, a well-respected, high-ranking official in the income tax department was very clear that he would not recommend his son to anyone and that Ajit Mama would need to get and keep a job on his own merit and hard work. This further soured the relations between the two. Ajit Mama borrowed money first from Nana to start a business—lost, borrowed more from others, and eventually left the debt for Nana to clear. He used Nana's contacts, drank heavily, and was locked up several times after street brawls. All in all, he had brought great shame to the family name. Finally, he was disowned—in every sense, except on paper.

Years after the ties had been severed, Ajit Mama came one day with his bride. Nana refused to meet them, but Nani's heart melted looking at the petite, petrified girl who came with her head covered and touched her feet. The girl had *sanskaar*s, Nani immediately decided, and hoped afresh that she would somehow reform Ajit Mama. She slipped her five-tola gold *kada*s into the bride's delicate wrists. The beautiful bangles that Naina so loved to clank on Nani's wrists—with elephant heads, their trunks raised to form an 'S' and eyes studded with rubies—sat clunky on the bride's thin wrists. The bride was from a wealthy family and her father had given her a big dowry—a flat and a car. It was also assumed that Ajit Mama would now be employed at his father-in-law's printing press.

But just like Amma's remissions, the periods of Ajit Mama's good behaviour were few and far between. The drunken brawls continued. The money at the press was misappropriated. There were talks of divorce, of his living separately, then of reconciliation. The drama was unending. Ajit Mama now had two sons and the wife seemed less likely to threaten with divorce. He was less brazen. Since Nana's death, he had again started visiting Nani and Amma regularly—almost every Sunday. He was received as family, because Nani with all her problems was grateful for all family ties in her old age. She had hoped that Ajit Mama would be of some support to Amma and the girls after her, but at the same time, had vehemently opposed any talk of dividing the property between Amma and him. She had told him clearly that what was his had been bequeathed to him long since and he had no claim on anything more. But Ajit Mama had kept trying and towards the end of Nani's days, the relationship was quite burdened with his intention of visiting them apparent.

Dark, heavy clouds scuttled across the morning sky, booming as they collided. Naina pulled the covers to her chin and lay snug in bed, looking outside. The *madhukamini* bush was shedding its snowy blossoms in a quiet circle under it. To lie in bed all day was all she wanted, but it was already 6 and she could hear Raju hum as he swept the porch. He was up early too. She sprang out of bed and was soon on the road—one foot in front of the other.

By eight, after a long, leisurely bath, she got into a well-worn green tee and jeans; it would be a do-nothing day. Amma and Tara were already seated at the table for breakfast. Neither responded to her 'good morning'.

Tara's dark, wet curls stuck in coils on her forehead, reminded Naina of Amma's. Amma's hair was greying fast. How grey, she noticed now. At forty-six, Amma looked much older with the creases around her eyes and mouth.

How beautiful Amma had been. The tattered albums with fading photographs that were now hidden away from all except her, flaunted a different woman. Young and bright, Amma with Papa. In Kashmir, both in overcoats surrounded by snowy slopes; Amma in a traditional Kashmiri *phiran* carrying a basket of apples; Papa's arm flung around Amma in red shoes; outside their government quarters with Preeti Aunty and her two sons, the group framed by the large-leafed money plant; and Naina, flanked by Amma and Papa with Tara in his arms outside the Taj Mahal—her eyes drawn out in kajal and white bloomers peeping out of her polka dot frock. That was perhaps their last photograph together. Some nights, when she found sleep elusive, Naina took out the old albums and spent hours looking at the photographs and wondering why things had changed. The Taj Mahal photograph always evoked some unease. Agra. It engulfed her heart with a deep melancholy.

Amma seemed to have forgotten last evening's episode, which was good, if only for a day. The change in weather had brought about a change of mood.

Whenever the skies darkened, Nani's household welcomed the sign of rain with pakoras. Raju had prepared pakoras for breakfast—

thin slivers of cauliflower, onion, potatoes, pumpkin, and brinjal dipped into a well-whipped besan batter and fried to a crisp, golden brown, the way only Raju could make.

Soon it was time for Tara to leave. Raju went to drop her to the centre, while Amma and Naina stood at the gate, waving, Naina calling out 'bye Tara' to no response. But she did turn to look at them more than once.

The heavy breakfast lulled Amma to sleep and she dozed off on the divan. Naina pulled a cane chair on the porch and sat reading the newspaper. At around 10, when she too was dozing off, she heard the phone ringing and scampered inside to answer it.

'Could I speak with Naina?'

'Speaking.'

'Hello Naina, this is Rajesh from Digital Wizards. I want to meet you today. Could you drop by sometime?'

'Yeah—sure. What time?'

'Can you come in within the next hour?'

'Um—okay. I'll be there.'

This could only be good news. She hurried into her room, opened her almirah and sat down on the bed looking for what to wear. The sky was at a tipping point, with the slate grey clouds rumbling on rooftops. She got into a pair of dark pants and shirt and was ready to leave.

Raju was chopping vegetables in the kitchen. 'Raju, I'm leaving. If I get late, you both eat. Give Amma lunch by 1:30 pm and make sure she takes her medicine.'

Then she went to look for Amma. 'Amma, the place I went to yesterday? For the interview? They've called me now. *Lagta hai, kuch kaam ban jaayega.* Something will work out.' Amma was sitting up, but did not look at her. Naina breezed out of the house holding Amma's unspoken blessing in her heart.

By the time she got off the bus near the bridge—this time on the other side, in front of the Hilton—it was pouring. The umbrella was of no help except to save her head. She took the short cut under the bridge and immediately regretted it. Slushy water seemed to gush in from everywhere and she had to hitch up her trousers to save them from the dirt, even though her clothes were now completely wet. The guard stood watching from his dry perch as she negotiated the stream that was the road, holding on to the folding-on-its-own umbrella, her wet trousers, and bag. Leaving the umbrella next to the guard, she walked down the dark staircase and, hoping she did not look as wet as she was, she entered the office.

Rajesh stood up and shook her hand when Naina entered his cabin. He was alone this time and looked a little surprised at her appearance.

'Naina, I must say, you write very well. I liked all your writings. Well, I'm happy to offer you the job. The requirement is immediate.'

'Immediate?—I mean, thank you.'

'Can you join tomorrow? Okay, I guess, I should tell you the details first. You will be part of a team of about six people, including graphic designers, programmers, and writers. You will report to the team lead. The working hours are 9 am to 6 pm, five days a week. You are not expected to put in extra hours unless the requirement is pressing and cannot wait for the next day. The project is already live, in fact, we've missed the first deadline. You need to work closely with the others as a team.'

Naina watched him transfixed. He paused to allow her some response and then, continued.

'Ah, and your salary has been fixed at 7000 during the six-month probation period and then we shall review it based on your performance. Anything else you'd like to ask?'

They are offering me 7000 rupees! No more tuitions? All the bills taken care of? It felt like a dream.

'Um—okay—I hope I'll be able to do what you expect of me.'

A hint of a frown creased Rajesh's forehead. 'You can write, right? All these are yours?' He pointed at the photocopies she had left with them the previous day.

'Yes, that I can.' She smiled.

Rajesh reclined in his chair.

'I think you'll be able to handle it. I think you have it in you, Naina. All the best. So, see you tomorrow morning at 9?'

'Yes, thank you very much.'

They shook hands and Naina walked all the way to Connaught Place in the rain that was now a steady shower, not bothered about her soaked trousers beating at her ankles, the locks of wet hair pasted on her forehead or the half-washed kajal.

All the way back home, all she had wanted was to get to Amma and share the news with her. She had wanted Amma to be the first to know.

'Amma! Job *mil gayi*! Very good job, Amma. They're paying me 7000 rupees a month! Imagine! *Ab sab theek ho jayega*, everything will be alright now; I'll take care of everything. Amma!'

Amma looked into her eyes like she did not believe a word, like Naina was lying. Naina pulled out the appointment letter from her bag and held it before Amma.

'It's true, Amma. See, here's the appointment letter.'

Amma pushed her arm away.

Why are you doing this to me? I am not the one who deserted you! I am not responsible for anything that is happening to us! Naina wanted to say. She wanted Amma to say something to her, express some joy, show some pride in her, but Amma was clearly adrift.

She thought of Nani, who would have embraced her and said, '*Shabbaash, meri laado*!'

This was all because of Papa. Where was he? Why did he never return? Why did he leave them? Questions that Bhabhi, Deepak's sister-in-law, had asked her that miserable day over the phone, two days after Holi.

Naina shut herself in her room again. After a good cry, she sat looking out of the window at the miniature pond forming under the *madhukamini*. The bushes, all washed clean, looked happy. It was a good day, she told herself. Her own problems were real. But Amma's? Poor Amma had to deal with all those imaginary people and the terrible side effects of the medicines without which even this semblance of a routine would not be possible.

Amma's reaction to the people on the roof vacillated between extreme fear and stiff defiance. Some days she threatened and hurled abuses at them and on others, she would not step out because of her fear that if she crossed the porch she would be in their line of vision from where they sat on the roof mocking her and telling her to do things.

Naina often tried to imagine what Amma saw and always visualized a row of little people, green as moss sitting on the wall, their legs dangling over the parapet. If only they were visible, real, she would shoot them in front of Amma. Bang, bang, bang with a pistol. Where would she get a pistol? Where did Nana get one?

No one knew.

Nana blew his brains out.

His head hollowed out by a single shot—a hole under the chin and another on the crown from where his brain shot out, splattering the lime-washed ceiling with blood and bits of flesh. His face whole, but only as a mask; his eyes shut, like when he slept in the middle of telling her a story. That's the image Naina carried from the hushed talk around her; from how she infused gaps in information with imagination. She had not seen anything. The room was sealed for almost a year—a big padlock hung from the latch covered in cloth with blobs of sealing wax that had also dripped and congealed on the floor under it.

For three days, after Nana shot himself, she did not know about it. She was at Gupta Aunty's house. Papa came to see her there a couple of times during the day. He asked if she had eaten, what she had eaten, or if she wanted something and then left, saying she must not trouble Gupta Aunty. Looking out from Gupta Aunty's upstairs window, she saw policemen and police jeeps outside Nana-Nani's house. On the third day, Papa came to take her back to their home and not across the street to Nani's.

When she went back to Nani's after a week, Nani looked like someone else. A little albino spot glistened in the centre of her forehead where the red, stick-on bindi used to be; the glass bangles were gone too. Naina felt awkward, almost afraid, and refused to go close to Nani, hiding behind Papa who turned around and glared at her, saying only, '*Arré*?'

Nani reached out and gathered little Naina in her arms, clutching her to her bosom so tight that Naina could not breathe. Then Nani looked at her face and smiled, though her eyes were still two streams, 'I will look after us all.' Never again did she say to Naina, 'Go, ask your Nana.'

Now, Naina would look after them all. The remaining all.

II

The coconut slid from her hands and fell. It struck the floor and broke into two. A hundred butterflies emerged from it—colourful butterflies, big and small that flitted about in initial confusion and then, certain of release, flew away in different directions. As she turned to look at it again, in place of the coconut shell, lay Amma's head—broken, empty.

Naina sat up in bed, wide awake. The dream, the horrible dream pressed down on her chest till she thought she could breathe no more.

'It's in her head!' Nana's angry words had boomed through the house, making its walls close in on her. Naina ran outside into the garden and hid under the guava tree so heavy with fruit that its branches drooped low, making it a perfect hiding place. With the sharp end of a twig, she cleaved into the smooth, peach flesh of its trunk. All her previous etchings were there, now dark and definite—apart from the conical hills with the sun wedged in between, there was Ramprasad's face with his big *lauki*-seed teeth; herself with long hair like Harpreet's; and a teacup she imagined blue in colour.

Naina began to tattoo her anxiety into an uncertain doodle when a scraping sound made her peep out. She saw Ramprasad, his body slanting forward like her cursive letter L, dragging the coiled hosepipe across the garden.

He spotted her just then and she came out walking up to him at the unspoken summon.

'*Arré, bitiya*, what are you doing hiding there? *Chup-chup ke* stealing my guavas? Let me see.'

He dropped his load and sat down on his haunches. 'Here's one,' he said, running his knobby fingers over her tummy. His fingers tickled her as he said, 'And—one more!'

She wanted to laugh, but Nana's angry voice would not leave her.

'Ramprasad?'

'*Bolo, bitiya*?'

'What's in Amma's head?'

Tapping his fingers on his head, exaggerating the gesture, he tried to gain time.

'Let me see—Chhoti Memsa'ab has beautiful things in her head.'

'Like what?'

'Like—um—,' he looked around, '*titiliyan*! Beautiful, colourful butterflies.'

'Do they fly? I want them to fly away.'

'Why should they fly away, *bitiya*? They are beautiful and pure just like Chhoti Memsaab.'

'You don't understand!'

'Then tell me, *rani bitiya*.' He put his hand on her shoulder.

Quietly, she disclosed her secret to him, 'If the butterflies fly away, she will become like everyone else's Amma.'

'*Arré*, *dekho* now, who will do all this work? Enough chit-chat, *bitiya*! *Chalo*, help me pull this pipe to the lawn. I'm getting too old for all this work.'

She stood away, watching him spray water on the lawn. On any other day, she would have taken the hosepipe from him and, squirting its mouth with her little fingers, turned round and round imagining rain.

'Ramprasad, I want another Amma.' And in that unburdening mood, she added, 'Not this one!'

Without waiting for his reaction, she fled inside.

Not this one!

With each step, her own cruel words thudded in her ears. She sprinted for a short distance and then slowed down to catch her breath. On some days, the physical movement forward did not help; reality dragged her back into the mire of memories, into her own guilt and shame.

The moment she reached the gate, she looked around for Amma. She was not on the bench outside. Amma was on the porch, trying to cross over an unseen hurdle. Someone watching her would think she was avoiding a puddle of water or something on the floor, but Naina knew. Blood? Fire? Glass? What were the people on the roof placing in her path now? In what new way were they terrorizing her?

Looking at her from the distance, Amma appeared so small, so scared as she changed her mind and turned to go back inside. Naina's throat constricted as she quietly followed Amma into the house.

It was her first day of paid work. Dressed in a dark teal coloured kameez and her favourite silver hoops in her ears, she sat down for breakfast with Amma and Tara. They ate in silence. A silence fragile like a makeshift escape route—they could go across without incident, but there was no guarantee that they would, that it would not give way, shatter, explode, melt, or be pulled away from under them. Like dust motes, nothing ever settled down in their lives; there was a constant whorl of disorder. Today was not a day to take a chance. Naina knew better than to trust her luck, even when all she wanted was to just be immensely grateful for times like these.

But when she looked at Tara now, she could not help smiling. Tara was starting to make streams of the butter melting on her hot aloo paratha. Naina gently rapped her knuckle; Tara looked up from her plate. Amma looked up too. And for the briefest of moments, they were all held together by an imaginary wisp she could call a family.

Just as she was slipping her feet into her sandals, ready to leave, the door of her room opened a crack. Amma flanked by Tara and

Raju stood outside. She had something in her hand, but she seemed to dither. Naina lifted Amma's palm covering what she was holding and asked, slightly irritated by her silence, 'What is it?'

In Amma's hand was a small bowl with sugar and curd. For luck.

A meals-on-wheels stood open, offering blanket-rolled sleeping people on its steel counters. A little ahead, in the main market, the mithai shops were stirring before the rest, even as portly, white 'On Government Duty' Ambassador cars with beacons were lining up to claim the first batches of sweets. Women in sarees, their heads covered, lean as the long broomsticks they swept the roads with, were raising miniature dust storms; and half-awake, half-clad *chhotus* vigorously washing shop floors were sending floods of water with sooty foam onto the street.

It took her only seven minutes to reach office through Bengali Market. She walked down the deserted alley to the basement. Thankfully, the reception was brightly lit and welcoming. But there was no one around. She settled into a chair. It was 8:40 am.

The place was so quiet that Naina did not think of looking inside the workspace. When she did, she turned away in a tricc, a little shocked. Through the glass partition, she had caught sight of bedraggled men in shorts and sleepwear gawking at her, as surprised as she was. A long sheet of foam was spread over the floor and covers lay on it in small mounds.

What have I gotten myself into? Naina panicked.

After about five minutes, the door to the workspace opened and a young man, now dressed in jeans and a tee, popped his head out and asked, 'Are you here to join us?' She nodded.

'Then come right in,' he said cheerfully and held the door open for her.

The work area had been cleared up. The bedding perhaps stuffed in one of the tall cupboards that stood in a corner. The young man introduced himself as Rahul. 'First of all, let me tell you, we're not always like this,' he grinned impishly. 'We've been staying back the past few nights to complete a project.'

Others started trooping around her. The feel of the black rubber slippers, she was required to wear inside, was unfamiliar.

'What about you? Where were you before this?' someone asked.

'Um,' what should she tell them, Naina wondered, 'I was with D3.'

'Wow!' Rahul exclaimed.

'Isn't that like—for want of a better word—coming down?' A chubby face whose name she had not caught, stared questioningly.

'I hope not.' And she changed the subject, 'Do you all—when do you go home?'

'Good question! Actually, *this* is home. When we go home, they refuse to let us in unless we show our IDs.' Everyone laughed as Rahul spoke. The office boy brought in tea.

'Don't freak her out, yaar,' someone remarked. 'Actually, girls don't have to stay back much as we would like them to.' More laughter. The jokes and backslapping continued. The office boys stole glances at Naina and smiled. The atmosphere was warm and friendly. DW seemed like a fun place, contrary to her impression of just a while back.

At 9:30 am, a girl with smart, cropped hair, dressed in tight black jeans and a tighter black tee walked in swinging a bright orange handbag. Everyone seemed to brighten up. She high-fived Syed about something and before keeping her bag in the overhead cupboard, took out a hairbrush and brushed her shiny hair vigorously. She was very attractive. Naina felt all eyes on them as Pari and she were introduced. Pari was as restrained as Naina was hesitant.

The workspace was divided into two sections—one side was for programmers and the other for the graphic designers, they explained, and continuing in the teasing vein, added that the 'content people' could sit anywhere.

Two other girls walked in talking animatedly with each other. Arundhati and Piyali were 'content'; both sharp and diligent-looking; and dressed typically in the image everyone has of writers and editors—ethnic kurtas, silver earrings, *jhola* bags, and elaborate bindis. Piyali shook Naina's hand and said, 'Welcome to DW', which prompted Arundhati to do the same, though not as warmly. The coldness of her light brown eyes was enough to keep anyone at bay.

It was almost 10 in the morning when Rajesh walked in. Lingering at the reception to check something, he looked inside the work area, and noticing Naina, smiled. Though everyone kept up the pretence as if nothing had changed, she sensed a certain straightening up—the laughter became a little muted, those sitting on the tables gently slipped down to walk back to their desks, someone remembered something to ask another, someone else thought it time to call for a meeting, and the place transformed into an office, as if an invisible hand had set the pieces back into their designated places on a giant jigsaw puzzle.

Later that day, Rajesh called Naina to his cabin and introduced her to Uday, the Project Manager, who had been away for a meeting in the morning. Uday, at first, seemed stiff and officious, speaking the precise welcoming words, answering Rajesh in a crisp formal tone, but he had a big laugh that seemed to balance it off. As they both stepped out of Rajesh's cabin after the meeting, he said to Naina, 'Let's go out for tea.'

He was her boss, Naina nodded and walked out with him into the hot afternoon.

'I'm wondering if I should introduce you to the adda right away or keep the pretence for today and take you to the chicer place in Bengali Market,' Uday stood thinking aloud, tapping his head with his index finger dramatically.

'Sorry?'

'Former.' He steered her to the left.

The adda was a *chaiwala* under the Hilton Bridge, where the breeze was cool. They sat on a stone slab propped up on bricks. Uday talked non-stop about work and Naina was thankful that this was not a probing session into her personal life like she had anticipated.

'I read all your writing.'

She looked at him in surprise. But he was not looking at her.

'I liked most—except that one op-ed about names. It had no soul.'

Oh my god! He's so direct. But imagine remembering? Naina smiled as she thought to herself.

'No defence?'

'No. It's your opinion. I liked it.'

'Wow! I would have expected a girl to argue this tooth and nail.'

'What do you mean *girl*?'

'Ah, there!' he said, smiling mischievously. She had bitten the bait. She liked him.

Back in the office, Uday gave her big binders to read. 'Let's find you a seat. Where would you like to sit?' he asked looking around.

'In a corner, please.'

'Okay, here.' To her dismay, it was right at the entrance of the bay—a corner one for sure.

'First rule: step out of your comfort zone.' He smiled and went away.

She read the binders self-consciously feeling all eyes on her all the time.

'Here, this is our style sheet. Read it *carefully*,' Arundhati tossed half a dozen sheets on her table.

By half past noon, everyone had gradually stopped working. Some ordered food from outside, some took out their *dabbas*. In the afternoon, they were all seated around a big round table to eat.

'Piya, you must discard this bit.' Arundhati held up the piece of tomato from Piyali's sabzi, its stem uncored.

'What! Gouge its eyes out?' Piyali asked in mock horror.

'Yeah, eating blind tomatoes is the least of my worries.'

Everyone talked about their food quirks for a while. As the conversation lulled, Piyali moaned, 'What a drag this project is!'

'You bet! I don't see it ending this year,' Arundhati said, stuffing bhindi into her mouth.

Uday spoke without finishing the food in his mouth, 'Two months max.'

A hush fell over. No one spoke. Uday's authority seemed undisputed. Naina had a feeling that he was disliked by most. After lunch, she resumed *reading carefully*. Shall I or shall I not? What will he think? What if he refuses? Let it be. Just try once—she kept vacillating, then finally, walked up to Uday.

'I had to join in a hurry. There was something I could not close. Is it possible that I leave a little early today?'

'Early like?'

'Four-ish?'

'You finished reading everything?'

'Yeah, I'll carry the style sheet to go over again later.'

'Okay, 4. Just today.'

'Yeah, thanks. Do I need to ask Rajesh?'

'Not required.' Uday said without taking his eyes off his computer screen.

The Malliks were sorry to see her go. 'Come and see us sometime,' Mrs Mallik hugged her at the door; the children along with the ayah stood waving till she came out of the gates.

Mrs Agarwal sat sunk in the orange velvet sofa, her shiny kameez at the brink of rupture over her distended midriff. Naina was not offered a seat and stood before her like a chastised child, as

Mrs Agarwal riled without looking at her, '*Pehle se batana tha*, *na*. Should've informed earlier. If money was a problem, we could have done something.'

Furious, Naina walked out of their place without taking the money due for the seventeen days of the month she had taught her sons. She clearly remembered having told Mrs Agarwal when her course got over that she would have to quit as soon as she got a regular job. At that time, Mrs Agarwal had said, 'Let's see when *that* happens'.

The editors met on alternate afternoons to discuss and review each other's work. Naina was part of the editorial team, but was a 'content writer'—still a rung below the editors, the more experienced. Before the first meeting, she was nervous all morning.

Pari had not returned from lunch, so the three of them met with Arundhati saying about Pari, 'Not that it makes any difference.'

Then, she began, schoolmarmishly, 'So this is about the local words for the travel project. Do we use 'e' for 'a' in words such as Banaras, kababs? B E N A R A S, K E B A B S? I prefer the 'e'?' she added decisively.

'Yeah, softer, more international.' Piyali agreed.

Naina nodded too. She asked, 'How much Hindustani?'

'Just don't use *chai, chappal, kurta, kishmish*...'

'Yeah, what's the point, if the user has to look up every word in the glossary?' Piyali seemed to agree with everything Arundhati said. Maybe they thought alike having been together longer.

'Oh, and Naina, why don't you start with the glossary? I mean, since you haven't started contributing any content yet.'

Naina singed inside, but nodded as they were interrupted by Sunita, the receptionist, who opened the door only so much so she could pop in her head and say, 'Hey, the HR lady from the head office is here and wants to see Piyali.'

'Tell her I'm in a meeting.'

'I can't tell her that. Go see her first. She's with Rajesh Sir now.' Sunita disappeared, banging the door for effect.

'Gosh, that HR woman is insufferable!'

'Tell me about it! Remember that meeting in the HO?' They began to giggle.

Not interested in their gossip, Naina attempted to bring the conversation back to the discussion at hand, 'What about words with double Os instead of a U? I am inclined to OO, as in ALOO instead of ALU.'

'Naina dear, sorry to disillusion you, but this thing we're working on is in English, so we aren't likely to write *everything* in *Hindoostani*—with double Os, if you please, so don't stress yourself so much.' Arundhati flashed an exaggerated smile and got up. 'Okay, dismiss! Get back to work.'

Pari entered office in low-slung striped blue pants and a white, tank top. She looked glamorous.

'Nice outfit,' Piyali said, admiring her genuinely.

'Thanks,' Pari replied and then for no reason, added, 'Sorry, can't say the same about yours.'

Silence. There was a complete hush for a long moment. It was Arundhati who spoke. 'You must be dispensing your style advice to complete strangers on the bus, no?'

There was a constant tug of war in the all-women content team, often not very discreet. Sparks flew about aplenty all the time, but within a week, Naina had become an integral part of DW. She was happy. Most of the male colleagues were friendly.

Her life too seemed to have settled into a neat schedule—regular and reliable, like Tara's. After she had breakfast with Amma and Tara, she helped Tara dress, because Amma, of late, though calm, appeared preoccupied. She left home at 8:15 and took the 8:20 chartered bus to Barahkhamba Road. Her seat was fixed—the first one on the right, just behind the driver. Now even the driver nodded and smiled at her. The others, all regulars, seemed familiar too. She reached office before 9. On most days, she and Uday were the only ones in office till around 9:30, when the others started to trickle in. Both enjoyed working in the morning quiet and getting a head start on the day. Others had the luxury of staying back late if they needed to, she did not. Uday stayed back late almost every day.

Back home too, everyone's routines were working well. By 8:30, Raju walked Tara to the centre. Amma spent her mornings looking at the newspaper or just brooding over some spot on the carpet, or trying to be out of the way of the roof people. The medicines made her drowsy and she usually slept after lunch. Raju picked Tara up in the evening. Tara was being initiated into simple, repetitive tasks. She was now wrapping chocolates made and sold at the centre.

There was a glob of flesh that moved up and down her right arm—a *gutli*, the size of a cherry stone. She moved her fingers over the skin and found it sometimes almost near the elbow, sometimes higher up. It was a game she played, running her fingers over her arm, feeling for it. She knew she should see a doctor, but Naina was not alarmed yet. She would be when it stopped moving, lodged itself into her flesh and grew root. Like things that take root in the mind.

Like little, green people. Green as moss.

She ran faster.

Amma was behaving a little strangely for some days now. Naina was on tenterhooks. Late for work, on reaching office, she found Syed and Uday bent over the morning newspaper.

'Away with the fairies—um…' Uday seemed engrossed. He sat on the table swinging his legs irritatingly and waved in Naina's direction when he saw her enter.

Arundhati walked in after her and announced, 'Piya isn't coming in.' Not getting a response from him, she shouted, 'I'm telling you, Uday.'

'Away with the fairies? Arundhati Ma'am?' He threw the question at her.

'Damn your crossword!' She shoved her bag in the overhead cabinet before walking up to him.

'Okay, what is it?'

'Eight. Second and third are N and S.'

'Insane—insanity it is, my dear Watson.'

'Yes! Done. So, what's her excuse?'

'Piyali is sick.'

'You mean *unwell*?'

'Yes, *indisposed*.' Arundhati imitated a perfect BBC accent as she sat down with Syed and Uday. Naina at her desk was not close enough to be part of the conversation and yet not so far that she could pretend to not hear them.

'There was a terrible jam on my way. A woman got hit by a bus. People were saying she won't make it. I used to see her around often,' Arundhati was telling them.

'Oh, you knew her?' Uday asked.

'No, I didn't know her, but she was—she was a bit "odd"—always standing somewhere in that area, wearing outlandish clothes and makeup. She had that strange look in her eyes. Away with the fairies, I would say.' There was a hint of a smile in the last comment.

'Where was this?' Syed asked.

'Near the Bhairav Mandir.'

Naina froze. She instantly knew it was the Big Woman. There was no point asking. A phone began to ring at the reception—its ringing reverberated jarringly in the relatively empty and now quiet office.

'Where's Sunita today?' Uday asked and went out to answer the phone.

'Must be caught in the traffic too, she lives in Sarita Vihar,' Arundhati said to Syed. The gathering had dispersed. The two of them went to their seats and switched their computers on.

How was it possible? How could a big woman like her not be seen by a driver? Naina realized that her hands were shaking. Who could she talk to about this? There was a meeting at 10; she had to gather herself before that. She quickly slipped on her shoes at the reception and came out of the office. Uday did not notice; his back was turned to her.

Was it the best way out for her? Death? How the passers-by had looked past her while she stood there, like she did not exist. On days that she was dressed more outlandishly than usual, or when she was talking to herself openly, loudly, weaving the air with her fingers, complete strangers smiled at each another, glancing at her. Everybody else—liars, cheaters, fraudsters, wife-beaters, husband-cheaters, paedophiles, addicts, bribe-givers, bribe-takers, doctors, lawyers, teachers, mechanics, mothers, grandfathers, beggars, rash drivers, people in fancy cars, rickshaw drivers, women wearing platform heels, women in Bata Hawai chappals—were together in their derision for her. All of them 'normal'.

An angry grunt escaped her lips and as the stress built up over the past few days began to surge, she began to cry. Then noticing passers-by staring at her, she turned into a quieter residential lane and stopped to wipe her face. That's when she sensed him behind.

'Whoa! What's this about?' Uday was panting beside her, not looking at her tear-stained face directly.

'Hey, is anything the matter?' Resting his palms on his knees, Uday bent down to look at her lowered face. Naina looked away.

'Do you want to talk, Naina?' he asked gently.

Naina's sadness, anger, and confusion tipped over. How long could she keep her secret from him. How long could she not talk of 'my mother said…' or 'my sister did…' before he and the others started wondering.

'My mother is psychotic. Schizophrenic. And my sister, she is autistic. *And* my father. He is not dead. He left us because he couldn't cope with it anymore. I live with them—my mother and my sister. I care for them. I love them. They never harm anyone. People make fun of them, tease them. They throw stones at our house at night. They write cruel things on our walls. They even hit my little sister with stones—brutes!' She broke down. Some people slowed down to look.

Gently but firmly, Uday caught hold of her arm and had her sit on a concrete tree ring. 'I used to see that woman too…alone and helpless,' she said after the storm inside had somewhat subsided. After long moments of silence, when she turned to look at him sitting next to her, Uday skipped off the ledge and offered her his hand, 'Let's get us a cappuccino.'

They took the longer route around the residential blocks, which calmed her. Uday spoke of the play he saw at Triveni and about bumping into Rajesh and his family there. He went on talking and she realized it was just like how she talked with Amma—he was speaking for both of them. She smiled. She also became aware of his hand still holding hers.

It was an oppressively hot and humid evening, as rainless monsoon evenings in Delhi are. Dilated pale, the summer sun lingered on the murky horizon, keeping the sky insipidly aglow. Switched on long before they were required, the yellow streetlights cast a fake sky-before-a-storm glow on the roads making people hurry over each other's elongated shadows. A meeting had delayed her; she walked as fast as she could and got on the first bus, packed tight with sweating bodies. When the bus broke down at the stadium and she had to look for an auto, she regretted not having taken one from the office itself.

It was almost 8 pm, when Naina reached home. Nothing seemed amiss as she opened the creaky gate and walked up to the porch, but then to her surprise, she saw the main door ajar. Open not as if someone had forgotten to close it, but open like it was meant to have been left so, for her to enter. Was there a visitor? Where were Amma, Tara, and Raju? There was no sound of anyone. Her heart throbbing in her ears, Naina stepped inside. As she turned to bolt the door, she saw Amma wedged behind it, her eyes wide. Fear gripped Naina's heart. And the next instant, she noticed the scissors—Amma was clutching a pair of scissors in her hand. Open scissors.

But she was hiding. She was afraid.

'What is it, Amma?' Suppressing her panic, Naina asked in a calm voice.

'Amma?' She repeated softly. *Where was Raju?*

'What's that in your hand, Amma? Give it to me. Have you eaten?' She edged closer and tried to divert Amma's attention, so she could take the scissors away. 'Let me see that.'

'They want the house,' Amma muttered, her knuckles turning white as her grip on the scissors tightened.

'Who, Amma? No one can take the house from us. I'm here, *na*. Why do you worry? See, now I have locked the door. No one can come inside, *theek hai*?'

Amma's glance shot behind her and Naina turned to look. She just caught a glimpse of Raju coming towards them and in a flash, Amma leapt forward with the scissors pointing at him.

Naina flung herself between them and caught Amma's hands with all her strength. Amma was frail, but when possessed like this, it was impossible to overpower her. Naina tightened her grip on Amma's wrists so hard that Amma had to let go of the scissors. Raju lunged forward and picked it up.

'You whore!' Amma hissed as Naina moved to pin her arms behind. She began to hurl the filthiest abuses at the two of them.

'*Dawai lao*!' Naina whispered to Raju, sending him off to get the medicine they gave Amma when she became agitated like this. Still holding Amma firmly by her arms, Naina pushed her towards the divan in the drawing room.

'*Haramzaadi*!' Amma spat at her.

All the years of listening to this—her own mother calling her names had not made her immune to it. Yes, Amma was unwell. Yes, she did not know what she was saying, but Naina had to really hold herself back from…hitting Amma. She tilted her head to her shoulder to wipe the spittle on her shirt, holding Amma by her bony shoulders. Very hard.

Every once in a while, Amma let out a shriek and tried to get away. She refused to eat or drink anything. It was 9:15, when she seemed to relax. Naina gestured to Raju to leave and waited for another few minutes before relaxing her grip on Amma's arms.

Naina followed Raju into the dining room. It looked like the whole room had been showered with shards of broken glass. The glass panes on the sideboard were shattered and every piece of crockery had been smashed. Among the broken glass were fragments of green. The lemon set was gone. Naina bent down to peer inside the sideboard and found one tubby green glass intact in a corner. She picked it up.

All through this, Tara had remained in her chair, rocking frantically at first and then falling asleep to its slowing rhythm as the chair came to a slow halt. Naina went into her room to freshen up quickly. She could not let Amma out of sight for long. Returning to the hall, she sat next to Tara and tried to wake her up, as Raju brought dinner in two steel thalis. He handed one to Naina and the other he held before Amma. Amma did not move, she was staring at a spot on the carpet.

'Chhoti Memsa'ab?' Raju tried to get her attention.

Naina coaxed her in a calm voice, 'Amma, *khana kha lo*. Amma, take your plate.'

Amma did not respond. Raju kept the thali before her on the table and Naina began to feed Tara. It was for herself—the mechanical breaking of roti, dipping it into dal, and taking it to Tara's mouth that slaked her anger and helplessness—stopped her from giving up.

Tara began rocking gently as she ate. She would soon doze off again. The thali before Amma lay untouched. Naina tried again, 'Amma, eat something. Shall I get you some more sherbet? Will you have some chai and biscuit?'

Later, after tucking Tara into bed, Naina ate in silence, watching Amma slouch on the divan. It was 10. They had mixed Amma's medicine in her favourite khus sherbet. Amma was tired and hungry and when Naina propped her up, she did not resist. She drank the sherbet and dozed off again. Naina let her sleep on the divan.

After locking all the doors, she walked into the dining room and picked up the lone green glass, washed it in the kitchen sink and rubbed it dry. Taking it to her room, she lay in bed looking at its tubby shape, its *khus*-green colour.

She had, one day, given up food and drink, demanding Nani let her drink from the green glass. Nani had relented. Nana brought the set down carefully, one piece at a time from the top shelf of the sideboard, placing it on the dining table. It was then carried by Nani on a tray to the kitchen sink where she rinsed it with vinegar and water till each piece sparkled. The old cook prepared lemonade and kept it in the fridge to cool.

That evening, chilled lemonade was poured into the green glasses and served on the lawn, where they all sat enjoying the cool, *madhukamani*-fragrant breeze. Nani refused to let go of Naina's glass. She held it from the bottom, while Naina sipped her lemonade. Nani must have declared a dozen times that she had bought the set for 30 rupees from Panchukuian Road almost fifty years ago and that she had cared for it for so long. She added that it was so delicate, it could break if held just a tad tightly. Immediately, Naina's grip loosened and the glass slipped from her sweaty palms into Nani's careful grip, '*Dekha*?' Nani was quick to admonish.

Uday slammed the receiver down as Naina entered the office. He looked angry, so Naina kept quiet. She switched her desktop on and began to clear her desk.

'You know what ergophobia is?' Uday was pulling up his chair close to hers. 'Aversion to work.'

'What happened now? Who has aversion to work, *ergophobia*?'

'What is your guess?'

Naina kept quiet. Uday continued.

'I think most people do. They want to get by with doing as little as possible. Infuriates me.'

'Pedagogy infuriates me.'

'Hain?'

'*And chimera.*'

'What's the connection?'

'None. Just wanted to let you know.'

Uday smiled at her matter-of-fact expression as she took out her things—pens, notepads, desktop calendar, a little box with stapler, scissors, and pins—and neatly arranged them without looking at him. The lines on his forehead fell off and he said, '*Chal*.' They stepped out for their morning cup of tea.

Uday could gauge her moods and make her talk. Naina was soon telling him everything about her life, family, and Deepak. When at sharp 6 in the evening, she would get up to leave for home, Uday walked her to the bus stop at Gopaldas Towers. She enjoyed this time with him. His quicksilver wit and practical outlook helped her stay balanced and view the day's irritants impassively. Also, Uday had a way with words that she found immensely engaging and funny. She loved it when she could help him solve his crossword.

There was a hushed silence when Naina entered office, late due to a meeting at Tara's centre. Everyone was working hard at appearing to work hard. At 10, her usual time, Pari made her film star appearance. She looked fabulous in a fuschia-coloured ankle-length skirt and a short white top. Fuchsia coloured, bangle-sized earrings hung precariously from her earlobes—elongating them to painful limits. Everyone seemed to avoid looking at her, though from the corners of their eyes, they were all watching her. Perhaps she was disappointed by this lack of attention, and because Piyali had kept her books in Pari's overhead space, she yelled, 'Get your stuff out of here, Piyali!'

'Office space is for office things. It's not your dressing table.' Piyali responded calmly, her allusion to Pari's personal paraphernalia taking up a lot more space than was allotted to each, apparent. She did not move to do anything.

'Uday, I want you to ask Piyali to clear her stuff from here.' Her screeching, sour tone jangled through the hushed room across to the corner where Uday sat with his head turned away from them. All heads remained turned away, deeper into their work.

Uday quietly swung his chair around to face her and said, 'Pari, you'll have to manage for today.'

Today? What was going to happen tomorrow?

The day was icy. No one joked. No one chatted. Tempers ran high over small issues. And when they gathered for a status meeting, Uday began by saying, 'And don't speak unless you have something to say.'

'Wow.' That was Pari—sarcastic like only she could be.

'Trust me.' Uday said, pinning her down with his cold stare.

At lunch, almost everyone sneaked out in groups. The few that remained ate in silence, an occasional laugh booming awkwardly. Everyone was trying to avoid something. Something that was looming menacingly over them. Naina was nervous, but she had learned to wait for things to unfold in their own time.

As evening approached, the morning's hushed silence became dense. At 5, just as Naina was stepping out for a cup of tea with Uday, she caught a glimpse of Rajesh and Pari through the half-open door of his cabin. When she left office at 6, they were still inside.

The next morning, the first thing she heard when she entered office was that Pari had quit. The big secret that everyone seemed to know was that she'd been asked to leave. But the next bit of news truly surprised Naina—Uday had got her thrown out.

How could he? How could Uday do such a thing? Shouldn't they have given Pari another chance, a warning perhaps? Naina wondered whether Uday was the nice, sensible, understanding person she believed him to be. When she saw him going about his work as usual, as if nothing had happened, as if he was not responsible for Pari's dismissal, she suddenly felt very unsure about him.

At lunchtime, when he came to ask her for lunch, she said she was not hungry.

'Come on, have some soup, at least,' he said.

Perhaps it would seem more professional if she just pretended that Pari's firing had not affected her. Perhaps he would tell her the reason for it.

They walked to Bengali Sweets, gave their orders and sat in silence till the food arrived. Naina swirled her pao bun in the steaming hot bhaji and began to eat, still silent. She watched Uday collect his pulao in a heap on one side of the plate, away from the runny raita aggressively moving towards it. After a bit, he gave up the effort and muddled the two together and began to eat. He talked of the morning traffic, the pollution of the Yamuna, his sister's wedding in winter, everything except office and Naina was soon responding, finding it difficult to doubt this person sitting before her, who she had begun to trust—and like. He must have his reasons, she told herself.

Back in the office, she continued to feel sorry for Pari. When no one was around at the reception, she asked Sunita how Pari had taken it.

'You know her, that bitch, she just came out, picked up her bag and left without speaking to anyone. Serves her right. She was so rude to me all the time.' But after a pause, she added, 'I think she had been crying. Her eyes were very red.'

Naina returned to her seat—imagine crying in public with fuchsia-coloured, bangle-sized earrings hanging painfully from your ear lobes.

October. The season of festivals. Of evenings glowing with string lights; of the volume of voices, radio, TV upped to hear over loudspeakers and bhajans set to film music. They had just bid goodbye to Ganapati Bappa and Durga Ma was at the doorstep. The markets were festooned with *Sale!* banners.

Naina was up to her nose in work and quite revelling in the involvement it demanded. She'd been with DW for almost three months and it felt like she'd been there forever. Steadily, she had picked up the other aspects of project development and a working knowledge of the production lifecycle. When she was asked to go through a CD due for release, she hesitatingly pointed out some issues she faced as a user and gave suggestions that eventually proved very useful. She had become an important 'resource'. Off record, the graphics and design guys began asking for her opinion. Someone would just call out, 'Naina, look at this, you think it looks nice with the solid blue background or shall I add a little gradient?' Because of her keen eye for detail, before long, she had become the unofficial tester as well. Whenever Rajesh sat down to look at a new creation, he would ask, 'Has Naina seen this? What does she think?'

In the monthly meeting, Rajesh announced that DW had bagged a prestigious government project. Everyone cheered and asked him for a lunch treat. With a great show of mock exasperation, he agreed. 'But before we leave,' he said, 'I want to congratulate our newest member, our "official tester" for her wonderful contribution, her diligence, and the speed with which she picked up new skills.'

Naina felt everyone's eyes on her and her cheeks felt very hot when she heard, 'Naina will now be head of the editorial team.'

There was an attempt at cheering—she could feel how subdued and insincere it was. Although the head of team was made on rotation, she was still new in the company and, for the others to accept this, would be hard, she knew. The content head automatically led the team of programmers and designers that worked on a project. So not only with the other two editors who did nothing to hide their displeasure,

Naina knew that with the other long timers too, it would be an uphill task for her to get work done.

They came out of the meeting room and the three editors got back to work. Naina noticed that they seemed to suddenly have very pressing work to resume. But then, Uday walked into the editors' bay, 'Hey, how about the new lead taking us out for a coffee?' Without waiting for anyone's reaction, he said, '*Chalo*, girls, let's go.'

'Gosh, you all! I could cut that silence with a knife. Like a piece of Karachi halwa,' he whispered to her as the other two got up without looking at Naina. They knew better than to refuse. The resistance had to be saved for more opportune times.

As the four of them walked to Bengali Market, a stray dog started walking with them, like he was part of the party. Arundhati constantly tried to keep a person between her and the dog. It was funny how she walked holding Piyali or Uday like a shield. When Uday stomped his foot at the stray to frighten it away, the dog bared its teeth and barking viciously, lunged at Arundhati who darted inside the nearest shop. Several passers-by picked up stones and terrified the dog into running away.

Once seated indoors, Arundhati relaxed.

'I am dead scared of dogs. You know, when I was in London, I used to see all these people walking their dogs and wonder how they were so calm. They never barked or attacked or chased other dogs…or people.'

'That's because they are all spayed,' she added when no one said anything.

'I think, it's rather cruel to suppress natural instincts. Imagine doing that to humans.' Piyali said looking thoughtfully into her ice cream float.

'But they do,' Uday said, calmly sipping his cappuccino.

'There is a big row in the UK about sterilizing teenage girls, you know.' Arundhati dispensed her knowledge.

'Temporarily?' Piyali asked.

'Of course, silly.'

They all laughed. Naina was beginning to feel uneasy about where this topic was heading.

'That's so Nazi.' Piyali blew at the ice cream with her straw.

'But what do you think about girls who are retard—,' Uday checked himself, 'Girls with neurological difficulties.' He chose his words carefully.

'That happens?' Piyali widened her eyes, pushing Arundhati's hand away as Arundhati tried to stick in a straw to sip from Piyali's glass.

'It is done with consent from parents—family.' He looked at Naina to add something, because she had been so silent and suddenly remembered. But it was too late to change the topic.

'What a shame! That's what I call a dog's life!' Piyali sucked the last dregs of her soda noisily.

When Nani took that decision for Tara on the advice of the counsellors at the centre, Naina had no idea there could be any opinion to the contrary. Now she felt the need to defend their decision. She could not let them, who knew nothing about what families such as hers go through get away with their quixotic ideas.

'It is not a casual decision for parents—or caregivers. They don't do it for their own convenience. It is in the best interest of the girls—those—um—who are "not all there".'

Naina spoke without looking at anyone. 'In our country where you and I, even with the help of all our faculties, education, lessons drilled into us, cannot protect ourselves from the perverts roaming the streets, in our homes even, how do you think these girls will take care of themselves?'

'You are right, but...,' Arundhati began patronizingly and for the first time ever, Naina cut her short.

'You know, it depends on the condition of the person, if they can manage their period, feel and enjoy a partner's love, become mothers, raise children, there is no justification, I totally agree. But mostly it's the family and caregivers who are the victims, really. So, reserve this empathy for them.'

There was an awkward silence.

Naina felt the need to diffuse the unease. 'My sister—Tara, has autism—non-verbal, which means she does not speak. She is eighteen and a beautiful person. Wouldn't hurt a thing. Yet there are those that won't stop to think of her condition before they harm her.'

'I'm sorry if I sounded rude. Didn't mean to. Totally understand,' said Arundhati.

As they filed out of the coffee shop, at the door, Uday placed his hand on her back. Naina realized she was beginning to come to terms with the realities of her life. She was glad for his support, his listening ear.

It was all over, before she reached the hospital. Amma had succumbed to her head injuries. There was nothing left to be done. Raju was looking at Naina in disbelief. Amma's body lay covered in a white sheet. The doctor, on being told that she was the daughter, lifted the sheet from one end. Amma's face was covered in a bandage. It ran over her forehead, head, ears, and under the jaw, as if trying to hold it all together. The rest of the body was unscathed.

Naina collapsed in a bundle on the floor.

Later, sitting on a very cold, steel chair, while the formalities of what she heard repeatedly as 'handing over the body' were going on, she kept wondering how Amma, sitting and stroking her hair in the sun that morning, had become a 'body' within hours.

Naina had returned from her run a little early and sat outside in the mild morning sun massaging oil into her hair. Amma came with her cup of tea and after several furtive glances at the roof, sat down beside her. For some time, she sat sipping tea and then all of a sudden, Naina felt Amma's fingers touch her hair. She turned around slightly to see Amma holding a crumple of her hair in her bony fingers. It was a caress. The only one. And now Amma was gone. Naina gasped for breath.

The police were there. Uday spoke with them huddled in a corner and then, came to ask her, 'Do you have any papers—prescriptions at home that say that she was—about her illness?' He fumbled. She looked up at him in disbelief, then at the policemen. 'It's a legal matter, Naina. We need to show them that she was unwell,' he explained.

'The papers are at home.'

Uday turned to the policemen, who were eyeing Naina all the time, and tried to steer them away from her a little. He came back to her with some papers to sign. Naina signed without reading. Two hours passed. The words 'mental case' were heard again and again, with no sympathy for, no apology to, her mother. Naina sat on the cold metal chair totally detached from the scene around her—doctors talking in hushed voices; uniformed policemen in a corner, eager to close the 'case'; nurses brisk on their feet and referring to people by their bed numbers; until Uday's soft voice drew her back into the new reality of her life, 'Naina, let's go.'

Desperately, she looked for Amma. She was coming along—all ready to leave, covered in a sheet, with Uday walking beside the stretcher on which she lay.

Naina sat with Uday and Raju next to Amma inside the hospital ambulance. Gupta Uncle sat in the front. As the ambulance weaved its way through familiar streets, she looked out at the world that seemed to go on, as if nothing had changed—a *paanwala* sitting on his raised perch creating perfect triangle bundles with practised ease, handing them out to waiting customers; a small, shirtless boy holding his oversized shorts with one hand running after a worn tyre he whacked; mothers busy in small talk, waiting at a bus stop to pick their kids off their school buses, a hand extended out of a car driver's seat, ashing a cigarette.

Naina closed her eyes and saw Amma sitting on the stone bench in the morning, when she was leaving for office. Amma was wearing her favourite lemon-coloured salwar-kameez, examining her toes. She did not look up when Naina called out, '*Ja rahi hun*, Amma, I'm leaving.' She was so used to Amma not responding that she did not wait for her to reply and walked away.

Naina had just entered Rajesh's cabin with Uday and Varun for a meeting when Sunita interrupted them. 'There's a call for Naina. It's an emergency.' Gupta Aunty was on the line, 'Naina, come home fast. Your uncle and Raju have just taken your Amma to Batra hospital. She is very badly hurt. Fell from the terrace. *Bas, tum jaldi aa jao*, hurry.'

They immediately left in Rajesh's car. Uday sat holding her cold hands at the back, while Rajesh sat next to the driver. On the way, Rajesh called up the hospital from his cellphone and was told that a woman named Naintara, who was brought into the Causality a little while ago, had been declared 'brought dead'. It was 10:30. It was all over in a couple of hours.

Rajesh and Uday made all the arrangements and informed Ajit Mama. The house was soon full of neighbours, all talking in hushed tones. They had taken care to change into white clothes. Women sniffed into their white dupattas from time to time. Ajit Mama came at 2. He wept aloud and touched Amma's feet. 'How much she suffered, my only sister,' he said to all and despite his reputation, got sympathetic pats and shoulder-squeezes. He came to Naina and for the first time in her life, she let him embrace her. She wept as he held her. Ajit Mama looked around and asked for Tara. 'She's at school,' said someone. 'We must call her', 'She might not understand anything, but we must call her for a last *darshan*', 'These things are important,'... the whispers around Naina grew, but she stayed adamant—she did not want Tara to witness this.

She saw Uday busy with the preparations for the cremation. He followed her into Nani's room when she went in to fetch a diya and finding her alone, he held her hand and whispered, 'Naina, I'm so sorry.' A sudden helplessness came over her and she sank on Nani's bed. 'I can't go through this,' she wept. Uday held both her hands, as she pleaded with him, 'Please bring her back, please. I can't live without Amma.' People gathered around them again and Uday left the room quietly.

At 4, the convoy left home, its porch still bespattered with Amma's blood—now dark and congealed—a strange rangoli at the entrance. The demons that leeched on her mind, making her incapable of differentiating between dream and reality had managed to prevail over her that morning as Amma walked down the parapet wall. Raju was returning home after dropping Tara at the centre. As he closed the gate, his back to the porch, he heard a loud thud and turning around, saw Amma lying on the floor, her body still, her head smashed. He called out to Gupta Uncle and they rushed her to the hospital. They knew she would not make it.

They had arrived at the electric crematorium. Naina kept looking at Amma's face, not knowing when the last glance might be. Is this how she would remember her always—dressed like she was now, against Naina's wishes? Like in life, in death too, the important thing seemed to be her married status. 'Yes, she is married, though God knows... But it can't be said for sure that she is widowed, so she is married,' the women had argued. Their decision prevailed and Amma was dressed in her wedding lehenga and sindoor applied to the visible part of the forehead. In death, she looked unlike how she had looked in life.

Naina prayed in her heart to be spared this. She could not allow them to take Amma away. And yet, there now, she was going away. 'But she's already gone,' they whispered as several hands held her back. 'How can she be already gone, she was here stroking my hair and not replying to me some hours ago?' she protested.

'I want to see her; I want to hold her. Please, not yet, don't take her away, please don't. What will I do without her? Please help me,' she pleaded with everyone.

People she did not recognize were holding her and murmuring incomprehensible, illogical things. She was slowly giving up the fight. She was too tired. She wanted to sleep. She collapsed again.

The porch had been washed when they returned. Amma's picture had been placed on a side table, dragged to the centre of the drawing room and a lighted diya set before it. Tara was home, sitting in her rocking chair, her feet tucked under her—a sign of anxiety that Naina recognized. Her expression relaxed when she saw Naina.

Naina patted Tara's head and hurried inside, choking on her tears. She just wanted to get into the shower, but stopped when she sensed Tara's footfall behind her. Naina turned and took Tara into her arms, trying not to cry. Tara stood like a mannequin, a reluctant receiver. She was all Tara had now, and Naina, her. Steadying her voice, Naina said what she needed to, 'Amma has gone, Tara. You will not see her anymore. Tara, baby, it's just you and me now.'

The next day, Ajit Mama, Tara, and Naina went to immerse Amma's ashes in the Yamuna. It was noon when they returned home. A congregation of assorted footwear—shoes and chappals had formed a strange pattern at the entrance.

As they stepped inside, Raju's gaze tried to convey something to Naina, and following it, she saw Deepak and Bhaiya sitting in the hall beside Amma's silver-haired photograph. Till now, she was mechanically doing everything she was required to. The parameters of propriety had just been lowered for her during this tragedy. The neighbours, who usually turned away their heads on seeing her and whispered behind her back, were outdoing each other to offer help and sympathy. But she knew that this was temporary; that they would soon put the tragedy behind and begin to castigate her for being too unfeeling, too practical, or the most scathing—being loose. There was no point worrying about them.

They got up on seeing her. Naina folded her palms and sat down next to them. Bhaiya spoke some comforting words that she did not try to comprehend, her eyes were fixed on the dusty footprints on the white sheets they sat on. She had stopped listening to what people were telling her. It only made it more difficult for her to hold herself together. She wanted to look into Deepak's eyes, to find comfort there. She imagined how Bhaiya and Bhabhi must have fought over their coming here. Bhabhi would have said there was no need for them to go. Bhaiya would have remonstrated that at such a time of grief, even an enemy would visit. She must have said that he could go alone, that there was no need for Deepak to accompany him.

Deepak remained silent and their worlds suddenly seemed too far apart.

When Bhaiya got up to leave, Deepak also rose. Naina walked them to the front door. Bhaiya nodded to acknowledge Tara's presence as he walked past her chair.

'Her sister is also like that,' Bhabhi's words reverberated in Naina's head. 'Her mother is completely *pagal*. It runs in her family!

You want Deepak's children to be like that? God knows, she too may become like that,' Bhabhi had spoken what others had, until now, only alluded to.

As Bhaiya walked out, Deepak turned to her, 'I'm so sorry, Nain. Let me know if you need anything,' he looked into her eyes as his own filled up.

No words came to her. People standing around were still saying how tragic it was that her mother should kill herself by jumping from the terrace and how difficult her life must have been after her husband left her and it was all fate and destiny and before she knew it, Deepak and Bhaiya were slipping their feet into their shoes and walking away.

She heard the women whisper, '*Kaun hai*? Who's it?', and then the sigh, 'Now who's there to ask.'

Naina came back to sit with Amma's silver-haired, diya-lit portrait and some women came to sit beside her. They spoke unfelt, repeated, rehearsed words of comfort. They cried, thinking of their own sorrows. Raju stood in the kitchen doorway, watching.

Naina woke up when she heard Amma's footstep. Amma was walking out of the room; she turned around to look at Naina for a moment at the door and, then, was gone. Naina looked around and realized she was sleeping in Amma's bed in the room Amma had shared with Tara. Tara, in the other bed, was fast asleep. She repeated the Gayatri mantra three times and then walked up to the door to peep out. The glow of the diya fell eerily on everything. It highlighted the dark spaces taken up by things. Raju was a bundle on the floor. She stepped into the lobby and then walked to her own room to check. Again, she felt Amma in the house, the low grunt that she made came from behind the door of her room. She turned to look and saw Amma behind the door looking at her.

'Who will marry her, Karuna?'

Naina overheard Nani speaking to Karuna Aunty who was visiting from Amritsar. Who could Nani be talking about? Naina stopped and quietly moving close to the wall, tried to listen.

'She'll be straddled with these two. And people will always know about Naintara and Tara, and say that it runs in the family. How long can I be around for them, I'm eighty-four now. You know, Karuna, even criminals and their families are not ostracized like this.'

What's wrong with Nani? Naina wondered. What is she talking about? There's also Nana, herself, and Papa, who are 'normal'. Why would people think of me as being Amma's daughter and not Papa's—the brilliant economist and writer? I must be hearing it all wrong. Anyway, I'll marry who I want to marry, and that person will not care about all this. Why would he care for anyone else? But Naina did not feel like going in to meet Karuna Aunty. And just as she was turning back, careful not to be heard, she saw Amma's face, her eyes looking at her as she too stood quietly behind the half-open door of her room. Amma was looking right at her and a chill ran down Naina's back. She retraced her steps back into her room and, bolting her door from inside, she came to sit on the window seat.

Was Amma also hiding? Listening to the conversation? How much did Amma understand? Did she hear and understand everything and just pretended that she did not? Was it because it was too much effort to make sense of the goings on, the way 'normal' people thought and behaved? Were people like Amma just tired of making sense of the world and its people?

A havan was held on the 13th day. Close to four dozen people came to pray for the peace of Amma's soul. Naina thought about them—Uday, Rajesh, Rahul, Varun, and Sangeeta from the office,

Shruti and Bhawna from Tara's centre—people who had never met or known Amma. Jai came with his mother. The pundits, neighbours and some of Nana-Nani's friends came too. Food was cooked for all—potato curry with pooris, sweet and sour dry pumpkin sabzi tempered with methi seeds, *boondi* raita, peas pulao, and rice kheer—all that she had seen Nani get cooked at every puja or festival. People were smiling and talking more today. Some ladies dressed in white, continued to sniff into their pallus and eye Naina's composure with censure.

Ajit Mama sat with Tara and Naina beside him for the havan. Smoke rose from the flames and filled the house with a pious fragrance. Amma's eyes from her face in the frame, watched everything.

Food was first served to the pundits. When they were all seated in long rows, Naina doled out ladlefuls of kheer into their slotted, steel thalis. The rest of the food was served by Raju, Ajit Mama, and his wife. Tara sat in her rocking chair, ignoring the spectacle before her and completely engrossed in munching pooris. Rolling a poori, taking a bite, and then opening it to look at the several half-moons, Naina seemed fascinated by the shapes she bit into.

That night as she lay in bed, trying to sleep, the questions that had bothered her for so many days, rose again in Naina's disquiet mind—Amma never went up to the terrace. Why did she go that day? What had happened there? Had she, in a false sense of bravado, confronted the green people? Did they terrorize her into jumping down? Mocked or challenged her? Had Naina missed some vital clue to Amma's mind that morning? Could she have paid more attention? Could she have gauged her mood and stayed back at home?

III

The respite from heat was now complete. Blankets and soft Jaipuri shaneel razais were out of trunks and lofts, smelling of mothballs. Sleep was agreeable. The winter smog hung low over Delhi's skies. Vehicle fumes, smoke from the small fires of fallen twigs and dry leaves that night-watchmen lit to keep themselves warm, and from the coal braziers on handcarts, hazed the horizon.

It was a sunny Saturday afternoon. Naina was volunteering at Tara's centre, something she had been doing for the past few weeks. She had just finished sorting the books in their small reading room and had gone to look for Tara, so they could leave a little early.

Following the muted strains of *Do-re-mi…* to the music hall, she saw from the doorway, the back of a man giving an affectionate tap on Tara's head, saying, 'I'm afraid that'll be all for today, love. I have to rush now.' Still turned away from her, he bent down, picked his bag and said to Bhawna, a part-time volunteer like Naina, who was sitting with them, 'Ask Tara's family to buy her a synthesizer if they can. Nothing fancy, a simple keyboard. It will do her a whole lot of good.' As he turned to leave, he came face to face with Naina. Pausing for a second, he smiled and walked away.

Michael! *Michael Jacob*!

Naina could not wait for Monday. On entering office, she saw Uday pacing up and down the hallway, deep in thought. Naina pushed her bag into the overhead cabinet and said, 'Guess what?'

'Can't.'

'Why?'

'Bad mood.'

'Why?'

'Just some stuff. Chai?'

'Let's go.'

The strong, boiling-hot concoction that the *chaiwala* under the bridge called 'tea' was very welcome as the winter's grasp tightened. Once they were seated on the cold stone slab, she asked.

'So, what's the worry?'

'Nothing. Some people will need to go. We are feeding parasites. Good for nothing.'

'What? Who?'

'You will know soon enough.'

'Hmm.'

'What now?'

'It just reminded me of something I don't want to think about.'

'Out with it then. *Do chai*,' he called out to the *chaiwala*.

'Gupta Aunty had come with a woman to take care of us and live in our house. She said that Raju must go now that Tara and I, "two girls", are alone. Raju was in the kitchen, probably listening. I felt very angry, but I know Gupta Aunty meant well. She said if I can "maintain" both, I could keep Raju as well.'

'I too have been thinking about this.'

'What?'

'I'm only asking you, Naina. Is it okay to have him around?'

'Okay? He's family. And it was not as if Amma was *protecting* us from him or something!'

'But you do understand, no one can be trusted. Do not you worry about leaving Tara alone with him?'

'You wouldn't say that if he were a male relative—a cousin or an uncle, no?'

They sat in her angry silence for some time.

'Tell me, what's running in that pretty head of yours.'

Naina swallowed her pride. She needed to tell him, talk to him, and have him approve.

'I remember that day like a picture. Raju used to run errands for us then. It was a freezing cold January morning. I came out of my bed and saw Nani snuggled into a razai on the divan in the hall. I ran and got under it too. She was so warm and soft. She held me tight. Just then, the door opened, and Raju entered with the milk. He carried it to the kitchen, leaving the main door open and an icy draft hit us. I shouted angrily, "Who left the door open!" He came running back to shut it and looked terrified. I noticed then that he was barefoot and wearing only a pair of shorts and a worn, oversized sweater. Later, I saw him sitting in a corner of the porch having tea and bread. I felt ashamed for my comforts then. We gave him warm clothes and soap to bathe. Nani grew very fond of him and I cannot even remember when he came to live with us. He's been part of our family. He genuinely cares for us, especially Tara. I cannot think of our home without him. That is, unless he wants to leave us.'

'But you admit, there is a risk?'

'Yes, same as it would be if the two of us lived with another male, even a blood relative.'

'That settles it then, doesn't it? As long as you know what you're doing, Naina. And in a way, I do think his presence around the two of you is good. Now tell me what was that big smile in the morning about?'

'Guess what?'

'Tell.'

'I met my school crush at Tara's centre on Saturday.'

'Which one?'

'Okay, be mean and I won't tell you anything!' she turned her head away in mock anger, but unable to contain the excitement, was soon telling him.

'I met Michael Jacob! The *god* for us in school. I was so crazy about him, everyone was. One day, Sister asked me to take a bottle of water to him. I couldn't believe my luck. He just looked up from his guitar and signalled with his eyes for me to leave the bottle next to him on the floor. Then, he mouthed a "thank you". I was gliding on air all day. How everyone envied me!'

'Hey, if you do not mind me breaking your reverie, who's this Michael whatever?'

The boy handed them grimy glasses of the sugary, milky tea.

'Michael, the musician! He came to accompany our Opening Chorus each Annual Day—he and two other guys with their electric guitars. Those two wonderful months when the rehearsals were at peak and they came in every day, all the girls in school swooned over Michael. I think he knew. During the recess, he would play popular numbers that sent everyone into a tizzy. It was a sight—girls leaning out of the upstairs corridors and windows, crying out for more the moment he stopped.'

'And now?'

'He's volunteering at Tara's centre. He is teaching Tara to play the piano and wants me to buy her a keyboard for her to practice at home. Said it would do her a world of good.'

'Did you tell him about your crush? Is it revived?'

'Do not be mean. You know how it is. It was so beautiful. Those days...'

'And these? What about the present, Naina? When will you begin to live in the present?'

He looked at her gravely. She looked away. Putting her glass of tea, still untouched, down on the stone slab, she paid the boy four rupees and stood up to go.

'*Chalo*.' Uday sighed and got up too.

Naina was looking forward to meeting Michael at the centre the coming Saturday. She took care to not mention it to Uday though. On Saturday, she tried to downplay her own excitement by dressing up casually in a pair of jeans and a navy t-shirt, but they still reached the centre early. Naina left Tara with her group and headed straight to the music hall. She went looking from room to room. Michael was not there.

When it was lunchtime for the smaller kids and she was halfway through patiently helping five-year-old Meethi learn how to eat with a spoon on her own, the grains of rice all over the table and on Meethi's person, the muted strains of a familiar tune wafted straight down the corridor from the music hall to her. Quickly handing the spoon to another volunteer, Naina ran towards the music hall.

'*People talking without speaking, People hearing without listening, People writing songs that voices never share…*' the words played in her head as hope and apprehension slowed her pace midway down the hall. There was a familiarity in the song that was more reminiscent of her little sister's frail, tentative fingers than her own school days.

Naina stood in the hallway watching from a distance. '*Hear my words that might teach you, take my arms that I might reach you…*' Tara played on.

Someone laid a hand on her shoulder. Naina turned to face Michael. The surprised look on his face transformed into a smile. Awkward as it was, she did not wipe off the tears streaming down her cheeks. Michael moved to the window ledge next to them and sat down, his face turned away, waiting for her to collect herself.

When she emerged from the washroom later, her eyes still very red, she came face to face with Poornima and Michael, waiting for her in the corridor.

Michael extended his hand. 'Michael.'

'Naina.' She said as she shook his hand, very lightly.

'Naina is Tara's elder sister and a volunteer here,' Poornima completed the introduction, smiling, but looking quite perplexed.

'Glad to meet you, Naina,' Michael looked into her eyes as if to check if the tears were spent.

'Tara is an absolute rockstar, isn't she?' he smiled and very abruptly, turned to leave, '*Chalo*, I'll catch y'all again soon.'

Naina smiled too, suddenly feeling quite light. There was no need to tell him about school.

Naina entered the claustrophobic Burma Bazaar in the heart of Lajpat Nagar Market. Cramped shops on both sides in a small alleyway flaunted gleaming imported ware—crockery, watches, electronics, and toys. Big-bosomed, perfumed Punjabi women in bright salwar-suits were haggling over imported cut-glass and baubles. Sunita had bought a keyboard from here last month for 1,800 rupees, but she thought she'd seen one that came for less.

Every year by July, Nani would start making enquiries. 'When is Rakhi?' 'Have you posted rakhis for Rishabh and Rohan yet?' 'Do it today or they'll never get it on time.' She was very particular about Naina sending rakhis on behalf of both Tara and her, to Preeti Aunty's sons. Preeti Aunty was Amma's second cousin, settled in Liverpool. In response to the rakhis, Preeti Aunty would sneak in a couple of pound bills into the envelope with her reply. This was one treat Naina looked forward to each year—her own money. Naina's list would be ready months in advance. That August when the money came, she had wanted to buy herself a hairdryer and a bag. 20 pounds—1,400 rupees! The hairdryer would cost 600 rupees, which would leave her with 800 rupees for the bag and something for Tara. But with how the finances had stretched this year, Naina had just kept the money away. Now it might be just enough for what she wanted to buy for Tara.

'Yes, madam?', 'Please come, madam', 'Imported perfume, madam', 'Lace bras, panties', 'Latesht, lycra, perfect fit', they roared in her ears. Naina avoided eye contact and searched for shop number 38.

'Keyboard,' she mumbled. What if Sunita had not heard or remembered correctly? She only had 200 extra, which she would much rather save.

'Here, madam. Yamaha. Best. It has…'

'How much is it?'

'4-9-9-9.'

'No, no. Show me something—cheaper.'

'Okay, here Casio. Only 3,000. And this model only 2,200.'

'You do not have anything cheaper?'

'Tell me your budget, madam. *Sab* adjust *karenge*.'

'Um...1,500?'

'Okay, here is one good model for 1,700. Fixed price.'

She shook her head and started to walk away.

'Madam, listen, *arré suniye toh*! Come, come. Tell me what you want. I have many more. See this one…only 1,300.'

Naina turned around; the salesman was holding it up for her to see. She imagined Tara's delicate fingers falling gently on those keys.

She was home much before Tara returned and had fallen asleep waiting for her. At the familiar sound of the gate opening, Naina woke up with a start and rushed to look out of the window. Raju was holding the gate open, letting Tara in. Naina watched her baby sister from the distance and noticed for the first time that her striking appearance—the mop of dark, unruly curls that hung over her large brown eyes and her luminescent skin—could no longer mask the stoop of her spine that was now becoming more pronounced and her wide gait was quite unmistakable too. Naina noticed how Tara's soft features highlighted by her innocent expression, made her look much younger than her eighteen years. How would she protect this harmless young woman from a world that only believed in what it saw and heard, but could not feel?

Tara stepped in quietly through the front door and headed straight to her rocking chair. Raju went into the kitchen to get milk for her in her yellow cup. Naina picked the keyboard from the table and placed it gently on Tara's lap and waited. Tara stared at it.

Naina pressed a key—tunn… Tara frowned. She waited for a few seconds and then pressed the same key—tunn… Naina pressed another—tunn… Tara pressed it too—tunn… Naina pressed three—tun, tun, tun. Tara pressed exactly the same ones—tun…tun…tun…. Then her face relaxed.

The cup of milk lay untouched on the table next to Tara, as she played her uncertain music for the next two hours. Naina and Raju went about their chores with their ears to the music, a little light of heart, a little joyful too.

Her computer was taking forever to boot. Sitting alone in the office, she missed Uday's company. He was on a week's leave for his sister's wedding. There was a lot of work and responsibility on Naina during his absence. Although he was on leave, he dropped by now and then to check on things. She hoped he'd come today. As she bent down to check the connections again, she saw him enter. His nose red and cheeks stained where the chilled breeze had made his eyes water.

'Hi, Rudolf!'

'It's biting cold!' He smiled and began to loosen the grey muffler around his neck.

'I love that colour—your muffler.'

'Harbour grey. I bought it only because the tag said that. It sounded nice.'

'Like I once chose curtains that the salesman called "leather brown". They appear so drab now.'

'Marketing.'

'Content.'

'Yes, that's why we'll do so well together.' Looking at her puzzled expression, he explained, 'Our company?'

For some time now, Uday had started speaking of "the company" they would start—he and Naina. Naina had taken it lightly, especially because he always added, 'when we grow up'.

'Tell me, what would you call the colour of your shirt?'

'Plum.'

'*Arré*, that's such a chestnut. Use Indian context.'

'*Shehtoot*.'

'Perfect. You shall be the "director of—names? Words". Now, let's get us some chai.'

'Puddle brown.'

'*Keechad*?' he said and laughed to see her grimace.

It was the day of the wedding. Naina had no plans to go for it. She had told Uday that she could not leave Tara and go out at night. But Uday had been very insistent. He swore that if she did not turn up at his home by 7 in the evening, he would drop everything and come to pick her up himself. He would carry her away just as she was, he had said.

The January evening was folding up fast and everyone began to leave early. By 6, the office was deserted. Prakash, the security guard, popped in to check and was surprised to see Naina at her desk. 'Madam, you are not going for shaadi?' Not wanting to explain, she said, not lying, 'I'm just leaving.'

She had just picked up her bag to leave, when the phone rang.

'Tell me, it's not true. Tell me, you're not in office. Naina, please! Come today, it's a request.' Uday pleaded.

In the background, she could hear the merry sounds of a wedding house, full of people.

'Naina?'

'I'll come, Uday. I'll go home, pick up Tara, and come for a short while.'

'Okay, please do turn up. And try not to take too long—please?'

'Bye.' She took an auto home.

It was 6:45 when she reached home. Winter darkness had wrapped itself eerily around the house. Slivers of light that seeped out of the kitchen window fell on the still plants braving the cold. Raju had forgotten to switch on the light on the porch again. Naina opened the gate and started walking towards the door, trying not to look up. Just under the porch, she shot a quick glance at the roof and began to ring the bell frantically. The line of the parapet was clear. But they could be anywhere in the dark. A chill went up her spine. Raju seemed to take forever to open the door.

'It gets dark early these days, do not forget to switch on the outside lights. Someone can hide in the darkness.' Naina tried to conceal her panic.

Tara was rocking her chair a little faster than usual, her eyes very red. Raju brought Naina a glass of water and said, 'Tara Didi did not eat anything, no lunch even.' She touched Tara's forehead. It was burning. Raju fetched the thermometer. 103 degrees. Naina gave Tara a paracetamol and started sponging her forehead. By 7:45, the temperature had come down. But Tara still refused to eat anything.

There were only two musambis in the fridge. Musambi juice was her favourite, so Naina sent Raju to get some more from the market and went into the kitchen to juice the two.

When the doorbell rang, thinking it must be Raju, she unbolted the door and turned away without looking.

'Naina?'

She froze at the sound of his voice. Uday stood at the door, looking very handsome in a dark suit.

'You here? Now? You shouldn't be. It's your sister's wedding. I can't come. Tara's ill.'

Raju entered with the sweet lime. 'Didi, you go. Now the fever has come down. I will give Tara Didi juice.'

Naina tried to reason with them, but neither Uday agreed to return without her, nor did Raju stop making her feel like her presence was absolutely unnecessary there. She helped Tara, who was dozing off, to bed before rushing to her room to get ready. Uday sat in the drawing room nervously tapping his shiny black shoes.

When she came back to the hall, dressed in a midnight blue silk saree, pearls in her ears and around her neck, and her hair neatly piled on top of her head, Uday gaped at her. She blushed, but with a wave of her hand dismissed his exaggerated look. Checking quickly on Tara and giving Raju a hundred instructions and assurances that she would be back as early as possible, she left with Uday.

As she alighted from Uday's car right at the entrance of the flower and fairy-lights bedecked house, Naina was aware that all eyes were on her. There were some mock disapprovals by the people waiting for the baraat, but the jovial wedding mood made it all agreeable. It was sheer luck that the baraat was late, they said, as they thumped Uday on his back, lovingly. That she'd been the reason for Uday's disappearance at such a crucial time was obvious. Naina was extremely conscious as Uday introduced her to his father and other relatives. An elegant white-haired woman came out of the house carrying a thali in her hands and stopped to look at her affectionately, 'So, this is your Naina? Welcome, *beti*, Uday talks so much about you.' A little surprised by all the unexpected attention, but warm with the feeling of belonging that she could not remember when she had experienced last, Naina followed his mother inside.

'Sneha will be glad to see you. She's a bundle of nerves right now. The baraat is also so late.' Uday's mother led her upstairs.

Naina braced herself before entering the ladies' domain. Heavily made up and jewellery laden mannequins chattered and giggled, some audaciously checked her out and others ignored her completely. Sneha could only muster a 'hello', but squeezed her hand affectionately. Naina sat there for a while; then excused herself and came out looking for her colleagues. She borrowed Rajesh's mobile to call home and Raju assured her that Tara was fast asleep and had no fever.

It was well past 11 when the dinner got over. Rahul was to drop her home, but he was still sitting with a drink in his hand, looking very high. Uday who'd kept an eye on Naina all evening—looking at her over somebody's shoulder, behind somebody's back, smiling at her while performing a ceremony—read her anxiety.

'*Chalo* Naina, I'm going your way to collect something. I'll drop you home. Rahul, you take your time, buddy, I'll be back in a jiffy.' He did not give Rahul a chance to respond.

The winter fog was wrapped around the streetlights like candy floss. The streets were deserted. Naina could not remember when she had stayed out so late last. She said the things-to-be-said to the host about how wonderful the arrangements, the food, his family were. And Uday added some interesting tidbits about his extended family and friends that she had met. Then Naina, a little stunned by the realization of her circumstance, suddenly said to him, 'It would be strange, wouldn't it, if a girl of twenty-three has not stepped out of her home at night ever? If I say, this is the first time I'm out on Delhi's roads at this hour?'

'Not at all. In fact, it is rather exceptional for a girl of twenty-three to not just be living independently, but also supporting and caring for a family of four.'

'Three,' she corrected him, but the praise lit her up. She realized that he had taken a detour and they were now driving towards India Gate, which looked surreal in the glow of yellow lights, grandiosely silhouetted against the darkened sky.

'Ice cream?'

Her first reaction was to say no, to remind him that they should hurry back, that she could not stay out like this, that there was a sister back home, probably still unwell. But before she could say anything, he asked again, 'If you're feeling virtuous, vanilla; if up to some fun, chocolate; and if you're really in the mood for mischief, a slurpy orange candy!'

'The last.'

When he got back into the car and handed her the orange bar, the wrapper dusted with frost, her conscience wavered again, 'You should be back at the wedding.'

'You'll always remain vanilla in your head. Come now, finish that; otherwise, Raju will see what mischief you have been up to at midnight!' He laughed and stepped up the speed as they rode through long tunnels of the tree-covered roads.

When finally, the car halted in front of her gate, Uday turned towards her, 'Good night, gorgeous,' his voice was a whisper and Naina felt a sudden rush of emotion as he leaned back and touched her cheek lightly with the back of his hand.

As she shut the car door behind her, the curtain moved in Gupta Aunty's window upstairs. It was well past midnight.

The house was divided into two. Ajit Mama came with his troupe on Sunday. The back gate that led in through the kitchen garden was repaired. The two rooms at the back were emptied and the common doors between the two portions were barred on Naina's side. Amma had signed the papers. Naina did not protest, accepting it as Amma's wish, but sorrow stalked her all day. When the night brought distance from the mechanical goings on, she felt it gnaw at her.

The only place she had ever called home, had been split into two. Her childhood, her memories lay scattered everywhere; shouldn't she have gathered them to her side for safekeeping? Was it possible to have ripped them from their roots and expect them to pulsate still? She closed her eyes and from some recesses of her memory, the smell of water on parched summer soil rose to fill her senses.

She heard Ramprasad sprinkling water on the summer-dry, concrete floor of the courtyard. Half a roti was still on her plate, she needed to hurry, or she would miss him. Lifting the bowl of *aam ras* to her mouth, she gulped it down at one go. Grabbing the remaining piece of roti, she ran outside to watch him cool the floor. He would fill the mug from the bucket and grabbing its wide mouth with his palm, sprinkle water, making swift up and down movements with his hand. Sprays, and from the larger gaps between his fingers, spouts of water fell on the floor exposed all day to the hot sun. The sweet smell of summer rain rose in the air.

Nani's loud warning—'Naina, do not get your clothes wet'—made Ramprasad turn to look for her. He caught the mischief in her eyes; she, his sanction. Naina ran and took the mug from him. They giggled as her grubby palm tried to cover its mouth in vain and when she took it upwards to gain force, the mug emptied itself on her. The feel of cool water in the sweltering heat; the tickle of defiance; a few moments of glee—short and fleeting; and the two were ready for reprimand.

When she came out later with Nana, the charpoys would be ready, covered with the white mosquito nets tied to tall bamboo sticks that stood with their long legs crossed. It would be her *ghar*, her house for the night. Lifting the tightly tucked net just a little to let herself in, Naina would slip in on the smooth white sheets. Nana would get in after her. *How come she slept with Nana and woke up with Nani? Are they one? Does Nana become Nani and Nani, Nana? Perhaps they take turns because Nani has so much work to do. But to be Nana must be difficult too—to sleep in the afternoon, to listen to the news, to take teeth out at night, and fit them back first thing in the morning?*

She would wait, lying perfectly still beside him, as Nana took off his spectacles, folded them and kept them on the little stool beside the bed and then begin his *kursi kahani*, his adventures on the flying chair. She imagined it to be like the one in his study, only with the seat covered in red *makhmal*, like he described. Nana would sit on it and command it to fly—over the electricity poles and the mango trees, over the Yamuna shimmering with the zigzag of streetlights, over dark public parks, where fountains that no one watched sprang in a gay, solitary dance. He would spin for her a funny, naughty tale each night. When he sat on the chair, he was a different Nana. A happy Nana.

Listening to him, her gaze would move to the yellow light of the windows; the clank and clatter of steel pots and iron kadais being scrubbed and kept away; the muted, night-voices of Nani and Raju. A cat silently trapezed the glass-edged boundary wall each night. Naina wondered, where the person who put the glass pieces in the wet cement got them. Perhaps he broke all the glasses in his house and asked his neighbours for those they broke—accidentally or by children. She was sure one morning that she would wake up to the sight of the cat dangling over the wall, impaled by a shard of glass. The blue one.

Nana asked her to count the stars when he began to doze. Besides the flying chair, she liked to hear the story of Alibaba—the sound of hooves, of the 40 horses riding towards the cave, towards them. Tab-rak, tab-rak—Nana would make the sound of the hooves and tap his fingers on his chest to keep the beat. Panic would rise in Naina's throat. She would look sideways at his closed eyes and the heaving of his chest—his loud breathing. His voice would slowly begin to trail. When it stopped, she waited. Sometimes it came back, but mostly Nana turned to his side, away from her and all she heard were soft snores.

Kitchen work over, Nani would come out and close the courtyard door from outside by latching it at three places and then putting a heavy, black padlock on the middle latch. As she slipped the keys under her pillow, Naina would realize it was her last chance. She had to go. 'Nani, *shu-shu*.' 'Oho! Couldn't you say a minute earlier? Just now I've locked the door. *Chalo*, come out quietly and sit in the corner.' Nani would propel her to the dark end of the courtyard. She'd hurriedly pee squatting on the floor near the drain and run back. 'Can I have some water?' Nani would tilt the fat-bellied earthen surahi to fill the steel glass covering its mouth with cool, earth-smelling water.

One big room with an attached bathroom and a small kitchenette was rented out to a Malayali couple—the Panikers. Both were working and returned home after 6. Every Sunday, they visited the temple. The aroma of sambar was the only distraction they caused in Naina's household.

The other room with a makeshift bathroom was rented out to a Punjabi bachelor—Chopra, thirty-ish. Chopra became a nuisance. It began with him requesting Naina to allow him to keep his motorcycle in the front porch, as the back gate was still quite rickety and he was worried his brand-new Yamaha would be stolen. She consented on the condition that if he came after their locking the front gate at night, he would have to park it elsewhere. Every morning, when he came to take his bike out, he would kick-start it and keep the engine running, while all the time looking at Naina's window. She fumed at the sound of his bike and started locking the main gate early. Sometimes he came, and seeing the light in her window, honked, but nobody opened the gates.

It was a beautiful Sunday morning. Immediately after his sister's wedding, Uday had flown off to London with a project proposal. Naina was waiting for him to return, so she could tell him about the partition of her home. Just as she settled down on the window seat with a book, Chopra appeared at the door.

'You lock the gate early these days?'

'Yes.'

'I was wondering if we can have another key made for the lock.'

'Definitely not.'

'I understand your problem, but my bike...'

'You should have thought about it before taking up the place. Sorry, I can't help you with this,' she was firm.

⁂

Uday and Naina were walking the rain-washed pavements of CP when the man came, calling, '*Naak, kaan chidwa lo!* Get your nose, ears pierced!'

'I've always wanted to get my nose pierced,' said Naina, her tone touched with regret as he passed them by.

'Why haven't you?'

'Why haven't I done all the things I have wanted to?' she sighed.

Uday caught hold of her arm, turned around, and steered her in the direction the man had walked away.

'What?' Perplexed, she asked.

'Bhaiya, *ruko. Chaidwale*, stop!' he called out. The man stopped.

'How much for the nose?' Uday asked him.

'Give me anything, Sa'ab.'

'I'm not getting it done!' Naina huffed, incredulous.

'Why not?'

'Here, in the middle of all this? What if I get an infection?'

'Naina, no one died of a nose piercing, for God's sake!'

'What if it doesn't look nice?'

'Then take it off, simple?'

'Sit, Bibi *ji*. See, all sterilized.' The man was spreading out his paraphernalia to one side of the corridor already.

'No yaar, Uday, this is insane!'

'Okay, leave it, Bhaiya; madam doesn't want.'

'*Naah—ruko*! You think it's okay?' Naina stopped the piercing man and sought assurance from Uday.

'Naina!'

The man smiled and took out a little stool from his bag for her to sit on. He squatted on the ground beside her and from a dirty, rusted bottle with an ancient spraying nozzle, he sprayed a strong-smelling liquid on her nostril.

'Bibi *ji*, you will not even come to know. Okay, with what shall I pierce, wire or pin?'

'Show me the pins.'

'These are gold.'

'How do we know it's gold?'

'*Arré*, Bibi *ji*, I won't cheat you for a couple of hundreds!'

'Wait...what couple of hundreds?'

'150 for this gold wire pin with diamond!'

'Diamond! Find someone else to fool!'

'It is diamond, Bibi *ji*; get it checked.'

'And for the piercing?'

'Give me 100.'

'I will give you 150—100 for this wire with the white stone, and 50 for piercing,' she told him firmly.

'There she goes—haggling to fulfil a lifetime's desire!' Uday sighed dramatically.

Passers-by noiselessly formed a loose circle around her to watch. Pale-skinned foreigners stopped to smile and nod.

When the *chaidwala* started to sharpen the tip of the wire on his shiny anvil wedged firmly between his dusty, cracked feet, Naina sought Uday's hand.

'An ant bite only,' the man said, and it reminded her of Nani, when she took her for the shots. Tears streamed down her face as the warm metal pierced her flesh and the man seemed to turn her nostril over in order to coil the wire on the inside.

'Done! Just heat some ghee and haldi, and apply on it for a few days. It will be fine. How beautiful you are looking, madam, *ekdum shaandar*!' He held out a plastic hand mirror for her to look. The nostril had turned red, but the little white stone that sat sparkling on it looked quite beautiful. She saw Uday handing the man 250 rupees. She kept quiet. The man salaamed him and began to collect his things.

'Hey, thanks.' She said to Uday, as they started back for the office.

'You're welcome. Is it hurting?'

'Nah.'

'Take a Combiflam if it does.'

'Yeah.'

Arundhati saw her first. She was at the reception. 'You got your nose pierced?'

'Yeah.'

Ratna came, 'Looks lovely, Naina. It suits you.'

'Show?' Sunita stood up to see.

Arundhati turned away mumbling, 'Some people have way too much time on their hands.' Walking inside, she announced, 'See what people do during office hours.'

Uday, in a calm voice from the other end, called her, 'Arundhati, hope you have put *your* time to good use. That report was due yesterday, you know.'

Sunita winked at Naina and Ratna smiled. But Arundhati's words had dampened Naina's joy.

'When she's not listening to me, I call her *matashri*!'

Piyali and Arundhati were giggling, talking about their mothers. The content team was having a late lunch.

'When I'm miffed with my mom, I call her by her name, Shwetambara.' Piyali said. Then there was an awkward silence. Under normal circumstances, it would be Naina's turn to speak.

How should I put the ease back into the conversation? Should I talk about Amma? Nani? Someone?

'What's your sister's name, Naina?' Piyali asked.

Sister for mother? A substitute. The living for the dead. 'Tara. My mother's name is…was Naintara.'

'Nice.' They smiled politely and turned their attention to their lunch boxes. Arundhati had got Naina's favourite jackfruit curry.

'My friend, Priya, made this.'

'You remember Priya, don't you? The one who eloped with Mr Moneybags?' She asked Piyali.

'Yes, you said, she's moved into your neighbourhood.'

'Yesterday she came to my house to give this curry wearing—guess what? A burqa!' Arundhati began to laugh.

'She's such a nut. Trust her to do such! It so happened that the day before, her mother-in-law commented on her clothes. She says she was wearing a perfectly decent pair of jeans and a shirt that was properly buttoned at the neck and fell under her hips. Still. So, she went and bought herself a burqa and told her mother-in-law that now she should have no cause to complain about her clothes. The mother-in-law was scandalized beyond words. Imagine!'

'But I admire her guts. She had the courage to run away with the man she loved, even with the families so much against it.' Arundhati added.

Naina thought of her own courage. Deepak's. Would he do it?

Uday who was sitting a little away from them, reading, but presumably overhearing their conversation looked at her, seemingly reading her mind. She looked away. She had not told Uday that Deepak had not contacted her after that day when he had come home with Bhaiya. It had been four months since then. But she had no time for any of this now. She drowned herself in work.

Naina was coming out of the office in quick steps. It was already 7:30. She would have to take an auto home; the bus would take too long and would be too crowded. As she waited to cross the road, a motorcycle came and stopped beside her. Even before the rider lifted the visor, she recognized his smiling eyes.

'Oh hi, Michael!'

'Hey…Naina? I'm sorry, I'm bad with names, but your face I would have recognized anywhere.' He smiled. Naina tried not to blush.

'What are you doing here?' he asked.

'I work here. In that building—with DW—Digital Wizards. Was just leaving.'

'You work so late?'

'Sometimes.'

'Can I drop you someplace?'

'Thanks, but no, I was just walking across to the auto stand.'

'In that case, I *insist* that I drop you. Say where?'

'Honest, it's okay.'

'Honest, it's my pleasure! Don't be silly. Hop on.'

It did not seem as if the tyres of Michael's bike ever touched the road. The cold breeze was on their faces as she leaned forward to talk to him. His manner was so unassuming that she felt completely at ease with him immediately. He told her that he worked as a graphic artist at Craftnet—in the big blue building very close to her office.

'How's Tara doing?'

'She's been missing you, I think. Poornima told me you stopped coming to the centre.'

'Yeah, it's been a crazy time at work.'

'Same here. I haven't been to the centre for a long time.'

'Have you had a root canal?'

'Sorry?' Naina was taken aback by the sudden change of topic.

'Root canal? The tooth thingie?'

'No,' she shouted to be heard over the wind.

'I had one done this morning.'

His visor was lifted. To hear him over the din, she had to lean really close to his face. She could see the curve of his long sideburns. Michael looked like someone.

'It was my first visit to the dentist. Before he looked into my mouth, he covered his mouth and nose with a mask, like my breath was going to kill him,' Michael laughed. 'Then he started prodding into my mouth. Now and then he'd say "spit" and I'd spit into the basin.'

They were now waiting at a signal and Naina could hear him clearly.

'He said he needed to take an x-ray. He fixed a film into my mouth. I believe, after fixing the film he calls out "shoot" to his assistant, who sits in a side room and controls the x-ray machine. Now this gentleman, after he fixed the film in my mouth, called out, loud and clear, "Spit!" '

They both burst out laughing. The light turned amber and Michael's kick-start tilted the bike to the right for a second. Still laughing, Naina caught hold of his jacket as they sped off ahead of a green Maruti. Two blurry faces inside it became people as she lost sight of them.

Bhabhi and Deepak.

The look on Deepak's face would remain fixed in her heart for the rest of her life. What was it—Anger? Regret? Scorn? How she wished she could tell him the truth. But what would it change?

Naina and Raju had started working in the garden. It had been prompted by the sudden blooming of frail lilies after several days of January showers. The hibernating bulbs sprouting long green tongues and the pale pink heads that struggled to keep themselves above the slushy garden had inspired hope.

They weeded and hoed the soil hardened from years of neglect. The brick edges around the flowerbeds were rearranged. A cartload of manure was bought and mixed into the soil. The *madhukamini* tree was trimmed. When the garden looked clean, they started planting seeds and saplings. It saddened her to see the trees of her childhood—papaya, guava, and pomegranate, which grew along the backyard wall—now in Ajit Mama's portion. They planted a lemon tree. It was therapeutic to work in the garden. She could not wait to get back from her morning run to see the plants sprouting new leaves and the garden slowly reviving its past glory.

She often thought of Ramprasad. He had continued to care for the garden even after Nani told him to look for another job. Gradually, his everyday visits stopped, and the garden became unruly. When he did come, his old hands pulled out and pruned, and every time, he had a new load of dried plants to carry away on his bent back. Then, he stopped coming except on festivals when he would sit looking wistfully at the completely dried out garden and would go away with some money that Nani handed him with a cup of tea and something to eat—a paratha or some biscuits.

Raima was a quiet girl. Hired as an apprentice graphic designer as she had no work experience she kept to herself. She was studying for her masters through a distance education programme. The boys often made fun of her and said there was only distance and no education in her degree. But Naina quite liked her. She was completely a no-nonsense person, very focussed on her work. Then one day, Naina felt a pang quite like jealousy when she saw Uday and Rajesh bent over Raima's desk, looking at her work. Uday was showing it to Rajesh who kept saying 'brilliant' and Uday seemed to gloat with pride like it was his own. When she looked again, she saw Uday's hand brush against Raima's as he took the mouse from her. Naina looked away. Raima was inconsequential, she told herself.

That day, while they were having lunch, she casually asked Uday, 'So how is Raima—as an artist?' She looked intently at him. Without betraying any sign of interest in his apprentice, Uday answered, 'She's very good. A bit raw.'

From then on, Naina associated Raima with that word. *Raw*.

'Naina! You are a godsend. Stuck on this one. Say, what's seven letters? A boon, a blessing?

'Um... try "Godsend", Uday.'

'Shit!'

Naina began to laugh, 'Isn't it like the "thunk" joke?'

'What joke?'

'A boy who had to write the past tense of "think" in school, tells his mother that he thought and thought, but couldn't remember, and wrote "thunk".'

'Okay, I'm done. The last word is…I know! Diaphanous.' Uday held up the completed crossword.

'I hate that word—diaphanous! I hear it and see a dinosaur in a diaper, somehow. It just does not convey the beauty of gossamer. Isn't it so—*unpoetic*?'

'Prosaic.'

'Like I wish *yellow* was something else. It's too beautiful to be called that.'

'Chal, let's go for chai, while your mood is so lyrical.'

'*Lyrical* is nice, isn't it? So like a song, ly-ri-cal,' she sang out.

On the way back, Naina's mood vacillated. She was not looking forward to the editors' meeting later in the afternoon.

'You know, I can't understand Arundhati.'

'Giving you grief?'

'Always. I wish I knew why she hates me so.'

'Not your loss, Naina. Arundhati has a story. I will tell you sometime.'

It was the Republic Day holiday. After an early breakfast, they came out in the garden. It was their big garden day. Tara sat on a chair in the sun, playing her music, while Naina and Raju began work.

Little but sure heads had emerged from the seeds they had planted all over the lawn area. They began to replant them in readied-flowerbeds just the way Nani had done for years—the tall dahlias next to the boundary wall, the gerberas along the main path, the lilies behind them, and the mogras along the edges of the lawn. Piyali had given Naina bougainvillea cuttings from her garden, neatly labelled, so they planted these along the boundary wall alternating the colours—magenta, white, orange, magenta…

All done, Tara and Raju went inside to watch the Republic Day parade on TV and Naina sat in the morning sun, oiling her hair. She could never sit with her back to the house anymore, always facing it. Always watchful. The mild winter sun was soothing on her skin and she relaxed, dozing off in the garden chair.

'Bonjour mademoiselle,' someone whispered in her left ear. She woke up with a start to find Michael standing before her with a brown, oil-stained paper bag in one hand and some kites in the other.

Before she could speak, he said, 'Got some kites. Where's Tara? Got hot jalebis for her.'

Kites on Republic Day! Only Michael could do this, she smiled.

'She's inside, watching TV.' Naina suddenly became conscious of her appearance—her faded black slacks, the green tee that hung at the shoulders, the oil in her hair.

The moment Tara saw Michael, she got up from her rocking chair and went to her room to get her keyboard. They had jalebis and Raju made some ginger tea. Then, they all went up to the terrace to fly kites.

Naina had not been on the terrace since Amma's accident. Now with the others, she felt safe. Clumps of dark, velvet green moss seemed to ooze out of the cracks in the walls. She pulled Tara away, when she got too close to it.

Michael was a complete failure at kite flying. Raju, who was assisting him enthusiastically, was no better. All three kites dashed into the garden below—tattered beyond repair. It was already 12:30 pm, but that was not the only reason why Naina asked Michael to stay for lunch. After a long time, there was some semblance of family life in their home.

Tara and Michael made erratically beautiful music, while Naina took a long, relaxed shower. She got into a pair of clean jeans and a red turtleneck sweater that reflected her bright mood. Raju had prepared peas' pulao, aloo gobi, and dal, and was about to start making the *phulka*s when Naina entered the kitchen. She quickly chopped cucumbers, radish, tomatoes, spinach, and adding drum-stick leaves with a dollop of hung curd, seasoning it with salt and roasted jeera, making Nani's favourite salad. Nani always said that there is never the absence of sorrow or grief in our lives or in the lives of others we know; so, we must never lose or forgo an occasion to celebrate, never let it go. Today was such a day.

How did Michael know Tara loved jalebis?

It was midnight and Naina was unable to sleep. After Michael left, all three of them had napped, waking up only after sunset. So, it was not surprising that she was wide awake now. She finished the report she needed to submit the next day and was generally feeling upbeat about everything. It had been a happy day. She went into the kitchen to make herself some coffee.

Taking the coffee to her room, she stopped to look at Raju. He was sleeping on the living room floor. He slept in the lobby during summer when the latticed west let in a balmy breeze, but now in winter, it was too cold there. Tara too was sleeping peacefully. The lobby was strewn with all the stuff they had collected from the two rooms at the back. Naina's eyes fell on a carton she recognized as the one that had Amma's things. She picked it up and took it to her room. Keeping it in the centre, she sat on the floor to look inside. There was Amma's bangle box. Red, maroon, green, pink, and two yellow bangles rankled inside. In a crumpled 'Gupta Store' polythene bag, there was a *chunri*—pink tissue with gold *booti*s—she remembered it as Amma's wedding *chunri* from the photographs she'd seen. There was one rexine covered black dairy, its pages turning yellow. It did not say who it belonged to, but the pages were filled with a familiar scrawl in green ink.

Today she held Tara, who's only 5 months, under the tap. It is freezing cold. I rushed to the bathroom hearing the baby's wails and rescued her. She offered no explanation.

Another attack. She kept yelling that I wanted to kill her. She hid inside the kitchen cabinet. It was only after I left home that her mother could persuade her to come out. She then went home to her mother, the kids remained with me. Tara is too small, but I worry about Naina.

I want to run away from all this. But what will happen to my kids? Who will take care of them? Their grandparents? They should. After all, it is their doing. Why did they marry her off to me when they knew her condition? They say they thought that marriage would cure her! Now what?—There are three more lives involved.

This was the first time she was looking at it from Papa's perspective. Yet her anger tainted her view. She had never wanted to know how he had felt. All she believed was that he had done a horrible, unpardonable crime in forsaking them.

Naina turned the pages to see if there was a beginning. The jottings were random.

Neurobiological brain disorder—schizophrenia.

15 mg of Stelazine with 2 mg Cogentin for side-effects.

The doctor has warned me that in the beginning, she might experience some side effects—drowsiness, muscle pain, rigidity, and EPS (extrapyramidal symptoms). With time, they would lessen. The delusions too.

Spoke to the psychiatrist again. Says it's her unwillingness. She needs to trust us and believe that she can be helped and that we're trying to do only that. But I'm really disheartened. I want to just go away. Leave all this and go.

She sits or stands in the same position for hours. Does absolutely nothing.

She's talking in a strange tone.

She never looks up when we speak to her. She's also sleeping a lot, which is perhaps the side effect of clozapine.

Naina dug deeper into the carton and discovered some more diaries—all with random notes.

I went to see her in Agra.

She is the only one in the world who understands me.

She takes care of my little things. She appears concerned about the family and how the kids are doing.

She came home today and met them.

The 'She' that was Amma till now was clearly someone else. A cloud of memories descended on Naina like 'her' soft as breeze, flower-printed, chiffon sarees, and the whiff of a familiar perfume.

There were guests in the house. *She* was helping in the kitchen. Naina wanted the lemonade that was going around on the tray. There was none left after the guests had been served. She crept into a corner of the kitchen, sulking. Who could she ask? Papa was with the guests in the drawing room. Amma was fidgeting with the dishes. Then *she* noticed Naina, and Naina was handed a glass of lemonade made especially for her with extra sugar.

The citrus taste filled her mouth now.

Leela?

LEELA.

She turned the pages. Leela? Papa?

A childhood instinct came back unbidden—a strong feeling of dislike that she had begun to feel for Leela. Where was she now? All the time that Naina was struggling to keep things going for Amma, Tara, Nani, and herself, were the two of them together somewhere?

Naina began flipping through the pages frantically. What had happened?

What am I to do? She does not trust me. Doctor says she thinks I want to kill her. She tells him that I will add poison to her food. Her delusions are growing.

Today I felt really wretched and frustrated. I was looking for a needle and thread in the dressing table drawer and there under the newspaper that lined it lay a whole handful of pills—medicines that I was religiously giving her, and she was hiding there instead of taking them.

It's all so futile.

I handed her the pill in the morning. As usual, she held it in her hand and waited. I got her a glass of water and waited for her to take it, but she just sat there. I again asked her to take it. She did not move. I was getting angry. I snatched it from her hand and forced it into her mouth. But she clenched her teeth. Then spat it out. I slapped her.

Naina knew this was the house. The huge space in front was vacant—no flower, grass, or weed, just a vast expanse of hard, russet earth. The white-painted, ancient house stood away from the road, embracing its canopy of tall trees. Two wide steps led to the main door. Closed. All the windows, a faded, peeling aqua, were closed too. She was shut out. Why had she come? How could she not, knowing he might be here? She phoned him. He was distracted, in a hurry. He was far away, someplace else, he said. She stood outside looking at the house then slowly walked away.

What was Uday's face doing in her dream? It was Deepak surely, and not him?

All afternoon, Naina sat sealed in his absence, refusing to believe he had forsaken her too. Unable to bear the tightness that thoughts of Deepak brought to her throat, she put her head down on the table and closed her eyes.

It was Saraswati Puja and most students had assumed it a holiday. The class was scattered, so Professor Chopra asked the backbenchers to move to the front. Amidst loud protests, exaggerated pushing and pulling of chairs, and shuffling of feet, they reluctantly moved to the front.

Her heart missed several beats when she caught sight of Deepak sitting down in the chair next to hers. Her fingers shook without reason and she begged her hammering heart to hush. The lecture remained a blur as she peered sideways at the blue plaid shirt sleeve, and the long, loopy handwriting. After the lecture, as she rose to leave, Deepak asked, 'Can I drop you home?'

'Thanks, but I'm not going home. I—I'm going to Maharani Bagh.' Then, as if she needed to explain why, she added, 'To give tuitions.'

'Okay, I'll drop you there.' He did not wait for her answer, picked up his bag and made way for her to lead.

'Wakie, wakie,' whispered Uday into her ear. Jolted out of her reverie, Naina looked at the time. It was almost 6.

'May I have the privilege of dropping you home?' Uday had missed the wistful look.

'Why? What's special today?' Naina was curt.

'Hey, why angry? I am going that way.'

'Okay.'

'I'll wind up in two minutes.'

Uday drove in silence. She was sorry she was rude. 'How did your meeting with the new CEO go?'

'It was okay.' He seemed preoccupied.

'What's he like?'

'Intelligent. Has amazing business sense.'

She did not look at him, but sensed a smile in his voice.

'Do you think we'll get another new project soon?'

'Let's see.'

Both fell silent again.

'Give me your hand.' He extended his hand. Naina gripped the bag on her lap tightly with both her hands. But he sought her right palm and held it firmly. Turning the car into a quiet lane, he stopped. Turning towards her, he took both her hands into his.

'Naina, I love you. I love you very much. I have great respect for you as a person. I've met and known many women. I've had all kinds of relationships, but Naina, I've never loved anyone like this before. Tell me, do you also care for me?'

Naina was quivering like a bird that had been caught. She did not want to hurt Uday. He was more than a good friend to her. 'Uday, I do care for you. You mean a lot to me. But that's all. I haven't really seen you…'

'Are you still waiting for Deepak?'

She did not respond. Uday pursed his lips and continued, 'Don't get me wrong, but from what I've learnt about him, I don't think he'll take that bold a step. Look at it from his side. You told me that his brother and sister-in-law have brought him up and he owes a lot to them. He would never go against their wishes.'

Uday's words stung. Yes, she knew all this, but Uday had no right to sit here and announce it so heartbreakingly to her.

'Look Naina, you have to think this through. If his sister-in-law is so much against your relationship that she says that she will never see Deepak's face again if he goes against her wishes, what do you think he'll do? Do you think he will leave them for you? Think about it. There's no hurry, but you need to have a clear head about this. How long are you going to wait for him?'

Who in the world gave him the right to speak about Deepak like this! How much did he know Deepak? How could he assume that Deepak is not coming back? It was all her fault. She regretted having confided in him.

Pointedly, she looked at her wristwatch. He got the message and started the car. For a while, he drove in silence, then began talking about office like the discussion of a moment ago had never happened. But Naina was still highly strung.

'Okay ma'am, here we are then,' he halted in front of her gate. 'I shall wait for the green signal,' he winked at her and lowered his tone to a whisper.

'Thank you.' She slammed the car door behind her.

'Naina, the graphics for the opening sequence are in the "D" drive. The file is "PCM concepts version 1", take a look,' Rahul called out from the landing. He worked from the office space they had extended on the upper floors recently.

Naina opened the files. 'No!' she moaned.

'What is it? Have you looked at the graphics yet?' Uday came by.

She was still angry with him, but this was work.

'It's just not working out. He's so out of sync with the entire concept.'

'Cool it Naina. This is how *he* sees it.'

'But it's not what I visualized and so painstakingly explained to him!'

'Too bad you can't do graphics and I cannot put your mind into the artist's.'

'But he can use his, can't he! I have to send this out today.'

'Cool it, lady. Let's work this out.'

He pulled up a chair and read through her brief. He seemed to approve.

'Obviously, He's not paying attention. Too bad.'

He got up, '*Chalo*, let's go.'

She thought they were going for a discussion with Rahul and his team. At the reception, he called out to Sunita, 'Hey Su, Naina and I are stepping out for a bit.'

She was not in the mood to go anywhere. But did Uday ever ask?

They walked the stretch up to Barakhamba Road with him telling her about a college friend who was setting up a cybercafé. Her agitated mind caught stray bits. Why was not Rahul getting it? She had been so precise.

By the time they stopped for tea, she was more receptive.

'You'd look amazing in an outfit like that.'

She followed his gaze to a girl in a powder-blue formal trouser suit. She knew it was a compliment of sorts and despite the unease, smiled.

'About Arundhati, you must know something. She's going through a very difficult time. She's in a relationship with an older, married man.'

'What?'

'Yeah, his kids are almost her age.'

'Why?'

'What do you mean *why*?'

'I mean, why a married man?'

'Does one stop to think?'

'But one should.'

'Think?'

'Yeah.'

'Reason?'

'Yeah, of course.'

'Did you? Easy for you to let go? Don't you think it's the same with her?'

Did one really stop to think before falling in love? What if Deepak married someone else? Bhabhi's sister? Would she stop loving him?

But Uday meant more. He meant himself.

'Why don't you write down the description again—in a more detailed manner?'

Just like Uday to never steer away too long from practical purposes. 'Also, you can have a meeting with the graphic artists if you want. So now, when we get back, start by making a list of what you don't like in the graphics or what you'd like changed. Call it "suggestions"—mild, right?' He got up to leave. 'I want a report in half an hour.'

'What will she do now?'

'She will find her way. All of us must.'

Raima took a two-month leave for her exams. Going for two months did not necessarily mean she was coming back. She may never come back. She may find a better job, or she may flunk and then her family might ask her to not work while studying, or she may get married and go away to America! The possibilities were endless and Naina was hopeful something would take care of Raima.

Later that evening, when Raima went around saying her goodbyes, and came to her, Naina could not miss the warmth and honesty in her words, 'Naina, I'm planning to come back, but you never know.' She was echoing Naina's own thoughts.

'I thought I must tell you that I learnt so much from you and you are an extremely gentle and patient person. I am so lucky to have a mentor like you.'

Not only did she feel embarrassed about her earlier thoughts, Naina felt a certain warmth towards Raima. But words failed her. 'All the best for your exams,' was all she said.

That was not the last she heard of Raima.

Michael called two days later.

'Hey, what's up? How have you been?'

'Okay. How are you?'

'Good. How's work?'

'Okay. Was just stepping out. Have to look up some references.'

'Where to?'

'British Council.'

'I was wondering if we could meet for coffee. How long will your work take?'

'I should be done by the evening. I plan to go home directly from there. Not coming back to the office.'

'Okay then, why don't we meet at BCL at 5? We'll have coffee someplace and then I can drop you home.'

Naina did not answer immediately. She was reminded of Deepak's gaze. But what did that have to do with Michael? He loved Tara. Tara loved him. He was good for Tara. And he was good for herself too, perhaps.

'I'll see you outside BCL at 5.' Michael did not wait for her reply.

'What if I'm not done? There's a lot of work and I must complete it today. Tomorrow is a holiday and the day after is my deadline.' She wanted to leave the door for a quick retreat, if the guilt got to her again, open.

'No problems, if you're not done, just step out and let me know.'

'Okay, done!'

Yanni! That's it!

'He looks like Yanni,' it came out a tad too excitedly than she would have liked it to, as she turned to tell Uday.

'Who?' Uday asked.

'Michael. I told you he looks like someone.'

'So, the crush is revived, is it?' he asked, his tone bitter.

Aghast, her voice trembling with anger, she retorted, 'Are you out of you mind?' and stormed out of the office.

Is the crush revived! Gosh, she could punch someone. This was insane. She was glad there was pressing work she had to complete. The long walk to the British Council building in the warm afternoon sun was meant to clear her head, but not anymore.

Naina flipped through books and took notes, but finding it impossible to concentrate, came out at 4:45 and sat on a stone ledge looking at the last rays of the February sun filtering through the trees.

'Señorita!' someone called out. She turned to find Michael bowing dramatically. 'And how are we today?'

He made her smile. He made her whole being come alive with his brightness.

'Are you done? Shall we go?'

'Yes, done. Where to?'

'Let's see, but first, is there drinking water around?'

Naina pointed to the water fountain. He went to it and made a huge pretence of figuring out how to turn it on; then, folded his palms before it as in prayer.

Michael and his histrionics! Naina laughed and shook her head.

'How does this damn thing work?'

Finally, he held his mouth open under the faucet, and with the water still streaming down his chin, called, 'Hey Naina, come and try this. It's great fun.'

She pretended annoyance and walked away.

They walked to the cafe. It was full and they had to wait.

'Come, I'll show you something.' Michael pulled her into the elevator. They were soon on the 8th floor.

'Where are we going?'

Michael took her hand and led her through a flight of stairs to an open terrace. Water tanks of various sizes were randomly parked everywhere. Electric cables lay strewn on the floor. But the sky was an amazing pink. It was beautiful and quiet—so surprisingly removed from the bustle below. They walked over to the parapet and looked down at the winding bands of the road with tiny vehicles barely moving.

She looked at Michael's silhouette against the western sky. His expression was so guileless. Michael was leaning over the edge dangerously. Alarmed, she moved closer to him. Too close, she realized as her hair flew over to his shoulder, but they were sealed in such a perfectly peaceful moment, she did not dare to move.

Michael was looking directly underneath—at a parking lot full of two-wheelers.

'Let's see where your spit lands.'

'What?'

'Come on, spit. Let's see where your spit lands.'

'Never!' Naina moved away repulsed.

'Try it once, Naina, it's great fun.'

'You must be crazy!'

'You miss out on some great stuff in life, you know. You are so—staid.'

'I think, I'll go home now, Michael. It's getting very late.'

At her insistence, he dropped her at the bus stop and went alone the same way, much ahead of the bus. She did want to go with him; she was trying to punish herself for something. Something else was also bothering her. *Staid.*

A bunch of white roses stood on her desk the next morning with a 'Sorry' note in Uday's untidy handwriting. He was sitting with his back to her, but turned around just as she read the note. He was holding his ears and searching her face for a softening of expression. A slight hint of a smile and Uday rolled his chair up to her.

'I was a little mad yesterday. I should not have said all that.'

'That's okay. Let's not talk about it.'

'Tea?'

'Yes.' She needed to clear out some things with him.

Sitting under the bridge on the stone-slab perch, she started to tell him, 'Tara was totally dependent on us. We fed her, we clothed her, we even brushed her teeth. "We", meaning, Nani and I mostly, and sometimes, Amma. We had so many challenges of our own; there was no time to think of how she could lead a better life. We always knew she enjoyed music as she would sit in her chair and rock for hours listening to the Gayatri mantra, or the songs on TV. At the centre, there was always some volunteer who took a music class—played some music on the piano or sang songs with the kids. Tara obviously loved these sessions, but no one could pay individual attention to her till Michael came and discovered her love for music. He spends extra time training her. I have never seen Tara respond to any outsider like she does to him. Last week, I saw coloured strips of paper that Michael had stuck on the piano keys for Tara to follow the notes. The volunteer told me he's been reading and finding out ways in which he can teach Tara better. Michael is a nice, fun person. He never fails to cheer me up. He has no family; grew up in an orphanage. Maybe that's the reason he's so giving and so eager to receive.'

Naina paused, a little tentative, then, continued, 'Very few people visit our home. No one who ever came to our house, came for Tara. No one treated her like one of us. Michael did. He came home to meet Tara and has kind of, made her a "person".'

Her eyes filled up and Uday took her hand in his.

'Everyone has a place in your life. It's not as if when a new person comes into it, the existing ones have to empty a slot,' she smiled, wiping her tears, thinking of parking lots.

'Which one am I? A shining new Maruti or the sturdy, old Ambassador? Don't tell me I'm a *phatphati*!'

She laughed, squeezing his hand. Both returned to work feeling much lighter.

Spring came with a burst of colour. By early March, the Purple Wreath that had confidently climbed the porch had delicate sprays of blue. The Easter Lilies stood erect on their long stalks like pinwheels in pots and the Portulaca planted in every empty space around the garden spread out their colourful faces to greet the sun every morning. The garden cheered Naina up like nothing else, but there were other things bothering her. And Holi around the corner was bound to bring with it that inescapable melancholy. She needed to tell Uday.

'You know I could be going Amma's way?'

'How is that?'

'Lately, I find myself—um, worrying about people.'

'Who?'

'Amma used to see people on the roof. They asked her to do things, mocked her, and frightened her. Now I always feel they are there. They are watching me and Tara and Raju. Yesterday, when the storm came and Raju was away at the market, I had to go upstairs to get the washing. I kept feeling eyes on my back but was too scared to turn around to look. And then, just as I reached out to pick a clip, in its place I saw swinging from the line, a small, green person. I swear I saw it, as I see you now. I could feel its soft body, I ran inside, terrified.'

'So?' Uday sounded as detached as a census-taker.

'I must be going mad. Sometimes, I am so convinced there are people other than us about the house. Amma saw them,' she hesitated, then added, 'I see them too.'

'Okay, did Amma say they were green and little? Isn't that a figment of your imagination? And you know that the people Amma saw were imaginary.'

'You don't understand,' Naina remained glum, 'I had all the clothes washed again. It felt creepy; them having touched my clothes.'

'Seriously, Naina, stop being paranoid. It's because you are overthinking so much that you can't shake the feeling off.'

'Uday, I'm so afraid that I may be going mad.'

'What nonsense! What is madness, really? You tell me, Naina? Amma was and Tara is merely...unwell, and they do things differently because their minds work differently from the rest of us. It's a pity that the world will empathize with you if you have cancer, but not if there is some error in the wiring of your brain. And what about the rest of us? I get mad at people. I get so mad sometimes, I have to stop myself from hitting them. Look at Arundhati—she's mad with jealousy. Syed is mad in love—he has slit his wrists three times because he cannot marry the girl he loves. Everyone has some quirk, some obsession. It's about how individual minds work—who decides what madness is?'

'But it runs in my family.'

The board game was a birthday present when she turned seven. She had to touch with the little plastic pointer a slot against a question and with another pointer, its answer simultaneously. If the answer was correct, a green light blinked. If incorrect, the red.

She had learnt all the correct answers quickly, but it was fun to tap the wrong ones just to see the red light blink. Then one day, she saw through a slot at the bottom, a maze of wires between the board on top and the cardboard box that held it. Carefully lifting it with her fingers, she tried to peer inside. The urge to find out was compelling and soon the box was prised open to reveal the wondrous network of wires. The game went kaput then, never to glow red or green again.

How simple Uday's rewiring theory sounded. Like she could reach inside Tara's head and pick the wires one by one and check for the wrong connections; pull one here and connect it with another there so the light of love would shine in her eyes; connect another so she could hold when held; and one more so she would speak—call out her name, 'Naina.'

'What is a sensory cross-wiring in the brain? Eleven letters. There is a "nest" after two letters.'

It was almost 10 and Uday was still doing the crossword.

'Synesthesia—S Y N E S T H E S I A.' Naina spelled it out for him.

Uday bent down to fill it in. 'Wow! I didn't know this, and Miss Crossword speaks like she's saying "potato"!'

'Hmm.'

'No really, Naina. That was awesome. You know so much.'

'Um... I happen to know a little about—the mind? Isn't surprising, is it?

'Tell me about this.'

'A kind of mix-up of the senses…the senses merge. People with synaesthesia see letters and numbers in colour, they can taste shapes.'

'Fascinating.'

'Buzz off now. I have work to do.'

'Yes, ma'am. And thanks!'

She was just shutting her computer down in the evening, ready to leave when Sunita called from the reception. She had a visitor. Naina wondered who it could be. Frantically hoping it was him, she walked to the reception trying not to look too happy. Sure enough, it was Michael.

'Hey, what you doing this evening?' Before she could answer, 'Let's go out? Bowling?'

He always began on a clean slate, no misgivings, no complaints.

'But Michael…I must get back home now. Tara will be waiting. You know that.'

'Whoever said anything about leaving Tara behind? Goodness gracious me! Some people think I'm as heartless as they are! *Chalo*, get your stuff, I'm waiting outside. The car is not parked properly.' Turning, he winked at Sunita, 'Thanks, love,' he said to Sunita, and walked out. Sunita, who was listening to it all, looked quizzically at Naina, but Naina was wondering about the *car* and did not tell her that 'thanks' was all Michael had meant. The 'love' bit, she could ignore.

A rickety, old, white Contessa stood at the gate. Michael leaned forward to open the door for her. The car chattered. The inside was musty.

'Come on! Stop looking like you're on a dentist's chair. Congratulate me, at least. This babe's mine!'

'Really? You've bought it?'

'No, I found it at the *nukkad* and while the owner was pissing in the bush, I drove away in it! Offo! Of course, I bought it—for 30 grand. Now, all of us can go out together.'

He became quiet, like he was embarrassed for having uttered the last sentence. Naina was so moved, she wanted to lean across and touch him, hold his hand, do something to show him how much this meant to her. Words, as always, failed her. Michael was busy negotiating sharp turns and manoeuvring his car between other vehicles. 'Easy, sweetheart', 'Way to go, baby', he kept talking to the car all the way home.

The project had been completed on time and the customer was pleased. Everyone badgered Uday for a treat. Ice-creams, they decided. So, at 3:30 in the afternoon, all twenty-two of them left for Nirula's. Boisterous like a group of students bunking class, each one ordered the largest serving of ice-cream. They lingered over it and it was clear that no one wanted to get back to work. So finally, it was decided that they would go bowling. Because, Uday added, with a desultory look towards her, 'Some people have been practising and it would be fun to challenge them.'

Naina felt the barb. She had not gone out bowling with Michael. He had received a call from work and had to go back to the office immediately after dropping her home. He could not even come inside for a cup of tea because Tara, if she saw him, would insist on playing the keyboard with him. But Naina had not thought it necessary to tell Uday all this.

She really did not want to go, but she did not want to be a spoilsport. Uday, as if sensing her hesitation, came to her and said, 'Come on, it'll be fun. See, it's only 4:30. We'll be back latest by 6, and then I'll drop you home. Come, it'll do you good.' He was trying to make up for that unthinking remark earlier.

She stepped into a bowling alley for the first time in her life. Everyone was talking over the loud music. She had wanted to sit and watch, but her name was flashing on the display. Reluctantly, she got into the shoes and Uday showed her how to roll the ball. *Thud*, it fell on the alley most embarrassingly. But two pins went down, and everyone clapped. Naina quietly slid to the back and sat in a corner. The din of the cheering and the music created an artificial vacuum around her. Uday seemed to be playing more often than the others.

A sudden loud cheering told her that the game was over and then she saw on the display her name—her team had won. Uday had played for her. He came to her and gave a high-five—a quiet moment before the others gathered around them talking nine to a dozen.

In an early morning meeting of the management, the decision was conveyed to her. Naina was to head the team on a prestigious project for the Ministry of Education. She was given complete charge of it.

'Hire people, fire people, do whatever. We have to give this project our 200 per cent. It *has* to be our best. Once we prove ourselves to them, there's no knowing which doors may open for us in the government,' Rajesh had been categorical.

Digital Wizards was expanding rapidly with new projects coming in, people being hired. Uday was away most days making presentations to prospective customers. Rajesh was busy hiring. Ten new people joined. Five of them, writers. Arundhati became the 'Ma'am' who would mentor them. An honour, Naina hoped she would consider more significant than her own.

Buoyed as she was, Naina could clearly foresee the trouble ahead—that of leading an all-men team. They already resisted her authority, challenging every small decision of hers, mulishly sticking to opposing ideas and ignoring deadlines. Now, I will not tolerate any tomfoolery, she decided as she stepped out of Rajesh's cabin. Everyone came over to her desk, congratulated her and the usual camaraderie seemed to return—at least on the surface. Naina was quite revelling in the attention, when in walked Raima.

In a black khadi kurta and a black dupatta with a wide red border, Raima looked stunning. The black and red set off the colour of her pale skin strikingly. She had become leaner, and her face seemed more angular. The gathering around Naina gravitated all at once towards Raima.

They were talking over each other asking about her like she was not the quiet girl in the corner, who they had bitched about endlessly, but a dear friend whose return they had eagerly awaited. Was it her imagination, tainted by jealousy, or was it true that Raima too seemed surprised by this warm reception?

The lunch hour crowds were milling into the corridors of CP. Couples holding hands; slow-walking Punjabi aunties coming in and out of plate-glass doors, office men with uninspiring jobs forming random groups to talk politics and berate their bosses, shabby foreigners with armpit hair and flapping thongs dodging beggars, and hundreds of others like her who seemed to be riding a wave carrying them all towards some fated destination.

The shirt seller in front of Regal was still putting up his display—hundreds of stark white, collared, button-down shirts that bellowed in the breeze like beheaded men—and calling out to young, job-seeking men, loitering the area. Silk ties, faux leather folders and shoes could be bought from this pavement. A man in tatters could, for a couple of hundred rupees, buy an 'executive' look right here.

Naina turned around discreetly. No one needed to know she was going nowhere. The walk was meant to clear her head, but the bustle was distracting. She needed to come up with the winning concept. The graphic artists and writers were meeting for a brainstorming session at 3. She hated it if she did not come up with the big idea. At best, others suggested some minor tweaking, but the basic concept was always hers—a fact accepted by all, so that most of the team had now stopped bothering to think up concepts.

It was 2 pm and her mind was absolutely blank. Purposefully, she entered Galgotia and walked up to the children's section. She was about to pick a book when someone startled her with, 'Caught you!' Michael stood leaning against a step ladder, smiling.

'Aren't you supposed to be at work?' Without giving her an opportunity to respond, he continued, 'And by the way, this is the children's section, no Romances here.'

'You know I don't read Romance.' She replied flipping through the book in her hand.

'What brings you here?'

But he did not wait for her answer; he caught hold of her arm and dodging his way through the bookshelves, carted her away to the other end. 'There's someone I want you to meet.'

Under *Cookery* stood a very tall and handsome, white man, in a formal jacket.

'Rob, meet my friend Naina.'

Not quite listening to him, engrossed in the books he was holding, Rob looked up. From over gold-rimmed, slender reading glasses perched precariously at the tip of his angular nose, eyes like blue glass marbles rose to meet Naina's.

Rob hesitated. She extended her hand.

'Glad to meet you…,' Rob looked at Michael.

'Naina,' she said.

'Naina,' he repeated, only it rhymed with 'hyena'.

'Naina, won't you help Rob select some cookery books?'

'Yeah, sure.' She smiled at Rob and asked, 'What exactly are you looking for?'

They stood talking for a while as Michael wandered off again. Rob picked up a book called *Red Hot Curries*.

'Looks nice, doesn't it? But might be too hot for you.' Naina smiled.

'No, no, it's okay, if it's nice.' Flipping through the pages, Rob asked, 'Do you think Michael will like food this hot?'

'I don't really know.'

'Aren't you good friends?'

'We are—friends,' she sounded unsure. She did not want to talk to a stranger about Michael and herself. Rob was looking at her closely. She looked at her watch. It was 2:30 pm.

'Rob, I need to get back to work. And I'm sorry I couldn't be of much help,' she held out her hand, 'Nice meeting you.'

'Same here, Naina. Be seeing more of you, I'm sure.'

She smiled and slipped out with not one minute to spare to look for Michael. He would come to her soon.

Raima joined office the week after. By then, Naina was nose-deep into her project, often staying back late. The last chartered bus home left at 7:30 and she tried not to miss it. The one kilometre stretch she had to walk to the bus stop was a refreshing walk at 6, but dark and secluded after 7. She missed Uday's company. One day, as she stepped out, Raima too was leaving.

'Where to?'

'Barakhamba.'

'Me too.'

'How did your exams go?'

'Okay. I messed up one paper, but I won't flunk.' She laughed.

'What time do you get home?'

'It takes me about an hour. What about you?'

'Yeah, same. Sometimes a little longer.'

'I love this weather.'

'Yeah, though the days are getting warmer.'

'Naina, peanuts? I'm so famished.'

'Yes!'

The air smelt appetisingly of peanuts roasting. They stopped by a pushcart. The vendor swishing the shelled peanuts in a large kadai, lifted his slotted scraper to sift the sand away and filled two newspaper cones that he handed them.

'Hey, that's my bus, got to run. See you, Naina.' Raima hurried away.

Naina hummed along with the film songs that blared in her bus and wondered how long it had been since she had had a girlfriend. She could not remember.

Soon they were making a routine of this. Raima and Naina. Leaving together, talking, munching on peanuts sometimes so hot that it scalded their tongues, and laughing at passers-by who made lewd comments, loud kissing sounds, or beckoned them.

They never discussed their personal lives, although Naina was more at ease with it now. 'I live with my younger sister,' she would say. 'And?' people would prod. 'And our house help.' 'Parents?' the intrusive ones would persist. 'No' was all she would say.

Uday was curious about this growing friendship. 'It'll do you good,' he said. One evening he came along with them, talking mainly with Raima. It was only when he asked Naina how Tara was and if the Christmas tree he got her from Bangalore survived, that she felt better. The two of them had things besides the office to discuss. Good, Raima was listening.

Michael called.

'Hey, sorry couldn't call. Been so busy with Rob here and all.'

'Is he staying with you?'

'Sometimes. But I take him out and stuff. He's been majorly shopping. And we've been eating out a lot too. He keeps asking about you. In fact, he asked if you'd join us for dinner one of these days.'

'I'd love to, Michael, but you know how things are. I don't like to stay out after work.' Then immediately sealing off the other possibility, she added, 'And these days there's so much work, I don't even get time to step out for lunch. Usually, someone gets me a sandwich.'

'Okay, no worries. I think he's gonna be here for some more time. We'll plan something later.'

'And how are things with you?'

They talked a bit about this and that and hung up.

There was something about Rob she could not quite pin. But she shrugged off the thought as she was not likely to bump into him again. Little did she know.

That evening, Raima put out her hand in front of Naina as they were walking to the bus stop. In the diffused yellow streetlight, Naina caught the glint of diamonds. A look at Raima's smiling face confirmed it.

'You got engaged?'

'Yes.'

'And you didn't breathe a word all day!'

Raima kept smiling.

'Congratulations! Who is he?'

'He's an architect in the US. He's come down for a month. The wedding is next week.'

'Next week! Oh my god, that's quick! I mean…this is nice—wonderful. Will you—like have to leave?'

Naina seemed so baffled, Raima smiled and said, 'I guess so.'

That night, Naina kept thinking about Raima. She had begun to like her. It was as if at last she'd found a girlfriend. Now Raima was set to leave.

'Did I tell you about Rob? Michael's colleague—and friend?' Raima had left early and Naina was glad for Uday's company after a long time.

'Don't tell me the old man's fallen for you.'

'No silly, I think he's fallen for Michael. You know what I mean?'

'Um—do I know what you mean? Would you be more specific?'

She could gauge the teasing, the slight provocation in his tone.

'Come on!' Naina had somehow wanted him to quell that little suspicion that had risen in her heart and that she did not want to recognize as a possibility.

'A little shocked, are we?'

'Obviously, I am. I'm not thinking about *that*, but nothing seems alright.'

'But why is it bothering you so much? These things happen. Michael is a mature person. He will know how to deal with it. And you never know...'

'What?'

'What Michael wants! Tell me, how much do you know Michael? Some swooning over him in school and some disastrous kite-flying now, that's all.'

'Michael *is* a friend.'

'I'm not denying that. But sometimes, we don't even know what's going on in our own family.'

Naina was absolutely sure that Uday's remarks about Michael stemmed from jealousy. Was not it natural? She was seeing

Michael almost regularly lately and she did have that crush on him in school. Now, though, he was just a good friend. A *very* good friend.

'Don't worry, Naina. Dilemmas unravel themselves. Anyway, there isn't much you can do. So why don't you just ignore what you can? *Chalo*, your bus is here. Go home and be a good girl. My troubled little sheep needs some rest and sleep.' Patting her back, he gently steered her towards the waiting bus.

The one in the red kaftan turned to look straight at her. The deep red yoke ran from her neck to waist with large elephants on the sides.

Leela. Leela in their kitchen, making tea. She watched as Naina walked in. Then, extended towards her a pencil—Flora—white with pink flowers. Naina, little girl, happy with a pencil! Leela caught her arm and took her to the bedroom.

Naina watched with her mouth agape as Leela lifted the ends of her kaftan and pulled it over her head. Too terrified to look away, she saw the elephants tumble over one another and disappear over Leela's head. There she stood, her heart pounding in her ears—looking at those breasts. Terrified, she screamed, but no sound came as in a dream-fright; she turned around to run, but Papa was standing in the doorway. He was laughing.

Naina pulled the shoelace tighter. She needed to buy new running shoes without delay. What would Raima do? Naina stretched herself as she came out of the house. It was cold.

Beneath the lamp the lady bowed,
And slowly rolled her eyes around;
Then drawing in her breath aloud,
Like one that shuddered, she unbound

The cincture from beneath her breast:
Her silken robe, and inner vest,
Dropt to her feet, and full in view,
Behold! her bosom and half her side—
A sight to dream of, not to tell!
O shield her! shield sweet Christabel!

A sight to dream of, not to tell... Naina had always imagined Geraldine's bosom to be extremely beautiful, unlike the rest of the class that wanted to think Christabel was repulsed by it. 'But Shelley fainted?' Jai had questioned.

'I need to talk to you, Naina.' Raima had whispered to her looking definitely careworn, something Naina had suspected she had been for the past few days.

'What's the matter?'

'Can we go upstairs?'

'Okay.' She saved the timesheet she was working on. This would break the train of her thought.

There was a large hall on the second floor that was soon to be renovated and readied to accommodate more people joining DW.

'Naina, this is very personal, and I have no one to confide in.'

Without waiting for her response, Raima turned to bolt the door from inside. She walked back to where Naina was standing in the middle of the hall and without looking at her, lifted her kameez. She pulled it over her head and removed her bra.

What she saw would remain etched in Naina's memory forever. Four. Two under two. It did not look human. And sorry as she felt for Raima later, at that moment she was repulsed, letting out a gasp, covering her mouth too late. Raima broke down.

Naina ran faster. She had confirmed Raima's fears. She had let Raima down. She hated herself.

Was it easier to live with a physical deformity than a mental one? Raima was considered the prettiest girl in the office. Most guys flirted with her and asked her out for dates. No one knew what lay under her shirt. And she did not need to live with it all her life. A surgery could easily correct it. Unlike a mental disorder. How does one hide that? It has to be carried like a branding on the brow. The glassy look in the eyes, the ungainly gait, the awkward social bearing—how naked, how totally stripped of dignity and worth.

And Leela? She kept coming back. When did they stop talking, thinking about her? How, as a child, did Naina know that it was not okay to talk about her? All the way to office in the bus, she tried to pin her memory to some incident or some time back then that had made her despise Leela so. Leela Aunty.

The early morning dream gnawed at her. When Uday came out of a meeting at 3 pm, having skipped lunch, he sought her. 'Okay to take a little sandwich break?'

'I'll take 10 to finish this review. Okay?'

'Alrighty!'

It was almost 4 pm when they stepped out.

'God! I'm hungry! Uday, I'm craving a dosa, man!'

They were walking towards Bengali Market already, but Uday hailed an auto.

'Come, I'll take you to a special place.' He got into the auto after her and said to the *autowala*, 'Jai Singh Road, Bhaiya.'

Protestors had blocked the road in front of Jantar Mantar, so they had to get off the auto and walk. A group of aggressive-looking protesters were shouting slogans and the police were wielding lathis in the air, trying to keep them in control. The Free Tibet and the Bhopal Gas Peedith groups that had taken permanent residence at Jantar Mantar looked with cynicism at the activity. Their own dharnas now gained momentum only on specific dates.

Uday and Naina turned left at the circle and just in front of the BJP office, across the road, stood a small eatery. A barely 10x10, asbestos-covered structure, inside which three men in mundus folded at their knees were ladling out food in slotted steel trays and outside, an energetic, young man with a heavy Malayali-inflected Hindi was taking and calling out the orders.

At 4:30, the place was surprisingly swarming with hungry office-people and the aroma of sambar hung for at least a kilometre around. Naina was handed a steel tray with a masala dosa, coconut chutney and sambar. The taste of authentic south Indian burst in her mouth. They ate standing up, balancing their trays in their hands. Uday only lifted his eyes from his food after polishing off his second dosa and smiled seeing her greedily lick the last of the chutney on her plate. 'Hungry cow!' he teased.

Sated and overfull, they decided to walk back to the office. The day's work was over for her, she just needed to check the status with the team before leaving and Uday had a call with a London client at 7, so they had the time. They took the short cut to Janpath through the small lane. Another day, Naina would have stopped to look at the wares lining the street, but the restlessness of the morning was again weighing her down.

'Let's sit somewhere for a bit,' she said.

'Tired? *Chal*, let's go to the office and have chai there. I need chai after this.'

They sat under the bridge, sipping tea and watching people leave for home.

'There was this woman in my childhood. Papa's colleague. She lived in Agra, but travelled to Delhi often.' As she spoke, a fog seemed to lift from those memories and Leela emerged clearer.

'She stayed in the guest house when she came. In the evenings, Papa would go there and sometimes he would take me along. She was very elegant. I think, I quite admired her. During work hours, she wore elegant chiffon sarees, but in the evenings, in her room in the guest house, she would be dressed in long, flowing kaftans, her hair tied high on her head.

Papa and she would discuss work—papers and lectures and I would sit there figuring out the fascinating patterns on her kaftan. I remember one with a yellow dragon. I sat wondering if it would come alive at night when Leela Aunty was asleep and lick her with that flaming tongue? Sometimes, I would wander off to the balcony to look at the passers-by until Papa was ready to leave.

Leela Aunty would make tea for the two of them and bring biscuits for me in the balcony—always the same—Sixer biscuits—six sides and six holes, one side smooth, the other, criss-crossed.

She would also get us packets of *dalmoth* and *petha* from Agra. I hated the gooey *petha*. I hated to see Papa scoop up, sometimes, two pieces at a time, from the pink cardboard box and gobble them down with so much relish.

I don't know what happened, if it happened suddenly or over some time, but I stopped going to the guest house with Papa. If I came face to face with her on the campus, I would run away or pretend I hadn't seen her. She, however, always smiled and called out to me. She even brought me a ruler when she came back from a conference in Japan—a 3D ruler—with names of countries and their capitals. Hold it straight in your hand and the dark grey strip displayed countries—Australia, Japan, China…all lined up neatly inside their boxes, tilt it and the grey turned silver and showed their capitals. It was amazing. I loved to hold it at an angle just between countries and capitals, so it showed a curious jumble of words—AUSTRALIA, CANBERRA half and half, ENGLAND with LONDON superimposed. I would sit engrossed in its wonderment for hours.'

Uday had been listening without making a comment.

'What are you thinking?' she asked.

'You know, Naina? You will never be able to look at what's happening in the present, because you're so caught up in your past. You're missing out on so much by just remaining sealed in what was. You have no clarity about your future. I understand you've had your share of troubles, but more people than you can imagine, do too. You have a choice. And what you make of your life depends on that.'

She had not expected this reaction from him. She had wanted to tell him what was bothering her and for him to show some empathy, some assurance that it was alright to feel this way. Here he was, lecturing her again. The deep melancholy the memories evoked gave way to anger. Uday sensed it in the way she seemed to stiffen up.

'Listen to me,' he said.

'Do I have a choice?'

'No, you don't!'

Naina kept quiet.

'Okay, sorry. But the fact remains. Just think about this—you have these ghosts from the past that keep haunting you—your father, your childhood, Deepak, now Leela.'

'They are not ghosts,' she retorted, her anger rising.

'Listen Naina, you know I'm trying to help you. Take small steps, but do this. Try and find out the truth about your dad, Leela, and whoever it is that does not let you move forward in life. Granted, you had no control over things that happened to you when you were small. But now? It's your life and the control is…must be in your hands.'

He made it sound like some kind of a remote she was holding—Press UP for Happiness, LEFT for Peace, RIGHT for Love…

IV

The bus entered the dusty town at 11. Naina was in a hurry. She had taken the day off and wanted to return home by late evening at any cost. It was important to come here on a weekday.

Till this moment, she had not been sure where she would go and now it came out of her mouth on its own accord, 'Dayalbagh,' she said to an *autowala*.

It could be Agra University or Dayalbagh. Somehow Dayalbagh had a familiar ring to it.

'*Mandir jayengi*?' the portly auto driver asked looking at her in the rear-view mirror.

'No, university.'

Once the auto came out of the bus-stand, her eyes began scanning everyone out on the streets, as if she would spot her on the road, walking among the bazaar crowds, carrying a *jhola* full of vegetables or perhaps sitting in the rickshaw that had halted beside hers. What would she look like now, almost 15…18 years later? Would she have allowed age to show gracefully on her—hair streaked with white and fine lines on that radiant face, her luscious figure slightly slack? What if she saw them together, Papa and her? What would she say to Papa?

Leela was her only lead to Papa. She had to find her.

Taut with anxiety, she suddenly became unsure of her decision to come to this strange city. She did not even know her surname, how would she find her in this town full of unknown faces?

Naina thought of Uday. She had been brooding for days and when she took the day off, he seemed to have guessed where she was headed. He had dropped a hint, unobtrusively, 'If you need any help, you know you just have to say.' He had looked at her closely, trying to read her thoughts, waiting for her to share if she wanted to. *No, not him, not anyone*. Naina was clear. She had to do this alone. But he gave her strength. She knew if there was need, he would be there.

They were now going past the majestic red turreted structure of the Agra University. Should she stop and ask? She hesitated as the auto zoomed past its gates. Panic gripped her again as they seemed to be headed straight to Leela or to some information leading to her. She wanted to stop and return to the bus stand. Back to Delhi. Back home. No questions asked, no answers sought. Life would go on as before. Nothing had to change.

To come this far and then give up? She could do this—ask at the university and return. She was already prepared for a dead end. Closure. She would then move on; she steadied her resolve. What would Nani have said about this impetuous expedition? But Nani was not her. Nani could not possibly have understood why it was so difficult for Naina to go on with life without finding out where her father was? Why he had *abandoned* them? Was he somewhere living a normal life with a normal family? It was imperative for her to find out.

It was almost an hour since she sat in the auto and the metre was speeding.

'Where in Dayalbagh?'

'University.' She repeated.

'No, which college, madam?'

Hoping her voice would not betray her nervousness, she said louder than necessary, 'Main office.' She saw him smirk in the rear mirror.

'*Pehli baar aaein hain*, first time?'

She did not reply.

'*Bahut badaa hai*. If you tell me the exact location...'

'*Aap chaliye*; I will tell you.'

As soon as the grand arched gateway of Dayalbagh Educational Institute came into sight, she asked him to stop. She could not take the risk of him knowing she had no clue where she was going. When she handed him the money, he looked straight at her, 'I can take you wherever you want—Taj Mahal, Fort, Masjid, Fatehpur Sikri. I will charge 500 rupees for the day.' A chill ran up her spine. He knew.

She flashed a confident smile and turned away purposefully. Arbitrarily chosen, she walked confidently in one direction scanning faces of passers-by for one that looked earnest enough to answer her uncertain question. A young man, probably a student, was coming right up before her.

'Excuse me? I am looking for the main institute.'

'Which institute?'

'The main office?'

'Registrar office?'

'Yes.'

'It's a little far from her. Take a rickshaw.' Without waiting for her reaction, he stopped a cycle rickshaw and told the rickshawala to take Naina to the 'registrar's office'. Before she could thank him, he had walked away.

The sign on the door read 'Records'. As she approached it, the peon sitting on a stool outside gestured her to go away.

'I have work in the office.'

'*Arré*, everyone comes for work here, not to watch films.'

'Please, let me go.'

'Can't you read? It's lunchtime. Come at 2.'

It was only 12:30. She came out of the building, and finding a bench in the garden to sit, she took out the tiffin box Raju had packed for office and began to eat.

At sharp 2 pm, she approached the door again. The peon was missing, so she opened the opaque half doors to peek inside. All the seats were vacant. No one had returned from lunch yet. At almost 20 minutes past 2, one gentleman came and occupied one of the seats. She walked up to him, her heart pounding. At her 'sir', he looked up.

'I am looking for a teacher here. Can you please help me, sir?' Her voice quivered with nervousness.

'*Hain*?' he said, looking up at her incredulously, as if people did not come with such requests.

Less nervously, she repeated, 'I'm looking for Ms Leela.'

'Who?'

'Leela…Leela ma'am?'

'Full name?'

'I don't know her surname.'

'Which subject does she teach?'

'I'm not sure.'

'No idea?'

'Sociology, Psychology—History?'

'*Hain*?' he waited for some reaction, then, 'Still here or retired?'

'I don't really know, sir. She cannot retire. I mean, she's not that old. But she could have left.'

He looked up some register. 'Sorry, there is no Leela on our rolls.'

She had to think of something quickly before he dismissed her, 'Sir, is it possible to know if she worked here, but has left now?'

'*Hain*?' again he gave her a puzzled look, but the 'sir' seemed to soften him.

'Misra *ji*,' he called out to a person with a single coil of black hair on his bald pate just settling into his chair. '*Koi Leela* ji *padhati thi yahan*, was there a Leela *ji*? Do you remember someone by that name?'

'One was there many years ago. What happened? Is she getting married?' he laughed.

'This girl is looking for her.' He gestured to her to go to Misra *ji*.

Naina knew from the barb about marriage that it was her. She thanked the gentleman and walked up to Misra *ji*.

'*Kahiye*?' he eyed her from the top of his glasses as his hands arranged files on his desk.

'Misra *ji*, can you tell me anything about Leela ma'am?'

'What do you want to know about her? She left this place many years ago.'

'Where did she go? There must be some record in the office or her address. Please help me.'

'*Aap hain kaun*, who are you? Why do you want to know about her?'

'I have come from Delhi. She was my mother's friend. I want to meet her.' The lie seemed like a betrayal to Amma's memory, but saying that she was her father's friend would not have worked with this man with the oily coil on his head.

'What's your mother's name?'

The question was not relevant but Misra *ji* had to be appeased.

'Kamla,' she lied just in case the rumours had reached here.

'What does Kamla *ji* do?'

'She's no more.'

'*Arré*, *arré*! Oh! So, you have come to bring her friend this news?'

She kept quiet. Her silence could not be misconstrued now. She was obviously grieving. He got up and went away. Naina kept standing at his desk. Other office staff had returned to their seats and everyone seemed to be more interested in looking at her than in attending to their work. Five minutes later, Misra *ji* returned with voluminous registers in his hands. He started turning the big pages one by one, repeating, 'Leela, Leela…'

When she pulled up a chair to sit, he looked at her as if she should have asked.

'Here it is!' he exclaimed. 'Leela Bharadwaj, F 22, Model Town, Idgah.'

With trembling hands, she noted the address down. 'Is there a phone number too? Sir…Misra *ji*?'

'No.'

She got up to leave. Then, with great difficulty, she brought herself to ask him, 'Did you know her?'

'Of course, I know everyone here. Have been here for thirty-five years.' Suddenly, he looked at her suspiciously, 'You don't know her?'

'*Nahi*, I was very small. Thank you very much, Misra *ji*.'

Just as she pushed open the half doors to leave, she heard an urgent, '*Arré suniye*, listen! Madam!'

Turning around, she saw Misra *ji* beckoning her, flapping his hand. He was looking at the register open in front of him.

'There is a note here.'

She peered to read. In the margin someone had scrawled, 'Address changed. New address not provided.'

'Oh!' the sigh slipped out of her mouth. 'Thank you, sir.'

Once outside, all her strength and bravado crumbled. The whole effort had been futile. She had come so close to finding Leela, also probably Papa, and now was clueless again. How would she ever get to the bottom of this? How would she be able to lay the ghosts of the past to rest? Could Leela be dead? End of story? Did she leave with Papa? Did they go away somewhere together to make a normal life for themselves? To live free of the responsibilities of a mad wife and daughter? To have normal children? Her despair turned into an angry resolve. She had to try.

She got into an auto, 'Model Town'.

It was a wide lane. A high boundary wall running along the left veiled whatever was beyond, letting her focus on the right side, which presented houses—shoulder to shoulder, each in a different colour, with a different façade, with no gardens, not even a patch of grass, just houses—concrete boxes that housed people. People like Leela. She asked the *autowala* to slow down.

'Tell me the number,' he offered to help.

'Is this F block?'

'Tell me the house number,' he insisted.

'22, F—F 22.' It felt as if she was letting him into her secret.

The numbers were haphazardly displayed. The *autowala* stopped to call out to a *presswala* running his heavy, coal iron box over water-splattered clothes that swished and let out a cloud of steam.

'*Ama kha*, where is this *aif twainty* two?'

The *presswala* gestured further ahead.

F 19 was finally spotted, peeping from over an oversized gate. Naina asked the *autowala* to stop. She needed to get to F 22 cautiously and inconspicuously.

An unkempt, covered porch overhung with creepers long dead, mint green walls, broken chairs and buckets, a tower of old newspapers balanced on a gas cylinder and no name plate—F 22 stood before her.

She pushed open the gate. The hinges squeaked. Her legs felt weak as she walked up to the front door. Would the kaftan wearing Leela open the door? Would it be someone else? Papa? Their kids? The house was too quiet, too derelict for scenes of such happy domesticity. Her mouth felt like summer earth. But it was too late, her hand was already on the doorbell. Before another thought could weaken her resolve, she pressed it. Feet shuffled inside and the door was opened a crack. An old lady, bent into half, her cheeks hollowed out, crinkled and strained her eyes to look closely at Naina.

'Is Leela madam there?' she asked as a student would.

The lady crinkled her eyes some more. Was she trying to catch some familiarity in her face? Did she see any? She mumbled something and turned inside. Naina peeked into the room. No trace, nothing to give off Leela's presence—no photos, no books on sociology, psychology—no Flora pencils.

'*Kaun hai*, Dadi?' a young man's voice boomed over the old lady's muttering.

He came out—a boy of 17 or 18 in a vest and green shorts. He showed no resemblance to Leela or Papa.

'I have come looking for Leela ma'am.'

'There is no one by that name here.' He looked annoyed.

'Leela Bharadwaj? Who taught at Dayalbagh?'

He frowned, 'We don't know anyone by that name.'

The old woman's mumbling grew louder. She caught the boy's arm, trying to tell him something, but he looked at Naina and gestured her to leave.

'I think she knows her. Please tell me what she's saying,' Naina requested him.

'She doesn't know anything. You please leave.' He looked so angry that it was impossible to plead with him. The door closed on her face.

Naina started walking back to the gate. Why was he angry? She was just a stranger looking for another. Unless—one of them was not a stranger to him; unless he had something to hide. To quit her search now would be difficult. But there was no way ahead. She had hit another dead-end.

From the corner of her eye, she sensed some movement and looking up saw a woman spreading out her washing on the terrace next door, become still. The woman gestured to Naina to wait. As Naina stepped out of F 22, the side door of F 23 opened slightly, and the lady beckoned her inside. Gingerly, she walked into another stranger's house.

'You are looking for Leela?' She continued, 'I heard you.'

'Do you know her?' The lady was easily forty-plus. There was a definite chance.

'Yes, I knew Leela. She lived there.' She pointed to F 22. Naina's blood froze. What did this woman have to tell? Was she prepared to hear it?

The lady continued, 'We were not exactly friends, just good neighbours. Chatting sometimes and exchanging dishes sometimes. Who are you?'

'I'm her friend's daughter. My mother died, so I came to look for Leela Aunty.'

'Oh ho! God bless her soul! What happened to your mother?'

'Cancer.'

'Oh ho, my mother-in-law also had cancer. God bless her soul.'

'Where is Leela Aunty?'

'But it has been so long since she went. Let me see—um—,' she counted someone's age and added some years on her fingers. 'It's almost seventeen years now. You all didn't know?'

Naina kept quiet, not wanting to lie again.

The lady shook her head, 'She ran away. With a man. Such shame she brought to the family, the university, this colony. The man was married and a father too. We have heard so many things about them. It's shameful!'

Looking heavenward in resignation, she continued, 'That is why this family does not want to speak about her. She was a blot on the family.'

Even though the woman had only confirmed what Naina had suspected for so long, Naina suddenly felt very weak, without being asked, she pulled up a chair from the dining table and sat down. They had done it. Run away. Papa from them and Leela from the half-bent woman, the boy in green shorts and perhaps others.

'Will you have some water?'

'No, thank you. I must leave now. Thanks for your help.' She tried to smile at the lady. 'Who lives in the house now?' She looked in the direction of F 22.

'Her mother and brother's family.'

'Her brother?'

'He committed suicide. Hanged himself from a fan after she ran away with that man.'

That man. Her father.

They were working in the garden. Raju weeded, while Naina pulled out the dry leaves and pruned the bushes. Soon they were tired, and Raju went in to make some ginger chai, while she slumped into a cane chair on the porch. Michael's motorbike came to a halt in front of the gate. Naina sat up, straightening her faded tee, aware of the mud and sweat clinging to her.

'Hi,' he came and plonked himself in the chair beside her.

'Hello, stranger! No Rob today?' She wanted to hear him tell her that Rob had returned to Australia.

He remained silent.

'Where were you? I came twice on Friday.'

'Some tea?'

'Yes, please.'

'Raju, one more tea.' She hollered for Raju to hear her in the kitchen.

'Where's Tara?'

'Inside, watching TV.'

'Michael, if you don't mind, can I take a quick shower?' She started to get up.

'Actually, I don't have too much time. I needed to tell you something.'

'Okay.' The way he looked and spoke, she was beginning to feel edgy.

'Rob—is my—partner—we're in a relationship,' he started suddenly. 'I'm moving in with him. To Melbourne.'

He was looking at the floor. 'Yeah, that's it. I've been seeing him for years. But this time when we met, we realized we…we want to be together.'

Naina held her breath, too stunned to speak, to say all the right things that would come to her later, after he'd left. Thankfully, he spoke again.

'I've thought about it. I've had no family—ever. Now perhaps life is poised for a change. And—he loves me.'

Naina was uneasy. Nothing seemed right, least of all, Michael's going away.

Raju came with the tea. Michael looked up at him and smiled feebly. He took the teacup from Raju. She curled her nervous fingers around hers, 'You will go—really? I mean, you think—'

'What is there to think, Naina? What do I have here? I could be here or in Melbourne or any goddamn place in the world, it makes no difference to anyone.'

'I wish—I hope you've thought this through. Perhaps—'

'No, Naina, I'm ready now. I have nothing to lose. Whatever will be, will be,' his voice trailed off.

'So, when—when do you…? *Go away?*'

'I'll leave as soon as the paperwork is complete.'

Naina wanted to be woken up from this nightmare to find Michael monkeying around the house, arranging coins on the floor with Tara, playing the keyboard with her, making Naina laugh, irritating her with his silly suggestions.

He kept his cup down. 'I must go. Rob's leaving on Wednesday. Loads to do.' He was avoiding her gaze. He turned towards the door to go inside, to meet Tara, but quickly turned back, deciding against it.

Naina walked behind him silently to his motorbike. Suddenly, there was so much she wanted to say to him, to tell him that he was perhaps being rash, and most importantly, that he could not just leave them and go away.

'Catch you, Naina,' he smiled a forced smile, not at all Michaelly, kick-started his bike, the sound of which boomed too loud today. And he disappeared around the bend.

Naina went inside and wept in the shower.

The landscape was faded and monotonous—dry, sun-bleached, stubbly fields dotted with flaxen haystacks. Spiky *babool* trees partitioned the train track from the fields. Enormous bridges over supine, sedate grey streaks that were rivers once, lay in wait amidst massive plains of caked mud. As the train clamoured over these bridges, people chanted 'Jai' and threw coins into the rivers, most of which fell on the rails. She thought of these—elongated coins under the rails. Nani had told her of how as children growing up in a railway colony, they would place coins and safety pins on the tracks. Naina never did such, normal things that normal children do.

Next to her sat an aged man whose face had been permanently set in a smile. He had helped her hitch up her middle berth at night. The rest of the people—a family of four had disembarked during the night and a group of college students—three boys—had taken their place. From their dialect, it was clear that the train had entered eastern India. The kind Uncle *ji* struck up a conversation with the students. They were travelling to Bihar, back after appearing for the Civil Services exam. One of them, a very thin, dark, young man, particularly jovial, said, 'I don't think I will be able to clear the ICS. I will just go back and start a coaching institute in Ranchi. I will have posters put up everywhere in the city that will say it has opened, three times—*Khul gaya! Khul gaya! Khul gaya!* Naina laughed with the others.

The lively conversation around lifted her spirits and the anxiety of the meeting ahead seemed to weigh a little less. The train's arrival time was at 7 in the morning, but due to the unscheduled stops and chain pulling, it was already 8:30.

The telegram from Benares had arrived even before she could steady herself from the two big jolts that came from Michael and Deepak. Like the scenery outside, the present was slipping away in quick flashes as she approached the end of her journey into her past.

Nibbling on the soggy cucumber sandwiches Raju had packed, she longed for a nice, cold bath. She had a return ticket for the evening and one for Sunday. Uday had arranged everything at a short notice. It was difficult to ascertain how much time her 'work' in Benares might take.

Her thoughts kept scuttling back to Tara. It was Saturday and she must be getting ready to leave for the centre. Maybe she was still sitting in her rocking chair. Any disruption in her routine led her to seek comfort in the chair's steady rocking. Shruti, a volunteer at the centre had agreed to stay with Tara for the couple of days that Naina would be away. It was the first time she would be away from Tara for so long. A lump rose in her throat thinking of Tara who might be missing her too, but would be helpless in articulating it in any way.

Deepak was also there somewhere. Someday he would return. Someday all would be well again. What if it was not? What if he never came back? Would she never behold those eyes, hold him close, feel his warmth? Her vision clouded over, and she turned to look outside, to what Uncle *ji* was pointing at, 'As a child, I learnt to swim in the river there.' A clatter of coins hit the rails again as the train traversed the bridge. 'Those children swimming there, dive for these coins and make a living from it.'

Each tree and pole that flashed past meant she was approaching him. Dithering between fear that dampened the palms of her hands; and a steely resolve to face whatever it was, once and for all, she shut her eyes to think of something other than what lay ahead.

The phone had rung past 11 at night. Naina was in bed, reading.

'*Ab chein pad gaya*? Happy?' Bhabhi had screamed into her ear. 'I tell you; you will never live in peace after ruining our lives. Such a happy family we were! He respected his elder brother and Bhabhi like his parents. But after you came, our lives turned into hell,' she accused. '*Ab woh hamein chhod kar chala gaya*, he has left us. If you know anything about his whereabouts, if you are hiding anything from us, I'm telling you, you bitch, my curse on you and your mad sister shall make you wriggle like worms in every birth!'

The verbal assault did not shatter her as much as the fear for what may have happened to Deepak. What exactly did Bhabhi mean? Did she actually say Deepak has gone somewhere? '*Arré*, do tell, where is Deepak? *Kha gayi kya*, have you swallowed him?' Naina kept the phone down. Off the hook. What if Deepak was really lost forever? Would she never see him again? When would people stop deserting her?

Naina had waited and re-dialled the seventh time, still, no one answered. Every day, the chowkidar came to open the office at 9:30 am, and Rupa, the receptionist, along with him. Bhaiya and Deepak usually came in around 10 am. At 10:10, when the phone was picked up, she stuttered, 'Chowkidar Bhaiya, can you tell me where Deepak Sa'ab is?'

'I don't know. Bade Sa'ab might come later. You can speak to him,' he was guarded.

'Yes, I will speak to him, but can you tell me something now?' she had nothing more to lose.

'*Aap* Deepak Sa'ab *wali bibi* ji *hain*, his friend?' He lowered his voice.

'*Han ji*,' she murmured, afraid he might disconnect. This was her only chance. Nobody else at Deepak's home or office would talk to her. It was Bhabhi's order.

'Bibi *ji*, *bahut bura hua*, Deepak Sa'ab has left home and gone away. It seems Madam *ji* was asking him to marry her sister. So, he said he was going away never to come back. Everyone is heartbroken. Bibi *ji*, if he calls you, please tell him to return home. Brothers should not be living like this—separated, in bitterness with each other.'

'Yes, Chowkidar Bhaiya, I will tell you if he contacts me, but you also promise me one thing, please? I will call you every morning at 9:30, and you must tell me if there is any news of Deepak Sa'ab.'

'Namaste, Sa'ab,' she heard his surprised voice, followed by the click of the receiver back on the cradle.

Every morning at 9:30, she had called Deepak's office and every morning for fourteen days the chowkidar had said, 'Bibi *ji*, *koi khabar nahi hai*, no news. Did you hear from him?'

On the fifteenth day, Naina had embarked on this, the most difficult journey of her life.

The train finally pulled into the railway station at 10. From the train, Naina could only see a sea of heads. She had never seen any place so packed with people. Holding her bag before her like a shield, she stepped out looking for the 'Exit', but realized there was no need. She was carried out of the station with the crowd. The TC at the exit stood helplessly waving at the crowds. No one cared to show their tickets.

She walked out of one chaos and into another—milling crowds, vehicle fumes, and buses moving arbitrarily; spewing dark smoke and gases; cleaners blowing shrill whistles and thumping the sides of buses; people sprawled in every available space—most of them seemed like permanent occupants with all the trappings of their public living strewn about them—dented pans, pieces of mirror, kerosene stoves, mineral water bottles opaque with dirt. Paan chewing, potbellied policemen wielding lathis moved among the crowd and arbitrarily tapped with the end of their lathis a bedding here, a *potli* there, asking for it to be opened and the fearful poor obliging immediately, forgetting the ignominy of laying bare their measly possession in the free-for-all.

Finally, she spotted the familiar red and yellow sight of a PCO. Raju answered the phone; Tara and Shruti had left for the centre. Raju spoke briefly, saying everything was fine and adding, 'Didi, *ja ke aao*, go and come.' He always said that. Every time she left home, Naina would call out to Raju, 'Raju, I'm leaving.' And every time, without fail, Raju would reply, 'Didi, *ja ke aao*'.

Outside, the sun melted down on her as she got into a rickshaw and asked for a hotel nearby. The *rickshawala* chose one called Broadway, a short ride away. Decent; it looked more like a lodge. Naina was relieved to see that all rooms on the two floors opened into a common courtyard, which served as an open-air dining space. The setting seemed safe.

'Room for a day. Maybe two days.'

The man at the reception eyed her curiously, but the moment she handed him the advance of 500 rupees, he handed over the keys of room number 56. Climbing up the stairs that had gained a dark sheen from use, she emerged into the hot sun at the top. A pair of middle-aged men leaning over the parapet wall, looked at her and smiled at each other. She turned the key into Room 56.

Mushrooms of damp covered the wall behind a single bed; a dresser next to it; and almost touching the foot of the bed, the door leading to the bathroom. 'God, please let it be clean,' she prayed as she pushed the door open and peeped inside. It was.

The water from the tap flowed in a booming cascade into a green bucket. For endless moments, she stood pouring cold water over herself. Slipping into a fresh salwar kameez, she took her time combing the wet hair, rubbing moisturizer, outlining her eyes with kajal and slowly walking up to the small terrace. Clotheslines bent under the burden of clothes long dry and now smelling of the afternoon heat, stretched from every possible nook. She spread out her towel in a corner.

Lingering over the humdrum, prolonging the mundane—all to keep herself from the thought of the impending action she would soon need to take, the decision she would have to make.

It was already 11. Naina collected her handbag and locking the door carefully, went down to the courtyard restaurant. A scrawny boy came over.

'What is there?'

'Chai, coffee, milkshake, cold drink.'

'Khana?'

'Sandwich, bread pakora, samosa, bread omelette.'

'Okay, bread omelette and chai. *Cheeni kum*, *doodh kum*, less sugar and milk.'

She could feel all eyes on her. She knew if she looked around, she would find strangers staring at her. Alien city, unknown people, I must see what is to be done, do it, and leave, Naina told herself.

Manik Mahal. The address had a regal and mysterious ring to it. The very first cycle rickshaw fellow nodded when she asked. For the first time in so many years, she was voicing something that was associated with *him*. It felt strange.

She had a choice. She could have ignored his request.

The rickshaw was pulling into narrow streets with houses on both sides. The streets were so narrow, passers-by had to stop, and sometimes even lean back on the walls to let the rickshaw pass. People seemed to be spilling out of their homes—sitting on doorsteps, filling water at the common taps, sweeping steps, buying vegetables. The rickshaw was speeding and grazed the walls, as it tried to avoid collision with sabzi vendors and other cyclists. No one seemed to mind. Suddenly, the *rickshawala* stepped on the brake and Naina lurched forward. Clutching the sides of the seat, she managed to not fall. A clucking hen scurried past the front wheel. The *rickshawala* spat out a couple of choicest abuses at the boys who stood looking on. They made dismissing sounds and gestures at him, '*Ja, ja*.' Challenged, he got off the rickshaw. She would have enjoyed the quarrel in chaste Awadhi on another occasion, not today. She called out to him, 'Bhaiya, will you go or not?'

'*Chaliye*,' he hitched up his dhoti and began to pedal forward still murmuring abuses under his breath. The boys smiled at her. The *rickshawala* was talking to the world at large, 'What if it had come under the wheel? *Sab hamka pakad lete*...they would've caught me.'

A short ride up the road and he halted. Naina looked around. 'Go up this lane and turn right. Manik Mahal is third on the left.'

She paid him and started walking up the narrow lane. The doors were all almost alike—old wood, with heavy chain latches hanging from their faces. None gave out any indication of the size of the dwelling on the other side or the status of the occupants like Delhi homes did. The third door on the left was as mystifying. It was painted a faded blue—peeling off, but serious looking. People on the street, neighbours stood watching her; whatever work they were doing, suspended.

Picking the end of the heavy iron chain-latch, Naina tapped the door. The self-conscious effort let out a faint knock—so feeble, it amplified her nervousness. A louder tap elicited some sounds from inside—the clank of glass bangles, the ring of anklets, a wooden chair or something pushed. A child began to cry. Surely there was a mistake. Someone would open the door and tell her this and she would go back home. To Delhi.

The door opened. A woman, her head covered, the end of the saree covering her face clenched in her mouth, looked at her enquiringly. 'Naina,' her voice rasped. The woman's expression changed like quicksilver—like they had not *really* expected her to come. Opening the door just enough to let her in, she closed it behind Naina quickly.

The woman led her through a long, dark, seemingly unused room into a brick-floored courtyard enclosed on the rest of the three sides with living quarters. Two stringed cots were occupied by this and that—an oily pillow, a rattle, a thali. Clothes on the lines were thrown carelessly. There was a tulsi pedestal in the centre, adorned with lines of yellow and red paint holding a withering tulsi plant; a few more shrubs and plants spouted chaotically from earthen pots and cracks in walls. Naina was gestured towards the sole chair. A very old man, his chin to his chest sat against a wall, talking to himself. He was probably blind. The crying child, naked waist down, was now clinging to the woman's saree, his nose running into it. The woman pushed him aside even as he bawled and calling out to 'Gauri', disappeared behind one of the several doors that studded the walls around Naina.

A girl of about four, pulling up the falling shoulders of her oversized frock came out shyly to pick the crying child and went to sit with him on the bare floor of the covered veranda. She started talking and pacifying the child while eyeing Naina all the time, showing off her maternal skills for Naina's benefit.

The woman emerged from another door carrying a tall steel glass on a small plate. She dragged a plastic stool before Naina and set the plate on it. It was probably lassi or *chhanch* and a piece of dry barfi beside it on the plate. Two women, their heads covered too, peered from behind the door from where the woman had emerged. Naina wanted to get this over with fast.

'Where is—*he*?'

'I will take you. He is upstairs.'

A shiver went down her spine as Naina imagined him looking down at her from some room upstairs. She did not look up.

It was a dark and narrow staircase. A thick rope with a knotted end hung from somewhere at the top. The woman handed it to Naina and led the way, expertly climbing the steep staircase without support, her saree hitched up to reveal her strong calves. Holding the rope, Naina followed her.

A long veranda joined the four sides of the house and opened into the rooms upstairs. A young man lay on the floor listening to a film song on radio in one of the rooms with its doors wide open. Most of the other doors were shut. A girl, with a towel tied on her head and a bucket in her hand, came running down the stairs from what must be the terrace. The woman entered the last door in the corner.

Naina had to bend her head to enter the low door which had a high ledge—like a window—probably to keep out rats or rainwater. The room was dark and at first, she saw nothing. The woman walked to the other end and opened a window. Light fell on a charpoy in the centre.

The body was shrunken and rose only as a slight heap under the sheets. Still. She moved closer and was startled by the expression she still recognized. His eyes shone for a second on seeing her, then tears welled up and flowed down the sides of his face into the pillow. Long grey hair and a longer beard gave him an ascetic look.

The woman brought a stool and Naina sat on it next to the charpoy taking care to not be too close and yet not look as detached as she was feeling.

'He cannot speak. Cancer in the throat,' the woman said softly and left the room.

Papa tried to reach out for her hand, but she sat very still, away, her anger and unease palpable. He drew back his extended hand.

Naina sat for a while, unable to find a single word to say. What was there to say to him? Her entire life was playing out before her like a motion picture. The one image that refused to leave her was Amma's body, her head held together with bandages. It filled her with loathing for this person lying before her. He had abandoned them. He was paying for it.

She sat still till she sensed that he had fallen asleep. There was nothing to do. She got up to leave. At the door, turning to take another look, Naina was startled to find him looking straight at her. He had no voice; his eyes were empty. She hurried downstairs and out of the house, not stopping to speak with anyone.

'I could not bring myself to forgive him,' she spoke after they had covered most of the distance to the bus stop in silence.

'Hmm,' Uday took her sweaty palm into his. An enormous storm that had been gathering rose inside and she longed for him to hold her. His hand on hers tightened. They were walking in a street full of office-leaving people. It was no place to seek the comfort she needed. Uday stopped near a low parapet wall and they sat down.

'It's okay now that you've done your bit. If you couldn't find it in you to forgive him, I guess it's alright. Eventually, you'll find peace.'

'Not in a thousand years!' She was so sure. And still so angry. 'I had so many questions. They remain unanswered.'

'Like?'

'Leela? What about her? Did she desert him? Where is she?'

'Maybe she never was with him. Maybe it's just your imagination.'

'No, no, they went away together. But then where is she now? I needed to know.'

'Don't you think it's all for the best? The answers could be more troubling. I think you should let this be. What has to unravel, will on its own when the time comes. Naina, I seriously feel it's time for you to move on. Look at the present—life's beautiful, seize your share of happiness and hope.'

He took her hands in his and continued, 'You are very courageous, Naina. And you are a beautiful person worthy of everything wonderful in life. Your time has come to shine.' They smiled at the mention of the song they heard together often, but Naina could feel the words coming from the depths of his heart and she could feel his love—the deep, loving concern of a close friend. He was right. They got up and started to walk towards the bus stop.

She moved to the back of the bus and slipped into a window seat. Fishing out the tattered copy of *The Inscrutable Americans* that had passed through everyone in the office and had finally come to her, she began to read. The bus was stuttering; it would be another five to seven minutes before it actually moved ahead. Until then, it would inch forward a little and then be pulled back by the conductor's loud thumping on its side as he tried to lure the passengers comfortably seated in the bus behind. The last seat was still not full.

'Do you mind if I move in there?'

Naina looked up and saw Pari requesting the gentleman seated at the other end of her seat. Pari sank in next to her, smiling.

'Hi, Naina, long time!'

'Hi, how are you?'

'Never been better. It's been two years!'

Naina was surprised that Pari remembered it so precisely.

'Do you take this bus every day?' Pari asked.

'Almost.'

'Then I think we'll be seeing more of each other now. I work with an event management company that has recently moved to this side of town.'

'That's great.' Naina was glad Pari had herself mentioned the job. It would have been embarrassing for her to ask and awkward to not.

'What are you reading?' Without waiting for an answer, she turned the cover in her hands. 'Oh.'

'You've read it?'

'Nah, we have a copy at home though.'

Naina pictured Pari in a cosy home with a doting father, a mother who looked as young as her daughter, siblings who squabbled, but talked and giggled after lights out. Pari, the name itself proclaimed over-indulgent parents and she did seem like a much-pampered kid.

'You know Naina, I never really got to know you in office. You were always so engrossed in work and stuck to your one friend.'

Naina ignored the allusion to Uday. Pari was wearing a beautiful white top with Kashmiri embroidery in hues of orange and pink over skinny jeans. Her perfume was strong. The man next to her seemed distracted as he squirmed in his seat, coughing nervously and pushing back his hair that did not require pushing back.

'Where do you stay?'

'Kailash Colony.'

'Neat! I stay at Masjid Moth. How is Uday? Is he still with DW?'

'Yes, he is.'

'And the others?'

'Good too.'

'And what have you become?'

'Um… Team Lead.'

'Wow, that's neat too. Hey, my stop is almost here. I'll start moving now. Catch ya!'

'Bye, see you.' Pari slithered between the standing crowd, her straight shoulder-length hair falling elegantly on her back; her lace bra clearly visible under her white top.

Naina lay awake at night thinking about Pari. Why was there this undercurrent of animosity between them from day one? Nothing had ever happened. What exactly was the reason they never got along? How had it become so evident to everyone else in the office, even without anything happening explicitly? When Pari was asked to leave, she had wondered if they thought she too had something to do with it, given her closeness to Uday.

Maybe she was in a bit of an awe of Pari—self-assured, fashionable, and extroverted. But Pari had been too casual about work and Naina bristled at her language; her indiscriminate use of swear words. 'But the girl has spunk,' was what Uday had said when she mentioned that Pari used 'sexy' for good, beautiful, bright, delicious, happy—everything. Naina had felt a twinge of jealousy.

One day, out of the blue, in the middle of a very unrelated conversation during lunch, Uday had started to smile and told her, 'You know what Pari did? She wrote a whole course without a single article. She said articles are redundant and content could still be intelligible without the 'a'-s, 'an'-s and 'the'-s. She just tossed the articles away.' He began to laugh.

'She was asked to go because of that?'

'Yes.'

'Is that reason enough?'

'Of course! She did that right at the closing of the project, she was warned, but she stuck to it. On the night before we needed to turn in the content—the course was already behind schedule—she went and deleted all the articles from not just her work, but the entire course! She was asked to go because of her stubbornness. We risked losing a big client, because of her pig-headedness. Imagine the stupidity!'

3:24 am—the neon digits glowed in the darkness.

Michael's flight to Bombay was at 9. He had to meet someone there before taking the late-night flight to Melbourne. Naina lay in bed looking outside at the inky silhouette of the *madhukamini* bush against the unlit sky.

Once, while playing under it as a little girl, she had spotted a pair of birds twittering above, fetching twigs, string, and grass in their beaks. When a nest began to form, she could not hold her curiosity and climbing on a stool, stood on tiptoes to peer inside the neat grass bowl. Three aqua-coloured eggs—each the size of a large grape; lay inside like a picture.

Excited, she ran inside to tell Nana.

After Nana had had a look, he asked her to get a notebook and write about it.

'What shall I write, Nana?'

'Write today's date and all that you've seen—the bird, the nest, the eggs—describe them. Then, every day write down what happens, the changes you see.'

He helped her identify the bird in the cherry-colour, leather-bound Salim Ali book. In her neat, round, cursive handwriting, she wrote—Red-vented Bulbul.

Every day at lunchtime, Nana would ask her about the birds. She drew the birds, the nest, and the tree in the notebook. Nana called these 'diagrams'. So, when Anjali called her to play house, feeling very important, Naina told her she was making *diagrams*.

One day, when she was standing on the stool looking at the featherless baby birds whose eyes bulged out of their translucent pink skins; wanting to touch them, Nana came and stood behind her. She could smell his Brylcreem. When he passed away some months later, and she slept with Nani on their bed, she could smell Nana's Brylcreem on the pillow.

She could smell it now.

Michael was leaving.

'Why me, Nani!' Seized by despair, she had burst out one day.

'*Laado dekho*, see, God has to distribute happiness and sorrow, success and difficulties among us all. He gave you these because he knows you are brave and strong.' Naina did not want to be brave and strong. She just wanted everyone in her house to be *normal*. Like it was for her friends. She wanted someone by her side when she did her homework; she wanted someone to get her a lollipop when they got home from the bazaar; for someone to tell the other kids that it was her turn on the swing; and when she wore her best frock, for someone to say she looked like a princess. Most of all she wanted to be called a princess.

What was it that she read in Michael's eyes as he held her hand for a fleeting moment last night when he had come to say goodbye? He kissed an unwilling Tara on the head and put his arm around Raju who seemed very sad to see him go. He had held Naina's hand, throwing his other arm around her in an awkward hug.

She looked long after him as he rode away; the sound of his Enfield kept reverberating in the distance.

Like drops of water on a hot griddle, the parched Delhi earth hissed when the first rain fell. It took several showers after the long summer months to douse the heat sunk into the city's belly. But it was cold today. Naina burrowed deeper into the covers. What should she do? She had an important meeting with a newspaper editor at 9:30 am. But Michael was going away to Australia. There was no knowing when she would see him next. If she would.

The *autowala* honked continuously and splashed the water in the potholes on passers-by. Naina had no inclination to ask him to not. The air was chilly; Naina pulled her jacket close and stuck her hands inside her cloth bag to feel the warmth of wool.

The muffler.

One knit, one purl, knit and purl…the long, grey knitting needles shone silver at their tips from use as they looped the wool and went back and forth. *One purl, one knit*...it went on till the yellow wool, the colour of lemon zest got over and Sister Anne asked her to use a *contrast*. Nani dug in again into the *Agarwal Sarees* polythene bag in her cupboard and came up with another ball of wool—a royal blue. It was a *good* contrast, she told Naina.

Michael was wheeling his trolley towards the departure gate. Naina dashed through the drizzle towards him, strands of windblown hair sticking to her damp face.

Standing in the queue, he looked surprised to see her as she leaned on the balustrade separating them. They were not within talking distance yet and he looked helplessly at people in front and behind him. When the queue moved and he came closer, both spoke at once.

'How did you come? When is the flight from Bombay?'

'By auto. At 11:30.'

'Tara must've left too.'

'Yeah.'

'What about office? You'll be late.'

'That's okay.'

'You leave now. I'm almost there and the rain… It will take you hours to get to work.'

But she lingered. He too did. Leaving five minutes early would not make a difference to her job or life. The queue before him began to shorten very rapidly. There was little time. She reached into her bag.

'Michael, this is for you. I made it in school…class six.'

Michael held the yellow and blue muffler in his hand for a brief moment and then he wrapped it around his neck. How bad it looked where the knit had become purl and the purl, knit and where one purl had dropped only to be picked up by a knit two rows later. But Michael wore it with such pride. His turn came too soon. As he showed his ticket, he grabbed her hand over the cold, wet metal rail and said, 'Take care of yourself, Naina. Take care of my Tara.'

And then he was sucked into the sea of people inside.

The flash of lemon zest yellow and royal blue was difficult to miss even in the crowd. He glanced back once and spotting her, waved back then walked away resolutely. Tears blurred Naina's vision and even though she strained her eyes, she could not catch him again.

How had Rob become family? Just like that, coming from nowhere and claiming Michael? Nani always said that being born in a family was not enough, more important was to make bonds that last. Sometimes family members turn sworn enemies, while good friends stand by like pillars in times of sorrow and hardship.

The sluice gates of the grey world above that were holding up, burst open.

Naina went to the telephone booth to call Mr Malhotra, to apologize for not keeping the appointment.

Stretched out on the cane chair in the porch, looking at the flowers that had shaken the recent rains off their faces and were preening in the morning sun, Naina turned at the sound of the gate being pushed open. An old man, bent over, came trudging up the garden path. Alarmed, she was about to call Raju, when she recognized him.

'Ramprasad!'

Ramprasad had aged immensely. 'Naina baby, *bitiya*,' for a moment, he was overcome with emotion, but quickly regained his former cheer, the pretence with which he had comforted her as a child, '*Arré*, you have grown so big,' he steadied his voice.

'Where were you all these years?'

'*Arré* baby, *apna kya hai*, wherever there is roti, we have to go.' He became silent.

'Heard about Memsa'ab and Chhoti Memsa'ab. *Bahut bura hua*, very sad…' his voice trailed off as he looked heavenwards. 'Where is Tara baby?'

'She's inside. Raju!' she called out and then turned to show him, 'Look Ramprasad, we're working on the garden.'

An anonymous joy descended on her the moment she opened her eyes. Naina lay in bed immersed in a gladness that seemed not to hinge on any particular source. Maybe it was Ramprasad. Memories seemed to buzz around him that he had not shaken off. For this blessing alone, she was grateful. In a flash, she got out of bed and wrote a check of 10,000 rupees in the name of Mr Advaith Singh, sealed it in an envelope and before another thought could cross her mind, wrote down the Benares address on it.

By the time she finished her run, the sunshine had covered everything with a gold foil. She whistled as she entered the house and Raju looked up in surprise, a little embarrassed. Girls do not whistle, Nani would say, it is *unladylike*. It had not helped being a lady. She whistled again.

Uday was mimicking a customer who said 'ph' in place of the 's' sound. He was hilarious. Naina was doubling up with laughter and asking him to stop. The two of them, along with Ratna, Piyali, and Syed were returning from the tea stall outside and as they piled into the office, their voices still high from the excitement, Sunita called out, 'Naina, there was a call for you from Benares.'

Naina's heart struck once inside her, ominous like a stopped clock. What now? No one else seemed to have heard, even Uday had walked inside.

'Who was it? What did they say?' She pretended to be calm as she walked up to Sunita's desk.

'He just said it was very urgent and that he would call—in another half-hour.'

'Who? When?'

'Um—they didn't leave a name,' Sunita looked at the time and estimated, 'At around 10.'

It was 10:30 already. Naina lingered at the entrance. If she took the call inside, at her desk, others would hear. Who was this? What did they want? Hope *he* is okay. I don't want to hear anything bad now, please God, she prayed, stiff with anxiety.

'Naina, I'll transfer the call. Hello,' Sunita picked the ringing phone, 'Just a moment,' she said and beckoned Naina who took the receiver in her trembling hand. Her faint *hello* did not reach the caller. 'Hello, this is Naina,' she attempted with more energy.

'This is Tarun. I have bad news. Professor Sa'ab has expired.'

Suddenly, there was no air to breathe, she gasped, tried to speak, but no sound emerged. Everything before her began to blur as she caught fragments, 'Late last evening—he walked—it was too late. The body—' Naina was falling backwards. 'Hey, what's wrong?' Sunita's voice seemed to come from very far away.

'Call Uday sir!' Sunita shouted.

Naina needed to sleep. Through the daze she felt people rubbing her palms, bringing a glass of water to her lips. She saw the hazy face of a very concerned Uday murmuring things to her and to others. Why was she floating like this? Life was demanding too much from her. She would do nothing now. And she shut everything out.

'Naina, let's go,' Uday was helping her to her feet. There were others. She leaned on whoever they were. They helped her into a car that trudged comfortingly; she reached home, the gate opened, bell rang, door opened, Raju stood agape; her sandals came off, the lobby floor felt cold and she was relieved to lie down in her bed. For some time, there was a buzz of soft voices around her, then someone held her arm, a little too tight and then there was a small prick.

A nurse had been called to give her a Valium injection.

She got up a few times in the evening to go to the bathroom, but did not eat. At 7, Uday held out a glass of milk, which she drank and fell asleep instantly. Uday had called up the centre and asked them to send someone home to care for Tara. Sukriti was with Tara till her bedtime. She would come back in the morning, she said and left. Asking Raju to call him if there was a need, Uday left too. Raju slept outside Naina's door, leaving it slightly ajar.

When Uday came at 9 the next morning, Naina was still sleeping. He dropped Tara and Sukriti at the centre on his way to office. Naina slept till noon. When Gupta Aunty saw Uday emerge from the house with Tara and Sukriti, she waited for them to leave and then came over to ask. Not believing Raju's word that Didi was running a high fever and sleeping, she came inside to check. Naina's forehead was indeed warm when she placed her hand on it and she went away convinced.

Uday came again at 3 in the afternoon. Naina was sitting by the window, her eyes glassy, her face relaxed. He sat across from her and held her hand. 'How are we?'

She did not look at him. It was many minutes before she spoke, her voice sounding strange to her own ears.

'He had held out his hand for me, but I came away.'

Uday entered her memory in padded feet, he had a vague idea about what had happened from the broken words she had been uttering in her delusion.

'He was unable to get up—so weak. But his eyes were the same.'

'Why did he do it?' The disquiet inside rolled out in tears. She had not imagined she would cry for him.

'When will my troubles end? Shall I also go jump to death like Amma? Or like him, run away? Who will care for Tara? Coward! Dead and gone. Free. All free except me.' Naina was suddenly so wild with anger, she banged her head against the grille.

In a flash, Uday held her away firmly, 'Calm down, Naina.'

'Leave me alone. You don't even know what happened.'

Without relaxing his hold on her, he gently asked, 'Tell me then.'

She leaned against the grille, crying. Her hands in his grip grew limp. He moved closer and putting his arms around her, drew her to him.

'He walked into the Ganga.'

His hold tightened as she trembled at the thought—Papa walking into the water—walking till there was nothing beneath his feet, nothing to bear him, the water rising above him, blinding him, he must have gasped for air to breathe—perhaps called out for help, not wanting to die and full of fear, perhaps he tried to save himself—the image tore at her heart. Why did he punish himself so? And her?

They sat in silence. Then holding her by the shoulders, Uday lifted her face. Such sad eyes, such sorrowful lips, for once he wanted to just pluck her away from this wretched life and place her into an easy, happy world. If only he could do something to help. Uday realized how much he had pushed Naina into doing all the difficult things. She had followed his word. How cruel and heartless he had been. Instead of giving, he had demanded love. He kissed her softly on her forehead and wiped her tears. Gently pushing her hair away from her face, he smiled to cheer her up.

When Raju came in with the tea, Naina got up to wash her face. Sipping tea, they sat looking out at the *madhukamini* bush and the little bulbuls that twittered playfully on the branches so tender they swung with their small weight.

'Do you want to go to the temple?' He asked hesitatingly.

She shook her head. 'Is Tara okay?'

Uday told her about the arrangement they had made for her. 'I have spoken with Rajesh, he says you can take a couple of days off.'

'What did you tell him?' she asked anxiously.

'Well, it was not possible to hide everything. I told him you have been stressed out completely. Piyali asked about the phone call, so I told them that you had lost a relative.'

Naina relaxed. Uday looked into her eyes as he spoke, 'The leave is granted, but I don't think it's a good idea to sit at home.'

'I have nowhere to go.'

'One of those times I wish I was a girl,' his eyes were making a half-hearted pretence at naughtiness.

'What then?'

'You'd come with me and we'd go on a holiday. But once there I'd be myself again, okay?' He was now smiling wickedly. Even Naina could not help smiling. They held hands and sat in silence.

'You know, he called me "Nadia"—it means *hope* in Russian. I never understood why. Now I think perhaps I was his only hope. And I turned away.' She grew pensive again.

'One day, there was a party in this house. There in the lawn the big table had been laid out—covered in a white tablecloth. The summer air was warm and pleasant. It was so beautiful—the mild fragrance of summer blooms mixed with the whiff of people's perfumes; everyone dressed so elegantly—especially the ladies in beautiful pastel chiffons and gossamer cottons; and the sound of laughter and friendly banter. The servants were walking with trays of iced lemonade. I was standing near the rose bed in my peach organdie frock—so stiff that if I got up from sitting, it remained sitting,' Naina smiled at the thought.

'Then Nani noticed me and called me over. When everyone's attention was on me, she urged me to sing. I was very shy. I looked around and saw Papa standing with a group of men. He was not listening to them; his attention was on me and what was being said to me. I felt all the more shy. But he looked happy. He winked at me as if offering me his support, asking me to sing. *Edelweiss* was his favourite. I started. Another aunty joined in. When I finished and looked around, he was clapping loudest of all. It meant so much to me. He seemed proud of me.'

'I can never understand how he did what he did. He used to shout and yell at Amma. Amma never shouted back, although she did all those frightful things. I still remember how fearful she was when he held her against the wall one day. He was choking her with his elbow pressed to her throat, her eyes were popping out with fear. I was so scared, howling and pleading, "Papa, let Amma go, Papa, let her go, please, Papa." '

Naina lapsed into a silence. After a few minutes, she asked him, 'Do you think I can be forgiven for what I did to him? I will never be able to forgive myself.'

'Naina, who are we to forgive or punish ourselves or others? Our actions are based on what we feel at the time. Don't hold yourself responsible for your past actions. You have to move on. You did what you thought was correct at that point of time. Maybe he was not justified in what he did and so he had to suffer so much.'

'*Maybe*? You still think *maybe*? You don't know what hell all of us went through because of him! He went away, but I could not, Tara could not, Amma could not, Nani could not. We were all trapped in this miserable life. Neither able to live nor die.'

'Yes, so I guess, you do believe in divine justice. He caused you all so much pain and he suffered for it.'

Clearly, she was torn between her conflicting feelings for Papa. She recalled everything she could about him, she cried, and she smiled thinking of him.

Raju peeped in at dinner time. Uday coaxed her to come out of her room. They went to the table where Sukriti and Tara were already seated. Sukriti asked how Naina was feeling and telling her that she was much better, Naina thanked her for her help. She stood behind Tara who did not look up from her plate. Naina bent down and kissed the top of Tara's head.

'Tara, Papa passed away,' she said, without emotion. Then she turned to Sukriti, 'So you see, we lost our father yesterday. I was a little shaken. Tara, as you know, will not understand. Anyway, she has no recollection of him as he—he *left* us when we were very small. But I have to let Tara know. Now if people ask me about my father, I just have to say he is *no more*. Simplifies a lot.'

Sukriti looked shocked and at a loss for words. After a few silent minutes, she said, 'I'm sorry.'

Uday refrained from saying anything. He knew how fragile Naina's emotional state was and how this seeming calm could at any moment flare into a rage or a breakdown.

They ate in silence.

The intoxicating scent of the *madhukamini* riding over the breeze wafted in. Naina seemed calm sitting by the window and Uday thought it was time to leave. As he got up, she caught hold of his arm; he sat down again. She moved closer to him and rested her head on his chest. Poor, little girl, Uday's heart brimmed over with love and concern for her. He wrapped his arms tightly around her.

She shivered in sleep and woke up. He held her. Floating on the threshold of sleep and dreams, she let herself go.

'Go as a river,' Nani would say. 'Resistance is futile. Life flows. Despite everything.'

Opening herself to the succour she sensed in their fused passion and desperate to not lose anything more, she drew him to her. He took her face in his hands and kissed her deep and long, unleashing all her bundled desires, the cravings of her restrained soul.

She thought of his car parked outside for all to see. She could not let him go. May it be night forever.

Naina stayed home the next day too, sitting by the window and letting thoughts, images flit in her head. Who were those people living with Papa? Why were they caring for him? She had left Benares immediately after meeting Papa. A young man had followed her as she breezed out of Manik Mahal that day. 'I'm Tarun. Professor Sa'ab is very ill. Cancer of the oesophagus.' Naina did not respond.

'Can I drop you to the bus stop?'

'No, thank you. Please, I don't want to talk.' She had walked away, her turmoil hastening her departure.

Tarun had called her now. *Expired*, he had said. Expired like a medicine? Like life had been put into Papa's body from this date to that. Date over, Papa had walked into the river. To drown. Expired.

In the evening, she went to the temple with Tara. A prayer rose in her heart and with all earnestness, she prayed for the peace of Papa's soul. Sad it was that there was no family to mourn him; no family to do pujas and perform other rites for the peace for his soul. Where was Leela? Papa was dead. He had paid for his failings. Back home, she tore off the check she had written for him and wrote another for the same amount, left the name blank, and sealed it in an envelope, writing the Benares address on it once again.

Uday had been gone seven months now. He was heading the DW office in London. Naina's only link with him were official e-mails. He copied all emails to Rajesh. Naina and he had never spoken directly with each other after that day.

Even before she opened her eyes, Naina felt the calm of a comforting, all-obliterating sleep. She wanted to linger in that languid state, soak in the bliss. But it was only a few moments before she became aware of an arm that cradled her head still, a warm breath on her neck—the sense of another.

With a start, she opened her eyes, waking him too. He opened his eyes; lay there looking at her for a second, then searching her eyes and finding no assurance, sat up. Awkward and confused, Naina walked into the bathroom allowing Uday privacy.

She forgot how long she stood still in the bathroom, reliving the night's events—each moment flashing before her like a slide show.

The room was empty when she returned.

'I'm sorry,' he said in the evening.

'Really?' stung, she spat out. All day she had thought about it. How easily her body and soul, desperately longing for love, yearning to be held and comforted, had yielded to his gentle loving. She had no regrets.

'You're sorry? Good.'

She had felt that he may be awkward from the awareness that he'd taken advantage of her in her weak moment. She wanted to tell him it was not so. But he had come to apologise. It was not love for him. It was a mistake.

'Naina, you know how I feel about you—despite knowing how you feel about Dee…'

'You think you are a saint? Giving to me only what *I* want? You accept things as they are? So much for all your liberal thinking! Oh please, stop it!'

'I am saying all the wrong things perhaps. I know you still love him.'

'Oh yes, God almighty, you know everything, don't you? Then why don't you just let it be? Why this drama?'

He was silent. Naina did not attempt to speak, she wanted him to feel the resentment she felt for him now. He got up to leave. Naina walked him to the door and without a word, banged it shut after him. Uday could not make himself to tell her that she'd been murmuring Deepak's name all the while they had made love.

He had held her face in his palms like a flower. He had looked into her eyes like only she mattered. The *madhukamini* had stood guard outside the open window, filling the night air with its heady scent to set them free. He had kissed her, and she had wanted more. He had squashed her slender body so tight in his embrace that she felt all her senses rip open. He was all she wanted. She let him take her as he cradled her willing body into his arms and lifted her to the bed like a baby. The memory made Naina tremble. Still without regret, she wondered if she had wronged Uday.

Naina had got home early as she was running a slight fever. Raju was making tea for her when the phone rang. Raju called out, 'Didi, there were calls for you earlier also.'

'Naina madam?'

Immediately she recognized his voice and her heart began to pound. 'Chowkidar Bhaiya?' She asked.

'Madam, don't tell anyone I called. I got your number from Savita madam. *Chhote Sa'ab ka pata chal gaya hai*, got news of him. He's in Himachal. Sa'ab spoke to him.'

'Thank you, Chowkidar Bhaiya. Anything more?'

'No, madam. Now I have to go.'

'God bless you, Bhaiya.' She was keeping the receiver down when she heard him again.

'Madam?'

'*Haan*?'

'One more thing, Madam *ji*, the marriage has been fixed.'

Her heart began to throb in her ears.

'Deepak Sa'ab's marriage with Memsa'ab's sister is this Wednesday.'

V

New Delhi 2000

Anand was of medium height, wore spectacles that constantly slipped down his nose and he kept adjusting with his right index finger, raising his eyebrows and pleating his forehead in the process. A satchel he carried at all times seemed like the extension of his right arm. He held it with both hands, close to his chest, when he sat. He looked older than thirty years, but had a pleasant smile and easy manners.

Preeti Aunty had arranged this meeting. Anand's sister was her neighbour in Liverpool. She had spoken to Naina about Anand and asked her to meet him. Preeti Aunty said that he was suitable for her in every way and at twenty-six, it was a 'stroke of luck' that she was even being considered for such an alliance. Anand's family knew 'all about her' and had no problems, Preeti Aunty had told Naina happily. Naina had not even bothered to give it another thought till Anand walked into her office one afternoon.

After a brief introduction standing at the reception with people watching, the two of them had walked to Bengali Market for a coffee. He spoke little; Naina, less. They had coffee, Anand walked her back to her office, and left.

Naina felt numb. There was no place for Anand in her life right now, yet there he was. Anand, the 9-to-5 college lecturer. How had he happened to her life? While she was doing extremely well professionally, her personal life was a constant trial. Was Anand, the satchel-carrier, her escape? The one man who would quietly walk into her life and close the doors on all others? Maybe he would even try and stick the label of 'nice girl' on her?

So, when Preeti Aunty called two days later, Naina listened.

'I'm so happy, Naina. Pallavi tells me that you and Anand met, and he wants to see you again. It will be nice if you call him home now. Only problem is, who will be there with you? Why don't you call Mrs Gupta? No—she will go around telling the whole colony. And—don't call any of your friends, okay? I think it's fine, don't call anyone. Tara and the servant are there, na?'

How Naina hated Preeti Aunty calling Raju *servant*! She knew she did it deliberately and there was no point telling her again. Preeti Aunty continued, 'Okay, *beta*, do call him over. Wear something dressy. Ask the servant to make something nice. I'll call you on Sunday. Bye, *beta*; give my love to Tara.'

Before Naina could make up her mind, Anand called. She knew the communication circle was complete, Preeti Aunty to Pallavi, Pallavi to Anand, and from Anand back to her.

Anand came on Sunday morning. Naina opened the door and was surprised to see him clinging on to his satchel even on a Sunday. He stepped inside and sat in the corner chair. Carefully, he kept the bag on the floor, wedged between one leg of the divan and that of a chair, so that it stayed upright, but hidden from view. Naina was ill at ease. She had not listened to Preeti Aunty—neither had she instructed Raju to cook something nice, nor had she worn 'something dressy'. She was wearing her well-worn brown corduroys, with a poorly matched and visibly faded sea-green tee. She called in Raju.

'Anand, what will you have?'

'I don't drink anything except tea. Teetotaller I am, since birth.'

Because Raju kept a straight face, Naina could control her smile.

'Raju, this is Anand *ji*. This is Raju. He lives with us. He has been here since he was little.'

Anand ignored Raju. Naina waited. He did not respond to Raju's namaste. To establish his standing in the household, she said, 'Raju, make chai for Anand *ji* and yourself.'

Tara sat cross-legged on the floor in the lobby, silently arranging coins in long rows. She refused to acknowledge Anand's presence.

'You cook, Naina *ji*?'

'Sometimes.'

'What is your speciality?'

Marriage interview. Staying calm, Naina answered, 'Actually Anand, I don't get the time. Raju takes care of everything.'

'I love to cook.'

'That's nice.'

'I live in a PG, but the owners let me cook sometimes. I make excellent Butter Chicken. Do you like chicken, Naina *ji*?'

'I'm a vegetarian.'

'Oh, I'm sorry, I'm sorry.'

'That's okay—just a matter of personal choice.'

'But later *toh*—you can have problems, I mean—if there is a problem, I can even think of becoming a vegetarian.'

Raju walked in with the tea and she was saved the trouble of finding a polite response.

There was a long silence as Anand dunked one Marie biscuit after another in his tea and ate. Once he was done, he asked, 'Don't you watch TV, Naina *ji*? Oh yes, you are very busy. But on Sundays?'

'Oh, shall I switch it on for you?' She was thankful for the distraction.

Anand watched the news for an hour, without talking. He got up once to use the bathroom, but paid no attention otherwise to anyone.

Naina pottered about the house. What a waste of a precious Sunday! It was getting close to 1 and Anand showed no signs of leaving. Raju quietly asked about lunch.

'Didi, shall I make something special, *kuch achcha*?'

Restraining her smile, she told him to not bother; then, decided to ask Anand.

'Anand *ji*, will you have lunch with us?'

'*Han ji*, I have no problem.'

'I meant—it might be your special lunch today, our vegetarian...'

'It's okay, I can sacrifice one day.'

They ate rice, kadhi, and aloo subzi in silence. It was only after lunch that they relaxed a bit and Anand started talking about his love for poetry. He wrote some himself and had been published too. Naina was impressed. He spoke at length about himself, his PG accommodation in Patparganj, his *miserly* landlord, his *excellent* college in Noida, and his *useless* colleagues. He spoke so much, almost as if the food had provided him with instant energy. All the while he had been watching Tara. Now he asked.

'So, what exactly is the problem with this child?'

Naina cringed.

'There is no problem. *Tara* is autistic. She does not have social skills and does not talk.' She spoke matter-of-factly, then added with pride, 'She's a great keyboard player.'

But Anand was not paying attention, he was already by Tara's side on the floor. Tara had resumed her coin play after lunch.

'*Ab dekho*, let me show you something.'

Before Naina could react, in one sweeping swish he had gathered into a heap the long trails of coins that Tara had been laboriously arranging all morning.

'Let's make something *meaningful*—'

His voice trailed off as Tara started to tear at her hair and hit her knees together. Naina rushed to her side and began to comfort her by softly talking to her and holding her arms down.

But she knew Tara would not calm down in Anand's presence. Furious with him, she still managed to tell him calmly, 'Anand, please don't mind. But can you—leave? I mean—perhaps wait outside? I'll just calm her and call you back. Please?'

He picked his bag and stepped out. Without saying anything, quietly, Naina began rearranging the coins. Her slow, repetitive action soothed Tara, who joined the task and was soon engrossed. Naina stepped out, half hoping he had left. Anand looked upset standing there with his bag, his eyes shifty. Something about him struck her then. A sense of disquiet came over her, lightly but surely. Abruptly he said, 'I must leave now,' and left.

That's it then, Naina thought. He's never coming back. Not able to distinguish relief from disappointment, she shut the door after him. It struck her then that he never even tried to say a simple 'sorry' as anyone else in his place would have. But she knew that it was not easy for most people to react appropriately when they first met Tara. She also couldn't help thinking that all morning Anand had talked only about himself—his likes and dislikes, but had cared little to ask anything about Naina.

So Naina? She asked herself. Good riddance, she decided.

But Preeti Aunty's call took her by surprise.

'Anand says, he likes you. And he seemed to simply love little Tara. I think Naina, *baat ban gayi*, it's done. *Beta*, I'm so happy for you.'

Naina met Pari almost every day on the bus now. She found herself looking forward to her company. For that half-hour they were together, Pari kept Naina totally wrapped in her fantasy world where there were no practical problems. She was totally unapologetic about her vanity.

'I will marry a very rich man. I'm very clear, yaar. *Pyar-vyar* kya hai? I want all the good things in life.' Pari was talking so loudly in the cramped bus that Naina was embarrassed.

'Naina, did you see my new earrings? Lovely, no? But this is *kaanch* only, maybe plastic,' she twisted her face, but brightened immediately, 'I love emeralds. I always see myself wearing emeralds and rubies. I want to party every single night of my life and wear designer clothes. This bus-wus, I totally hate! I want a chauffeur-driven car at my disposal at all times. I want a husband who wears a suit every morning and plays golf in the afternoon.'

Naina laughed, 'You're impossible!'

'Okay, laugh. But one day when you are standing at the bus stop waiting for your 525 or whatever, a shiny, black BMW will stop by and madam Pari "so-and-so" will offer to drop you home.'

'Naina, I will pick you up every day,' she added so sincerely that Naina felt a tightness in her throat, a loss for words. Pari was already half standing, getting ready to move to the front as the bus approached her stop.

'*Chal*, catch you.' She looked back once and was gone.

Naina was a little nervous when Sunita transferred the call saying it was Uday.

'Hi.'

'How are you?'

'I'm good. Did you get the report I sent this morning? Is there a problem?'

'No. Just wanted to hear your voice. You okay? All well at home? Tara?'

'Yeah. All well,' her voice almost cracked with emotion, but she checked herself, 'How are you doing?' And then she could not keep herself from adding, 'It's been years.'

'Who's the guy?'

'Who?'

'You know—the guy you're seeing.'

'I'm not seeing anyone. He's a family friend, my aunt's acquaintance.' When she realized, she did not owe him an explanation, anger got the better of her. 'Are you spying on me?'

'No, just trying to stop you from doing anything foolish.'

When she did not speak, he said more calmly, 'Just wanted to let you know that I'm here if you want to talk. Let me know and I'll call.'

Naina remained silent, torn between love and anger.

'Take care of yourself, Naina. I will always protect you whether you like it or not.' He paused for a moment and then hung up.

Naina locked herself in the washroom and wept. She wanted to tell him to come back, tell him that she missed him, and she couldn't go on without him.

At work, when others asked her about Anand, Naina said he was a family friend. But she could sense their curiosity. Then one day, when Naina was held up in a meeting, and he sat waiting for her at the reception, Anand introduced himself to her colleagues as 'Naina's fiancé'. When she came back into the office after seeing him off, everyone began congratulating her.

Naina was dazed. Should she just let this happen? Should she flow with it? Her heart grew heavy as it all seemed so imminent. Just when she had gotten back to normal life—a bare life with no upheavals, here was one staring her in the face.

Three deep lines of worry were beginning to form firmly where her eyebrows met. At work, she still maintained a steely veneer, but alone at home, late into the nights, she stayed up agonizing over the gauntlet life had again thrown at her. Sometimes, in the stillness, finding herself utterly alone, she let self-pity take over and wept.

Three nights later, as she sat ruminating over her circumstance, Nani's words, 'go as a river' rang in her ears like the sign she had been waiting for. She got up and started writing in her journal. Having listed all the pros and cons of her situation, she sighed. The odds seemed against her personal desires.

On the evening of the fourth day, when the doorbell rang and Anand walked in, she knew the time to take her toughest decision was at hand.

Anand stayed all evening—drinking two cups of tea, watching Channel V and making inane comments. Naina tried very hard to not be unpleasant, but she could not make herself to carry on a decent conversation and did not ask him to stay for dinner.

After he left, she began to see things from his perspective. What was Anand's fault in all this? He seemed like a harmless person. Willing to marry her even after learning about her family history, something even the one who claimed to love her, had backed out from. Anand had told Preeti Aunty that he would move in with them and nothing needed to change for her; that Tara would be like his little girl and Raju could continue to take care of the house; that Naina could also continue her job. It was all so thoughtful of him. She was being unfair. Then, again—*harmless* really? Did she have to choose harmless over love? Would she find love again that would encompass her being that was tethered to the responsibilities of a home and family; and the deep social stigma?

She decided that she would say 'yes' when Preeti Aunty asked her on Sunday.

Anand had called on Thursday evening to tell her that he would come over on Saturday. Soon after, Rajesh informed her that the client from Malaysia would be visiting on Saturday and she had to make the all-important presentation. She called Anand to tell him this. Anand said that he too would be busy in the morning and would come only in the afternoon. So, on Saturday morning, she asked Raju to make something nice, although she didn't bother to ask what he planned.

At 11:30, when the discussion was going on after her presentation, Sunita interrupted the meeting.

'Sir, there's an urgent call for Naina.'

Naina tried not to panic and, excusing herself, came out. Raju was on phone.

'Didi, Tara Didi is not okay. Please come home.'

'What happened?' she panicked.

'She is troubled. Please come, Didi.' Then, after a short pause, he added, 'Anand *ji* is also here.'

Naina froze. She went back into the conference room, mumbled a quick apology, and ran out of the building, hailing the first auto and jumping into it before it could stop completely. What is Anand doing in our house at this time? Didn't he say he had meetings in the morning and would come only by lunch?

Tara's forehead was turning blue from where her fists had hammered her head repeatedly. Naina held her in a tight embrace, pinning down her arms to her sides. Softly she spoke, with clear, snappy words, looking straight into Tara's eyes. 'It's okay', 'I'm here', 'You are okay, Tara'. From the corner of her eye, she caught sight of him. Anand, sitting in the corner chair was completely unperturbed. Seething with anger, she wanted to get up and slap him across his silly face. Was it a *tamasha* he was watching?

Naina helped Tara into her rocking chair. She knew Tara would be okay in some time, but furious at Anand and not knowing how to send him away, she decided to leave with Tara.

'Raju, get an auto, we'll go to the doctor.' Half-turning towards Anand, she said, 'Sorry, we must go. I'll just get her file.' She went inside hoping he would leave. But he did not.

The auto was waiting at the gate. Tara got in and as Naina followed, Anand too slid in quietly beside them.

Tara was calm by the time they reached the clinic. Her counsellor talked with her and distracted her with her favourite cube game. They applied ointment on her bruised forehead. Anand sat with Naina, as she reported the incident to Doctor Malti, who they had been consulting for many years now. Naina felt Doctor Malti eyeing Anand all the while.

'What was happening at the time Tara became agitated?'

'I have no idea, doctor. I was at work.' Lost, she looked at Anand. Perhaps, he could tell them something. But he kept quiet.

Then the doctor looking at Anand, asked, 'I'm sorry, I don't know you. Are you a relative?'

'Friend,' Naina quickly answered, 'Anand.'

'Anand, nice of you to have accompanied them here. Please, would you mind waiting outside, while I talk to Naina?'

Without a word or gesture in polite response, Anand walked out.

'Who was at home at the time?' Doctor Malti turned to Naina.

'Raju...and perhaps Anand. I have no idea. I was at work. I didn't have the time to ask.'

'Hmm—Naina, Tara would not get so agitated without a reason, you know that. I must tell you that you need to be very careful. You have a huge responsibility. Tara is a grown-up girl now. You must not let your friends—especially your male friends—visit Tara in your absence.'

Naina felt so ashamed of herself then. She knew the doctor was right. Unwittingly, she had put her little sister in a vulnerable situation.

'I understand that, doctor, and it never happens. It's just that—Anand and I are getting married. We'll all be living together, and I know he thinks of her as a child.' Even as she spoke, her heart was gripped by cold fingers of fear and the last bit came out sounding hollow and without conviction.

'Naina, how and where did you meet Anand? How much do you know about him? Do you know him well enough to marry him?' Doctor Malti was frowning.

'My aunt has arranged it. She knows the family.'

'Naina, don't get me wrong. I've seen Anand visiting my professor regularly. You understand me?'

She stopped to look straight at Naina to gauge if she understood.

Doctor Malti sighed and spoke slowly, 'He came as a patient. I may be wrong—I hope I am, but please do find out about him properly, before you get further involved.'

There was another long pause. Naina felt numb. Doctor Malti came up to her and took her shaking hand into hers.

'Naina, you two are like my children. I feel responsible for you. I cannot see any harm done to you. Let's find out about him. I will try to do everything to help you, but till then, keep a little distance, okay?'

When she gathered enough strength to come out to face him, Anand was nowhere to be seen. Relieved, Naina led Tara to the waiting auto. The auto had just turned onto the main road when she spotted Anand waiting at the bus stop. Their eyes met for a brief moment and as the auto zipped past, both looked away. Naina's heart was beating very fast. She was scared. What was happening to her life? Who was Anand? Why was he consulting a psychiatrist?

Raju was waiting at the gate.

'Anand *ji* did not come with you?'

'No.'

'He should have come, no? Left you alone?'

Naina lost her cool, 'Why should he come with us? Who is he? Am I a child? Haven't I always taken care of us?'

Her male friends. Angry and agitated, she slumped on the sofa, as Tara began to gently rock in her chair. Raju stood by, eyes downcast. She knew he must be feeling guilty for not having taken care of Tara in her absence. But she was in no mood to placate anyone.

'Tell me now what happened. When did he come here?'

'Around 10. He was sitting and reading the newspaper.'

'Where was Tara?'

'Tara Didi was playing on the floor with the coins.'

'Did he talk to Tara?'

'No, he just said he was waiting for you. I told him you will come only by 2. I said I will call you, but he said you know.'

'Then?'

'I was sitting here cutting vegetables. Then he asked me to make tea for him and I went into the kitchen. I was straining the tea when I heard Tara Didi shout and when I came here, Anand *ji* was sitting there, next to her.'

'And?'

Raju looked very uncomfortable, 'Um—he was holding her from behind, telling her to stop. Then she started banging her head on the floor.'

'You didn't stop him?'

'Didi, I told him to let go. I told him it will trouble her more.'

'Then?'

Raju looked away. 'He said, "*Tum chup raho*, shut up! Stay in your limits".'

'Raju, listen to me now! You are my family—you and Tara. When I'm not home, you are the only one to take care of Tara. No one else, no Anand *ji*, *no one* will come near her, okay? You have to keep this in mind. It's your responsibility. Understood?'

Raju nodded. 'I'll get lunch.' He went into the kitchen. Naina stretched her legs. Her feet touched something next to the divan. She got up to see. It was Anand's satchel. She glanced at the main door. It was bolted from inside. With trembling hands and a pounding heart, she opened the bag. It was full of files and papers. Thick files, poems in a minute scrawl. But there were other writings. Some letters.

All letters were addressed to 'Doctor Sahib' and mentioned 'difficulties' and 'illness'. His profile, background, all filled into forms. She quickly glanced over the personal details and then began to read.

Interests: Started writing poems at the age of seventeen.

Academic performance: I was a science student, but I did not study. My parents always feared I would fail. I got 88% in higher secondary with distinction in two subjects.

My inspiration was the life and works of Mirabai, Ghalib, Dinkar, Pant.

I did not want to go into the science stream, but as I was a brilliant student and surpassed all other siblings in studies, my family wanted me to be a doctor or engineer, which was not difficult for me, but I wanted to be a poet or a psychologist. I wanted to take up arts, but as science has more scope; so I was forced to join the science stream.

My poems were so good that often I was asked by other students: 'Where did you copy this from?'

I got my masters in biochemistry.

Started teaching in a higher secondary school.

Became biochemist at a leading pathology lab.

Lecturer for the last four years.

Mental Health: Sometimes have a vague feeling of having seen the place I am visiting the first time. It happened at the National Gallery of Modern Art.

Fell ill when I was twenty-three.

Diagnosis: Unspecific schizophrenia

History of treatment:

- 5 years—Trinicalm plus x3, Tancodep 1-2, Anthensol deconotate injection with phenargan, monthly.
- Shock treatment in March 1998
- 1999 till date: La calm Forte (25 mg) x 3 tabs, Hexidol plain x 2 tabs, Flumap (weekly)

The disease is now almost under control.

In 1996, I was working as a lab technician in a hospital. There were two more girls working with me at the same post, but their salaries were lower than mine. They were jealous of me because of this. They were good at making friends with all the doctors. Once they organized a party in the hospital, but did not invite me. I was very hurt and started hating them. I am not good at making friends. I cannot stand office politics. I did a lot of good work at the hospital. I standardized their methods and established the biochemistry lab within 15 days. But these two women started talking ill about me to everyone. One day there was a huge argument with a doctor and some misinterpretation ensued and they got me suspended. I became very depressed. I had to wait endlessly for the inquiry.

About one week before I was suspended, I had a feeling that everyone at the hospital was keeping an eye on me. If I saw anyone in a black coat, I thought it was a lawyer for the hospital who was trying to frame me. I kept trying to fool him by changing buses all the time and going as far away from home as I could and then taking an auto back home. On reaching home in the evening, I would ask my family if 'they had come?' They would ask, 'Who?' I would say, 'As if you don't know!' They would say, 'We do not know what you are talking about.' I would say, 'Don't fool me; I know you are hand in glove with the hospital people.'

Gradually, I stopped stepping out of the house. I felt scared of people. Even after taking Calmpose, I could not sleep. Time seemed to have stopped. I started feeling scared of the wall clock. Started feeling scared of red colour. Scared of my brothers also. I started sleeping away from the wall where the clock hung. I used to make a swastik sign on the wall which is the sacred sign of Ganpati. One day, someone drew a circle around it and I thought I would be killed as Ganpati could not move. I stopped talking and looking at people coming and going.

I was afraid of plants, which had serrated leaves. I kept my distance from these and thought if I went near, the sickle (as I saw the serrated leaves) would kill me. I kept looking for the number plates of scooters and autos. If I did not like the number, I believed that they belonged to my enemies.

When I first started taking treatment, I had to go to the general hospital to take injections. We could not afford to go to a private clinic. Since the injection contained Phenargan, I used to start feeling drowsy on the way back. I was always feeling drowsy, sometimes the brain felt numb, sometimes my legs. I took up a job in another town. Somehow, I used to get onto the bus and once at work, go straight to my seat and go off to sleep. People would shout at me and ask, 'You get paid to sleep here? Get up and do your work.'

I had to go for shock treatment. There was some improvement with the new drugs and my brain did not feel numb. But nightmares did not leave me.

Today I am asymptomatic, although I cannot do much physical or mental exertion.

With trembling hands, she put the papers back inside the bag and kept it back exactly where and how Anand had left it wedged between one leg of the divan and that of a chair, hidden from view. She got up and locked herself in her room. The doorbell rang and she heard the main door being opened. Raju knocked at her door, but she did not answer. From a tiny parting in the drawn curtains on her window, she watched Anand's back as he walked back to the gate hugging his bag.

In the evening, Naina checked Tara's forehead. It looked better. She needed to be on her own and since Tara was watching TV, she went out alone.

Naina walked away from the bazaar, but the temple bells seemed to call out to her. She resisted, feeling very angry, torn, and tired. Why had this been meted out to her? Hadn't she been through enough? What kind of test was this?

The sound of temple bells followed her. The further she went, the louder they seemed to peal. She turned and went into the temple. It was time for the evening *aarti*. She prayed for guidance. Slowly, the bhajans calmed her and she thought of Tara and herself and of Anand. It was not Anand's fault that he was schizophrenic. Just as it was not Amma's. Was she going to shun Anand like Papa had done Amma?

They were on the terrace. He kissed her lower lip again, sucking it between his lips. He was drawing all the love, desire, need from her body into his. Brimming with unspent love, she let herself go, her body, his, when the sound of large raindrops falling brought her back. It had begun to rain. Reluctantly, she released herself from Uday's embrace to get the clothes drying outside.

As she pulled the last sheet from the line, there they were. Little, unwet, green—they stood in the pouring rain frowning angrily at her.

Naina woke up sweating. It was 3 in the morning.

Anand continued to visit them regularly as if nothing had happened. Naina also pretended that nothing had and tried to forget all she'd read that he carried protectively around in his satchel. It seemed to Naina that Tara was troubled when he was around. But she was sure Tara would soon get used to his presence in the house.

It was Sunday evening and they were all watching a movie on television. It was time for Preeti Aunty's weekly phone call, but the phone was dead. When the doorbell rang, Naina expected it to be one of Raju's gully friends, but it was Gupta Aunty's maid. Preeti Aunty had called at their place. Naina rushed across the road to be greeted by Gupta Aunty. 'Preeti said she will call back. You wait here.'

Naina sat down next to the phone thinking of what she could speak of in front of the Guptas. As time passed, she grew anxious. Tara was with Anand. Should she go back? What would she tell Gupta Aunty? She remembered Doctor Malti's warning…*your male friends.* In desperation, she picked up the phone to check and was relieved to find it dead too.

Thanking Gupta Aunty, she dashed across the road. No sign of anything amiss. As she drew closer, she did not hear anything unusual—only the sound of the television. Entering, she saw Tara slowly rocking in her chair. All fine. Raju was smiling at a love scene in the film.

'Where is Anand?'

'Bathroom,' Raju replied without moving his eyes from the screen.

She peered into the lobby. The bathroom door was shut but the light was not on. However, a band of yellow light edged the closed door of her room. Fear gripped her as she tiptoed towards it. A faint sound from inside set her heart thumping and she pushed the door open, bracing herself up.

Anand was standing before her open cupboard. Her clothes were strewn all over—on the bed, on the floor and in his hands. He turned around to look at her.

'I'm sorry, *beta*. I didn't know. You know what that Pallavi said? She said, "I thought Naina would be more sensitive. After all, she's lived all her life with such people. Preeti *ji*, do you think any normal boy would come forward to marry her? Naina has to see all that also, *na*? Who would want to keep Tara always?" '

Now clearly, it was Preeti Aunty speaking behind the guise of Pallavi. Naina hung up.

Pari got off at her stop. Naina waited for the bus to move. It didn't. There was some commotion in the front and before she could make out anything, she saw Pari entering the bus again. 'Sorry Bhaiya, I left something,' Pari was coming back to where she had sat next to Naina. Naina looked around for what Pari may have left behind. Pari came up to her, caught Naina by her arm and pulling her up from the seat, steered her towards the gate.

'Oh wait! What?'

'Come, come, no time to explain. Naina, you're holding up everyone.' As they got down, Pari turned and shouted pleasantly to all and to no one in particular, 'Really sorry!'

'What is all this?' Naina was more dazed than cross.

'*Arré*! You always say you'll come home to meet my mum, but you never do. So!'

'This is crazy, Pari! You know, I can't do this!'

'You can't? Why not? Where is it written that you cannot come to my place to meet my mum?'

'Not that, you know it. But like this? I'm like—totally not prepared!'

'Oh ho! Come now. You are so—*controlled*, Naina! Sometimes, you must just follow your heart. Or mine.'

She smiled and completely disarmed Naina, who threw her hands up in mock exasperation.

Pari caught her arm and led her into a bylane. Kids were playing badminton and cricket in the street and surprisingly, when cars and pedestrians came by, they patiently waited for the children to move to the side. It seemed like a nice neighbourhood. As they walked ahead, with Pari still holding Naina's arm, several people standing outside at the gates chatting, smiled and nodded when she greeted them in her loud and cheerful 'Hi, Aunty! Hello, Uncle *ji*! *Kaise ho*, how are you?' and kids called out 'Pari Didi' to her.

Pari stopped in front of an apartment block—a neat, white, three storied building with washing hung out in the front of each floor on what seemed like its outstretched arms. The ground floor looked the neatest with clean windowpanes and Naina was glad that was where she was being led.

Pari rang the doorbell twice, without waiting. There was a sound of movement towards the door, but it was not footsteps. The door opened and a woman, her hair generously grey, sat before them in a wheelchair.

'Yo girl! Why are you always in such tearing hurry, *ghode pe sawaar!*' she chided Pari, pleasantly.

'Shame on you, Mum, talking like this in front of our guest.' Pari continued in the same vein and bent down to plant a kiss on her mother's cheek.

It was then that the woman, Pari's mum, looked up at Naina. Naina saw her. Unmistakable. Here she was. Those large brown eyes, that fair face still unmarred by wrinkles, the mole just where her lips met.

'Mum, this is Naina. Ex-colleague, bus-mate, and now my best friend!'

'Naina?' Leela looked into Naina's face.

'I just remembered—I'm expecting someone at home. Sorry.' Without looking at either of them, Naina turned around and fled.

What more was life going to unravel? Naina lay awake thinking. Pari is Leela's daughter. It was obvious why Pari had never mentioned her father. Pari was her half-sister.

Naina left office early. She got down at Pari's bus stop. For the past three days, she had taken an auto home to avoid meeting Pari.

At 4, the place bore no resemblance to what it had looked like the other evening. That crazy, motor-mouth Pari had led her into a street she could not find now. She turned into the first lane and was lucky to spot the neat-faced apartment block after a short walk. Her heart was pounding in her ears. What was she going to say?

The doorbell rang loudly inside. She listened for the sound of the wheelchair, but heard footsteps. A girl—the house-help, opened the door and waited for her to say something.

'Aunty?' haltingly, Naina murmured.

'Come inside.'

Presently, the sound of the wheelchair approached her as she sat in the neat, sparsely furnished drawing room.

'Naina! I was so confused the other day by how you suddenly left. I asked Pari to bring you home.' She came close to Naina and held out her arms. Naina felt revulsion rise inside her like vomit. She stood away.

'Naina, how are you, *beti*?'

That did it.

'Don't call me that!' Naina unfurled her rage. 'You father-stealer! You took Papa away from us. Were there no other men left in the world? Why *our* father? Do you know what he meant to us? To me? Do you know what you put us through by snatching him away? Because of you, my Nani died, my Amma died...'

'Oh!' Leela let out a gasp, as she covered her mouth with her hands and looked terrified.

'What—what happened?'

'Don't pretend you know nothing! You destroyed our family. I'm glad he left you too and died repenting.'

'Who died? Naina, *beti*, tell me, who died? Not *him*?'

'You don't know then? Good. You deserve nothing better. I'm glad he had the courage to free himself of you. He died lonely and sick. He killed himself. But no, you know what? I think *you* killed him. *You* killed everyone including Papa.'

Leela covered her ears with her hands.

Shaking with anger and emotion, Naina got up to leave.

Leela's feeble voice came to her as she opened the door, 'The last I heard of him was that he had gone missing. I never met him after that.'

Naina stopped in her step. 'You were not with him?' She said, turning to look at Leela. Leela sat slumped in her wheelchair, her head in her hands, crying softly.

'Tell me? You and Papa did not live together? Are you making this up?' Naina turned to face her as Leela composed herself, wiping her tears.

'No.'

Naina waited.

'Your father and I were very good friends. He shared a lot of his problems with me. But it was not I who took him away. I talked with him, listened to him. Gave him whatever support I could. No Naina, you are too harsh on us. It was a beautiful friendship. I respected him a lot. Such a wonderful person, such a gentleman! And now you tell me that he is no more.' She searched Naina's face, her own eyes vacant and sorrowful.

'Pari? Tell me. I need to know.' Naina was desperate. 'Not my father's daughter?'

'No!' Leela sounded indignant. She seemed to grapple with her emotions before she began to talk.

'I was in love with a colleague in Agra. He was married. I didn't know this till the family moved in with him—wife and daughter. I tried to move on, but he had become very possessive of me—something that had been very flattering in the beginning, but was becoming increasingly threatening. He just would not let me leave him. I used to confide in Advaith. He always gave me sensible advice.'

'Then, my brother came to know of my relationship with this man and was mad with rage. He put me under house arrest, literally. I escaped and came to Delhi to seek Advaith's help. But I was in for another blow. I was shattered to learn that he had gone missing. I stayed in the guest house that night, meaning to get your Nani's address the next day and go to meet you all. I felt so lonely and dejected. I missed Advaith so much then—his sane advice, his gentle words. Wondered where and how he was, your Papa. Oh Naina, he was such a wonderful man. My best friend.'

'The next morning, my life changed forever. I got ready to leave for your home and came out of my room to be confronted by my lover. He was distraught, almost hysterical. I loved him so much, but I was determined to leave him. It had to be done, once and for all. I told him he had to return to his wife and child.'

'He ran to his car and came back with his wife. The poor woman clutching her child looked terrified. He had dragged them to Delhi from Agra. He threatened to commit suicide if I did not leave with them. His wife implored me. There was such a scene. The last thing I wanted was a scandal on the campus. I could not think clearly. It was best to leave with them then and think of something later. I got into the car with them. He drove like a maniac. The baby would not stop crying. The mother looked too shaken and tired, I in the back seat, took the child from her. The child calmed down and slept as I held her to me. All I remember after that is there was a loud crash and I was thrown off the seat.'

'We'd hit a truck headlong. Its two occupants and the two in our front seats had died instantly. There was blood and fumes and shattered glass everywhere when I was rescued.'

The recounting weighed her down with loss. Her grief was tangible.

'Both my legs were stuck in the mangle, but the child in my arms was unscathed.'

After a pause, she let out a deep, forlorn sigh, 'What was there to do? It was a scandal. No one wanted anything to do with me or the baby. I would be in a wheelchair for life. I stayed back in Delhi and brought her up.'

Naina would need time to have it sink in and make some sense to her. She wanted to be alone. Leaving Leela sobbing in her chair, she left.

Just outside the door, in the gathering dark, stood Pari looking stunned.

Naina walked past her and away.

It took her three days. Naina returned to their house on Sunday. The three of them sat in an oppressive silence in the drawing room. Pari looked broken, her mother worse. Naina knew she had to return this family's peace back to them somehow.

'Aunty, I'm sorry. I'm really sorry for judging you so harshly for all this time. I could not forgive Papa when there was still time. When I realized, it was too late. Maybe he killed himself because he could not stand my rejection.'

'Oh, Naina, no, *beti*! Don't say that.' Leela came closer and Naina got up to kneel by her wheelchair.

'I'm sorry, Aunty.'

Leela hugged her and held her close. All ill-feeling vanished as they came together in their grief for Papa and the terrible tragedies their lives had witnessed.

Naina sensed Pari getting up to leave.

'Wait, Pari,' she got up and caught her arm. Pari, the peppy, careless, impulsive girl she knew seemed to have changed irrevocably in the last three days.

'I'm sorry you had to go through all this because of me, Pari.'

'My mum is not my mum? Why did she never tell me? What should I do?' Suddenly, Pari seemed like a little, lost girl, abandoned by all. Leela Aunty was silent. She looked tired and defeated. She must have tired all her convincing, explaining already.

'I know how you feel, but being born into a relationship is not enough, Pari. One may never get the love and care one looks for there. I had everyone. Think of your life before all this—how wonderful it was. Who created this? Why, if you meant nothing to her? Don't you see how she has nurtured this bond with you? These are the bonds to be cherished, to live and die for, girl. This is all that matters in life.'

'Pari, please understand! We're all in this together—you, your mum, and I. I can understand how you must be feeling. All of us have been through so much. But it's healing time now. It might take you longer, because it's only now that you have discovered cracks in your picture-perfect life. But sweetheart, know that we're with you, no matter what. She's your mum and she loves no one else in this world more than you.'

As she spoke, she let her hemmed-in tears flow. The other two listening to her words were crying too. Together they were purging away the hurt, the anger. Naina got up and pulled Pari to Leela Aunty and all three sat holding each other for comfort.

Naina began to laugh.

'What?' Pari smiled too, wiping her tears.

'Stupid girl! See what mess you have landed us all in! Don't drag anyone else into the house again like this!' They were all laughing hysterically now.

New Delhi, 2012

Like an ice-cream float, the evening was softly sinking. The windows in the west looked out at a lingering crimson that blended with its soft glow over the glass and steel township at its feet. Soon the darkness would congeal and silhouette the skyline before withdrawing gently behind the sequined towers. This was the hour she coveted. It was not every day that Naina could catch these hushed, fleeting moments. On most days, she only caught the lighted cityscape and looking down from her 22nd floor office, long ribbons of vehicle lights below.

The chair reclined quietly as she leaned back to feel the release of another rewarding day. She tapped the phone buzzer, 'Tea please,

Sapna.' Walking towards the windows, she kicked off her shoes and slumped into the sofa that faced the skyline.

The weekly call with her team in London had been encouraging. The project was sailing smoothly. The project lead was certain that the initial contract of one year would be extended and the clients were seriously considering two other proposals of theirs. She might have to travel soon.

Sapna padded in, careful not to disturb, but finding Naina at the window, relaxed. As she poured the tea, she assayed Naina's mood from her stillness and placing the cup on the table before her, left her silence unruffled.

It had been an eventful day. First thing in the morning, Naina had written her last cheque for the loan she was repaying for their home. Their house was now theirs—hers and Tara's and Raju's. In five years, she had been able to pay off the loan, which she took to buy the portion from Ajit Mama. It hadn't been easy. Ajit Mama was not ready to part with it and had quoted almost double the market price, but eventually the lure of ready money had been too much for him to resist.

These last five years, Naina had slowly restored their childhood home, the home that resounded with memories of all those she had loved dearly; the home that never failed to offer succour when she returned to it tired of life's travails. Restoring it hadn't been easy. Many interior decorators and architects came and showed her overwhelming renovation plans—to break this wall and wood panel that; install glass and marble; turn the kitchen into study, and the living room into kitchen. Naina agonized over the plans. What they called the structure, lived for her—the walls held stories, the windows embraced the garden outside, the floor rooted her.

To retain this haven that made her soul sing when she came to it, Naina decided that the basic plan would remain. The old teak doors and panels were sanded and polished. The floors were tiled. The smaller windows overlooking the garden were replaced by large bay windows, so the garden extended indoors. Wall colours, light fixtures, drapes, and upholstery were changed to add warmth and cheer. Only the kitchen was modernized and the front gate, which still proudly proclaimed Nana's name, now slid noiselessly aside. The house stood elegant in white, surrounded by the lush garden.

The splintered fragments of her life that she had struggled to piece together had in the past few years all settled into their destined slots. Tara was now working in a library for two years where she had been placed by the centre after training in cataloguing. Raju and his young family lived in the large room that was once Nana's study—it had an attached bathroom and its own entrance too. His wife Sati was a magic housekeeper and a cheery presence. So was their gurgling two-year-old, who Raju believed was Amma in her current birth and who he had named after her.

Naina's internal line beeped. 'Ma'am,' Sapna was animated, 'the invite for the Indo–French Initiative Forum has come. There was a call from the Consulate earlier.'

'Great! Sapna, is there anything else? I need to leave now.'

'No, Ma'am, nothing else.'

'Good. Take care, Sapna. And you too get home at a decent time some days.' They both laughed.

The traffic stood still at the toll plaza.

'Not a good idea to leave early, no, Mohan Singh?'

'Peak traffic, madam, *jaam hai*,' Mohan Singh craned his head out to see why the cars in front hadn't moved an inch.

Naina was desperate to get home now. In the crowded bus next to her car, a young girl sat leaning her head against the window, a faraway look in her eyes.

What is she thinking? Who waits for her? Does she dream of—love? A career? About twenty years ago, she could have been her; Naina felt a rush of emotion at the thought.

As the car moved ahead of the bus, she couldn't take her eyes off the girl. For one passing instant, their eyes met. Naina smiled, but the girl stared back. The traffic in their lane slowed down and the bus caught up with them again and as it slowly overtook the car, very discreetly and casually, Naina turned her head hoping to catch another glimpse of the girl.

The girl looked right back at her and smiled.

A sincere, silent prayer rose in Naina's heart, 'May you have courage.'

This is what she taught her kids—those with the big, happy smiles, those who wanted to sit at touching distance from her, their eager breath upon her; and their wide eyes that did not leave her face even for an an instant, while she talked to them of life, living, and relationships. Courage is what she talked of the most—courage and hope—every Saturday at the school for destitute girls, supported by the company.

Courage that had come to her late.

'*Degi kya*?' Naina heard the usual lewd comment, as she started jogging. She had never looked at him. She was not even sure it was the same person all these years, calling out as she sprinted across the bridge. Naina had never stopped to question why she allowed him or others like him to do this to her—why that man under the bridge opened his fly every time she passed him by or why the grocer touched her hand while handing her the change every time. She had become an expert at turning away; at pretending to not see. That was the norm.

In the beginning, fear would clutch her heart in its icy talons, like when that man on the bus shagged on her. She could never wear that black and white kurta again, because it carried shame—shame and fear that she fought against day after day, alone, with no one she could ask or confide in; no one to tell her that it was not her fault. Too scared to even move her weight from one numbing leg to the other or do anything that would indicate that she was aware of what was happening to her, she had sat at the edge of the packed bus seat, while he rubbed himself on her shoulder as he stood pressed against her.

'*Degi kya*?' She heard him holler again. Louder, emboldened, provoking.

Seething with rage, Naina slowed down. Lifting her arms over her head, aware that her tee rode up the safe length, she turned sideways, stretching herself; then bent down to touch her shoes. Time ticked away; she had no clue where he was or if he was watching her.

'*Jalwe dekh rahe ho*, enjoying the show?' It was a cyclist riding past her, pretending to talk to someone, his intention clear. Without stopping to consider, if there were others with him on the lonely stretch, Naina charged at him with all her might; pulled him down and as he fell over the cycle, landed such a resounding slap on his face that it staggered her.

'Let's go to police and see *jalwe*,' she held him tight by his arm. He tried to run, but she kicked him hard on the shin. He howled and fell on the road.

'I—I was talking of someone else.'

'Let's talk to the police.'

No one called out obscenities at her anymore. Sometimes, she heard people whisper 'Jhansi ki Rani' as she sprinted past.

EPILOGUE

She was in the bath when she heard the cellphone ring in her room.

'Sunainaaaa! Answer the phone, must be dad,' Naina called out and waited till she heard the hurried scamper of Sunaina's fluorescent green flipflops across the lobby and the ringing stop, before slipping quickly into the bathrobe and winding the towel around her wet hair. With all the hurrying too, Naina was late. It was time for Uday's Saturday morning call. She could hear Sunaina talking now.

—Dad! I'm wearing mehendi! It's awesome! And we bought lehengas—pink and gold. Similar ones for me and Tara Aunty.

—In the evening, when Tara Aunty is back from work, we're going to model in our new lehengas. Dad, shall we Face Time then?

—Yes! And, Dad, we're also going to see a film tomorrow.

—In the shower. Will you call back later?

—Yes, I spoke about it with Mum.

—Yes, Dad. Okay—wait, wait, here she is! Looking like your Madhuri Dixit, wet hair and all. (Sunaina giggled) No dad, I don't think so. Yes, I will tell her that. Love you, Daddy!

Naina pulled Sunaina's ear in mock anger and took the phone from her. Sunaina ran away laughing.

—Good morning, *Amreekan*.

—Hey beautiful, what's for breakfast?

—Hmm—*chhodo*, let it be; it would be cruel on you—kachoris and aloo curry for brunch.

—Uff!

—Hahaha! I'm taking Sunaina to the mandir now. All of them had so much fun at the Kingdom of Dreams yesterday.

—Why didn't you go?

—You know how that project was going.

—Over? How did it go?

—Very well. Your inputs were very helpful. Thanks, Uday.

—Wonderful!

—It's so lovely to have Sunaina over; thank you, Uday.

—Seems like we're in the business of 'thank yous' today. So kindly be accepting mine for taking the brat off my back for a bit. Hey, whose turn is it this week? Mine, no?

—Yes.

—Here's a dog's chance you know what a cat's cradle is.

—Tut-tut! That's an old chestnut, Uday. *Amreeka* is no good for you.

—Bengali Market is?

—Yes, but—

There was a long pause, his sigh inaudible.

—You take care. We must hurry or the temple will close. Give my love to Pallavi.

She waited for him to disconnect. He for her. She did.

Hurriedly, she dressed and called out, 'Sunaina, let's go!'

'Coming!' Sunaina came running out of the kitchen having pinched a kachori.

'Couldn't wait! Sati Aunty makes the best kachoris in the world! But you don't worry; I'll wash my hands before entering the mandir. I know where the tap is,' she said earnestly, juggling the hot kachori in her hands.

Naina tried to maintain a straight face even as Sunaina flashed a conciliatory dimpled smile. They came out in the winter sun. Closing the gate behind them, Naina turned to look at the roof. Clear. They must've ducked on seeing her.

As soon as they turned into the street, Sunaina sought Naina's hand, wrapping her little fingers around hers. She's going to be tall like Uday, thought Naina. How time had flown; Sunaina was eight already.

'I will also rinse my mouth if you like,' Sunaina looked up to see if Naina had been sufficiently disarmed. The disapproval Naina was feigning, evaporated. Her grip tightened on the child's moist hand. Sunaina skipped in the air and continued her chatter.

'And yes, Daddy asked me to tell you "it doesn't run in the family". Whatever does that mean, Aunty Naina?'

ACKNOWLEDGEMENTS

I owe this novel to Anando, who knew I would write it, even when I did not, two decades ago. To him, to Dinesh, and Shibani, who read every draft and give disparate opinions that made me find my way, many fist-bumps.

This second book journey with Niyogi Books has been as gratifying and pleasant as the first because of their wholehearted support for their authors and their commitment to creating fine books. Nirmal *da*'s reassuring words on this manuscript will remain my beacon in times of darkness during my writing journey, always.

Thanks, as always, are due to my literary agent, Preeti Gill. Arunima Ghosh's insightful comments on the manuscript and eye for detail during editing are much appreciated. Finally, the person who is entrusted with the job of making the book leap out at readers, Misha Oberoi Chakravarty, I'm grateful and much in awe of your craft.

About the author

Shefali Tripathi Mehta's most recent book is *Ek Koshish: The Story of Arushi* (2019). This is her fifth book and the second work of fiction after *Stuck Like Lint* (2017). She has published short stories and poems in anthologies and online. She writes on disability awareness, social issues, travel, and parenting. For close to ten years, Shefali wrote the cover story for the Sunday supplement of the Deccan Herald.

She lives in Bangalore and works at the Azim Premji University. Shefali volunteers with the disability organization, Arushi, and curates Gond art to support tribal artists.